The Lobster Pot Café

A seaside novel

Barry Dore

This is Barry's debut novel. He and wife Jakkie live in rural Staffordshire, splitting their time between home and Aberdovey on the Welsh coast.

Barry is a leadership coach and facilitator, has published two leadership books, runs a programme for 50 young leaders, writes and broadcasts extensively on leadership, chairs a conservation charity and presents two local radio shows.

Also by Barry:
Lead Like Mary
Building a Community

www.barrydore.com

To all of our children

Remembering those wonderful summer holidays

Chapter 1

The incessant ring of his mobile penetrated Stephen's sub conscious. He groaned, willing it to go away, rubbing his throbbing head. The phone stopped momentarily then began again.

Rolling over on the sofa, his duvet dropped to the floor. Peering blearily at the screen, he tried to focus on the caller's identity. His mother! Jesus, what time is it? He focused his aching eyes. 8am? For goodness sake! The ringing ceased again. Six missed calls!

Turning onto his back, Stephen tried to concentrate. He had no recollection of getting home but it must have been the early hours. His clothes were strewn across the floor, next to a half empty bottle of whisky. The previous day was a hazy memory, as far too many were recently. He had vague memories of several pubs, a club, dancing...then nothing.

Something else was bothering him, something he had forgotten, his parents, what was it? Damn it, he had been supposed to have Sunday lunch with them, it had completely slipped his mind.

Dragging himself out of bed he staggered to the bathroom, examining the sunken face that stared back at him in the mirror. He felt dreadful. Opening his schedule on the phone, he realised it was Monday. He had a meeting at 11am, just time to pull himself together.

The mobile rang again, his mother. Wearily he pressed the answer button.

'Mum, I'm sorry about lunch, I for...'

'It's your father.'

The panic in his mother's voice forced Stephen fully awake.

'What's the matter?'

'He's had a heart attack.'

'Oh my god, when, is he...'

'Last night, I don't know, I'm at the hospital now, they won't let me in, I'm so scared.'

'I'm on my way, half an hour.'

Driving in a daze, vaguely aware he was no doubt still over the breathalyzer limit, Stephen felt numb. Images of his father flashed through his brain, sitting in his favourite chair, carving the joint on a Sunday, on the beach on holiday, together along with much more unsavoury pictures of his own life over the last few months. He parked outside A&E and rushed in, urgently seeking directions from the receptionist.

His mother was in the corridor outside the emergency rooms, her head in her hands, sobbing. Stephen sank down, his arm around her, fearing the worst.

'Is he...?'

'No, I don't know...'

They sat together praying their husband and father was clinging onto life. The waiting was interminable, harried doctors and nurses rushing past, in the distance machines bleeping.

Eventually a young doctor appeared, sitting next to them, looking hardly old enough to be out of medical school.

'Tell us...'

'It's okay, he's stable, he's going to be okay, we've had to carry out emergency surgery.'

A wave of relief overwhelmed Stephen.

'Thank goodness, can we see him?'

'Maybe later, he's only just come round, he needs to sleep.'

A couple of hours later, after too much plastic coffee from plastic cups, they were shown to his bedside. Stephen stared down at his father, connected to various machines with a plethora of wires and tubes, looking gaunt and grey.

'Are you ok?'

'I will be son, I will be.'

Over the next week Stephen and his mother were daily visitors to the hospital, as his father slowly recovered. They talked about everything and nothing, childhood memories, family holidays. By the weekend he was well enough to go home, Stephen supporting him as they made their way to the car.

His father was delighted to be home, sinking down into his

favourite chair. Relieved that his father seemed on the way to recovery, Stephen felt able to return to work, but leaving early enough to spend a couple of hours with his parents. He was pleased they lived so close.

On his second day home, as they sipped coffee, his father quizzed.
'You never came to lunch.'
'I know, I'm sorry.'
'Stephen, what's happened to you?'
'What do you mean?'
'You know what I mean! Was it the divorce?'
'I don't know, that's done with...'
'It's not though is it?'
'What do you mean?'
'Stephen, we might be getting on but we're not stupid. You never call, you miss lunch, when you show up you look dreadful and stink of alcohol.'
'But apart from that..'
'Stephen I'm serious, we're worried.'
'I know, so am I...'

Over the next few days Stephen took stock. His father's heart attack had frightened him. Racked with guilt over missing lunch, he may never have seen his father again. He tried to piece together his life over the last few months. He and Helen had separated a few months ago after over fifteen years together. They had met at university and married soon after graduating. The divorce had recently come through. Was it that? Maybe, but it hadn't been acrimonious, it had been right for both of them to go their separate ways and there were no complications and no children.

Maybe it was more the pressure of work. He had a responsible job in a demanding industry where excessive hours and stress levels linked to high rewards were the norm. He was good at it, liked and respected, but it had taken its toll.
Stephen's life had slipped further and further out of control.

Sometimes he had the feeling he was watching himself in some psychedelic parody of his life, a film where the lead actor bore only a passing resemblance.

Maybe splitting with Helen was the trigger? Maybe it was some kind of mid-life crisis? Maybe the pressure of work? Maybe it didn't matter why.

Stephen's job had always been demanding, long hours, countless meetings, never ending crises- with each promotion the pressure increased. He stayed later and later in the office, drifting to the pub with colleagues to pick over the remnants of the day. Previously a moderate drinker he took to consuming more and more every evening, returning late to the now empty marital home for a microwave meal washed down with whisky. Several times he never made it as far as his bed, waking in the early morning cramped up on the sofa with the taste of stale whisky and a splitting headache.

Then there were the women. Tall, good looking and still in his thirties, Stephen had always attracted interest from the women at work. He began to date more than one, causing a cauldron of office rumours and petty jealousies. He started leaving his colleagues in the familiar drinking haunts, moving on to pubs and clubs, seeking out groups of women out for the night, or singles, as lonely as him. Several mornings he woke in a strange bed with the most hazy of recollections of who lay beside him. He used dating sites, leading to liaisons with increasingly more women, moving from one to another, obsessively.

All of this inevitably began to have an impact on Stephen's performance at work, and his health. Going to the office later, missing meetings, struggling with deadlines, too often arriving bleary-eyed and unshaven.

In the rare moments of logical thought, he stared in the mirror in disgust, hating the hollow-eyed stranger that stared back. At those times, he longed to get off the conveyor belt, to become himself again. He just no longer knew how.

Things reached a crescendo. He'd only intended to have one drink, a hair of the dog, after a typically heavy Saturday night before heading off for a pre-planned Sunday lunch with his parents. One drink turned into two then countless more as he staggered from pub to pub, lunch date forgotten, unaware of how he got home, collapsing on the sofa, eventually awoken by his mother's frantic calls.

Now sitting with his father, looking at the frail figure next to him, guilt, self-loathing and a sense of helplessness pulsated through him.

He and his father had grown apart over the years. Work had consumed him, but their bond was still strong, built on empathy. As he recovered his strength his father, who had watched Stephen's behaviour change over the past few months, broke the taboo, gently prodding

'What's been the matter Stephen, what's gone wrong?'

'It's a heart attack dad, the doctor explained you're going to...'

'Not me son!'

'What do you mean?'

'Your mum and I aren't stupid, we've watched you fall apart, what's happened?'

'It's nothing, I'm fine, I...', an overwhelming feeling of remorse coursed through Stephen, 'I don't know, I'm sorry. I hate myself.'

Stephen's head collapsed into his hands, sobbing uncontrollably, his body shaking, months of pent up emotions coming to the surface.

It was only when the sobbing subsided that his father spoke.

'It doesn't have to be this way.'

'Dad we almost lost you.'

'Son...we thought we'd lost you.'

The next day, after his first alcohol free day in months, Stephen knew he needed time to think. Heading out into the country, he parked at a popular walking spot. Over a long walk he reflected deeply, examining what had happened to him. His break up from Helen had hurt, but more through sadness, not for what had been, but what might have been.

Reality slowly dawned, he had known it all along. He hated

his job. It wasn't so much the long hours, the pressure, the daily crises. It was the constant demand for results, for increased revenues, bigger profits, always about the numbers, shareholder returns. Always about money, nothing else but money. He had been sucked into the game with everyone else. What had happened to the idealistic twenty something fresh out of university ready to change the world?

He hated the stranger he had become. What had happened to the kind, smiling, down to earth person he had been all his life? It was time to rediscover the real Stephen before it was too late.

It really didn't have to be this way. Not the drink, nor the women, not even the job. He could take control, make any choice he wanted! He felt liberated, happier than he had been in months - maybe years. The first chinks of light were appearing through the thick veil that had consumed him for too long.

Over the next few days, his father back home rebuilding his strength, Stephen took more and more time to think. Much to his colleagues' surprise he booked long overdue holiday. Using the gym, he changed his diet, stopped his drinking, deleted numerous names from his contacts. Most of all he walked, lost in thought.

Stephen realised he could quit his job, it was his choice, he had ample resources to survive for at least a year. He held healthy share options together with savings. He could take his time finding the right job for him, something that would fulfil him.

Why rush into finding a job? Why not take maybe a year out? At the back of his mind he remembered a long held ambition that faded away, his dream of being an author, writing a novel! Increasingly it had become a distant fantasy but could he rekindle it, maybe devote the year to researching and writing?

As the next few days passed Stephen's plans began to take shape. His dream was fanciful but possible. So much of his previous decisiveness, the clarity and action bias that had propelled him up the corporate ladder, returned. The following week found him explaining his decision to an incredulous CEO, who had been well aware of Stephen's deteriorating performance in recent times but chosen to tolerate it. He and Stephen went back a long time. This news was extraordinary!

Stephen's colleagues were equally bemused. There were coffee machine whispers of dismissal, an office pregnancy, but a few weeks later, his notice served, he was given a warm and rousing send off.

With time on his hands Stephen turned his attention to his future plans, feeling reborn. A year it would be, but not here. Anxious to sell the marital home, bury the past, move far away from the rat race Stephen decided on a year by the sea. It would provide the ideal creative environment. But where?

He had distant memories of childhood holidays, blissful summers full of crabbing, ice cream and beach cricket. Memories of a beautiful harbour and beaches. Stephen struggled to remember the name of the village- mid Wales, he was sure of that. Studying the map his finger traced the coastline until he found it. Aberdyssyni!

Now all he had to do was find somewhere to live!

Chapter 2

Stephen checked his watch. 10pm. Was it too late to call tonight? He glanced down at the advert, a shiver of excitement passing through him. It sounded perfect.

'To let. Aberdyssyni. Old Coastguard Lookout. Panoramic views. Unmodernised'.

After only a moment's hesitation he dialled the number. The phone rang several times and he was about to replace the receiver when a soft Irish accent answered...

'Hello, Rachel Saunders'

'Hi I'm Stephen Blanchard, I'm sorry to bother you so late at night. I've just seen your advert for the property to rent in Aberdyssyni. Is it still available?'

'The Lookout, yes it is, how long do you want it for, a week or a fortnight?'

'I was thinking of a year actually'

There was a pause at the other end.

'A year, are you sure? It's not modernised you know?'

'How not modernised?'

'Well, it's not been lived in before, there's no electricity apart from a generator, no bath or shower, only cold water.'

Stephen was already intrigued.

'Tell me more about it, is it really a coastguards lookout?'

'It was, for over a hundred years. It's got a great view of the estuary and sea. There's many stories of shipwrecks over the years.'

'That's amazing.'

'There's so many legends. Fires being lit to confuse ships into thinking they were in safe water. When they ran aground the crew were set upon by smugglers. That's why the lookout was built.'

For several more minutes Stephen listened enthralled as Rachel described the building and its history. He was captivated by the enthusiasm in her voice, and her love of the Lookout and

Aberdyssyni. As she finished, generators and hot water sounded irrelevant details. He knew he had found his home for the next year.

'I'll take it.'

'Really, are you sure?'

'I'm sure.'

'That's great. We'll just have to sort out a couple of details and a reference. Why are you coming here for a year, I hope you don't mind me asking?'

'In a nutshell a new start. I'll tell you more when I get there.'

Moments later Stephen put the phone down, unable to suppress a grin. He rarely acted impulsively but this just felt right.

Days later, formalities complete, he transferred to Rachel a small amount for the first three months rental.

A few short weeks later, after a quiet Christmas spent with his parents, Stephen heaved his large holdall into the taxi, glancing back at his former marital home for the final time. It was a cold, crisp morning in early February.

Easing into his seat, Stephen gazed from the window as the taxi threaded its way through the Birmingham traffic towards the station. At last he felt his adventure had begun. So much had happened so quickly, his divorce from Helen, slipping off the rails, the shock of his father's heart attack, the decision to quit his career, to make a new start. The plan to escape for a year to fulfill his dream of writing a novel. He couldn't believe that only a few weeks ago he had been a highly paid executive, with all the rewards. His new life lay ahead.

The taxi screeched to a halt shaking Stephen from his memories. Hoisting the bag onto his shoulder he went in search of the train. Even in the middle of the morning, Birmingham New Street station was busy, a mixture of workers, shoppers and students threading their way across the concourse like a colony of ants. Striding down the escalator onto the platform Stephen climbed onto a four coach train. He settled into his seat and looked round the carriage. It was nearly empty, two middle aged women with shopping bags deep in conversation, and a young girl listening to music on her headphones, were his sole companions.

Minutes later the doors closed, a whistle and they were underway, snaking through multiple sets of points as the train left the busy station. A surge of excitement passed through him, the adventure had begun!

Stephen relaxed, closing his eyes briefly then gazing out at the old industrial landscape of the West Midlands, lost in thought, passing long closed factories with crumbling walls and broken windows, ghost lands long deserted, abandoned to graffiti artists and pigeons.

The announcement of arrival into Wolverhampton shook Stephen from his daydreams. He stood helping an elderly lady struggling with a large suitcase and voluminous handbag.

'Here let me help you', hoisting the suitcase onto the luggage rack with some difficulty.

'Thank you dear, that's so kind of you', the woman replied, settling down into the seat opposite Stephen. He watched fascinated as she took a crossword book, a magazine, a pair of glasses, her knitting, a wrapped sandwich and what appeared to be a hip flask out of her handbag.

'Just something to keep out the cold', she confided, noticing his stare. Moments later she was knitting furiously.

The train emerged from the harsh urban conurbation into soft countryside. A weak winter sun illuminated the landscape. Stephen caught a glimpse of the Welsh mountains in the distance. Another shiver of excitement!

At Shrewsbury the two women disembarked, still chatting non-stop, to be replaced by harassed parents with three noisy young children. They settled at the far end of the carriage, the eldest child indignantly demanding to know why they had to visit his aunt and uncle while the younger two energetically devoured the picnic their mother set out on the table.

The elderly woman opposite Stephen put down her knitting,

glancing at the family, where a squabble had broken out over the last sausage roll. She took a quick swig from her hip flask.

Stephen felt compelled to break the silence. 'Where are you off to?'

'To see my daughter and family in Welshpool, she replied, pulling a photograph from her handbag. 'This is Diane, my daughter, and Mark, he's a teacher you know, clever as anything, this is Susan and Michelle, and this...' she paused to pull another photo from her bag, 'is Toby, my new grandson.'

Thrusting the photo at Stephen she added proudly 'I can't wait to see him he's just a month old, the cardigan's for him.'

She gazed affectionately at the photo one last time before returning it to her handbag and picking up the knitting again. Soon the needles were clicking furiously, she was obviously intent on finishing the gift before they arrived in Welshpool.

'How far are you going?' she asked Stephen, taking another swig, looking at him over the top of her glasses.

'Aberdyssyni.'

'What a wonderful place that is, my late husband and I used to go there when Diane was young.'

Stephen smiled and closed his eyes. He did not want to appear rude but was desperately anxious that his vision of what lay ahead was not shattered before it had begun. His mind wandered, still disbelieving how his life had changed over the last few months. At times the dream of taking a year out to write a novel seemed ridiculous. He still had no idea of the subject of the story despite spending hours scouring the shelves in his local book shops, downloading best sellers, delving into thrillers, romances and historical fiction. He was no closer to deciding on a genre, let alone creating characters and formulating a plot.

After Shrewsbury the train crossed the border into Wales. Stephen watched the countryside change from flat fields bordered by hedges to a terrain of rolling hills and tall trees.

At Welshpool he said goodbye to the elderly woman, helping to carry her suitcase off the train while she rammed her belongings back into her handbag. As the train pulled away he watched her drown her new grandson in kisses, a beam of delight on her face.

At Newtown the family departed, the children still complaining noisily about the enforced visit and the lack of food at their picnic. The train picked up speed heading deeper into Wales, the carriage now deserted. Stephen imagined that in summer it would be much busier, families heading for the coast with suitcases, buckets, spades and excited children.

He watched the countryside change once more. In the distance gorse covered mountains with snow-capped summits, sheep dotted across the landscape. High above a farmer traversed the steep slope in a red tractor. Stephen's mind wandered as he thought about all those years cooped up in the city in his office or apartment, he already felt more alive, he could almost feel the fresh, clean air.

He tried to imagine what lay ahead, thinking about the Lookout, wondering what it was like, feeling apprehensive and excited at the same time. He had rented a place he had never seen from a woman he had never met on nothing more than a whim and far off childhood memories. So out of character with his previously organised life. His head full of images, he dozed.

Stephen woke with a start as they arrived into Machynlleth. Now on the last part of the journey he began to pay closer attention to his surroundings. Tall pine trees covered the surrounding hills, and the road snaked along the hillside above him. The train crossed a tidal river with boats marooned on the mudflats. They rounded a bend and Stephen took a sharp intake of breath as he caught his first view of the dramatic river Dyssyni estuary. The train ran along a narrow path cut into the hillside. Oyster catchers, herring gulls and lapwings swooped over the water.

Ahead, in the estuary mouth, a number of fishing boats at anchor, some tilted to one side by the low tide. The train swung sharply, gliding dramatically above the roofs of the first houses, the wheels seeming to almost touch the chimney pots, creating an illusion of flying. They passed through a tunnel, emerging to a brief glimpse of the jetty and sandy beach before the train slowed and pulled into Aberdyssyni station.

Stephen quickly grabbed his bag and climbed down onto the deserted platform. Seconds later the train doors closed and it was on its way again with a loud hoot.

Putting his bag down Stephen looked around. In the distance were sand dunes, the mouth of the estuary and the sea beyond. He could hear waves breaking on the shore, above gulls swirled in the pale blue sky, screeching to each other. The air was chill but the platform bathed in winter sunshine. Childhood memories flooded back. He breathed deeply, feeling alive and exhilarated.

To his left lay the village, a colourful array of houses lined the shore, a pleasing pastel mix of blue, yellow and cream. Rising above them a prominent blue building with a balcony looking out over the estuary.

The station was long, red bricked and Victorian with tall windows and no obvious entrance. Stephen pulled a piece of paper from his pocket. Rachel Saunders, Beach Cottage, Aberdyssyni. No road name or directions but it couldn't be hard to find. He'd head for the village and find someone to ask.

As he picked up his bag a woman appeared around the side of the station, tall and distinctive with a shock of blonde hair. She waved, calling his name, bounding down the platform to meet him.

'I'm Rachel', she said, grasping Stephen's hand shaking it vigorously, 'welcome to Aberdyssyni!'

Chapter 3

Before Stephen had a chance to return her greeting Rachel grabbed his bag and marched off down the platform. He hurried after her, struggling to keep up.

'I didn't know where Beach Cottage was' he shouted, 'I was going to get a taxi.'

'Don't worry, it's not too far.'

They turned left at the end of the platform, then through the door at the front of the station. Rachel dropped his bag on the floor and grinned.

'Welcome to Beach Cottage!'

'Well that didn't take long' Stephen laughed, as he realised, he was now in the converted station.

'Sorry, I never tire of that joke.'

Stephen looked around. He was in a cosy sitting room with white walls and dark floorboards, furnished with a comfortable looking sofa and armchair, piled with cushions, a large dresser and an old oak table. On the walls hung colourful pictures of seaside scenes. He recognised one as the harbour he had passed moments ago. Open magazines, books, paints and half-finished pictures gave the room an untidy but homely air.

A large, reddish brown dog bounded into the room hurling itself at Stephen barking madly and wagging its tail, almost causing him to lose balance.

'Get down Bryn,' ordered Rachel, 'I'm sorry Stephen, he's harmless, just a crazy Irish setter!'

Recovering his dignity Stephen smiled, already invigorated in Rachel's company. He looked at her more closely. About forty, a few crinkly smile lines around her eyes, maybe a couple of years older than him, tall and attractive in a very individual way. She ran her hand through her unruly shock of blonde hair, which seemed to have a life of its own. She was wearing a thick woollen jumper, faded jeans and, strangely for mid-winter, a pair of open toed sandals.

'Cup of tea? Make yourself at home.'

Without waiting for an answer, she disappeared into the kitchen closely followed, to Stephen's relief, by Bryn. Moving a pile of magazines, he sank into the armchair looking around. An open fire burned in the grate giving the room a warm glow, driftwood piled by the hearth. He gazed at the paintings on the walls, pictures of the sea with dramatic swirling waves, the harbour and a picture of children crabbing from a jetty, once more stirring early memories.

Rachel swept back into the room carrying on her tray a teapot, two odd chipped mugs, a milk jug and a plate of biscuits, which Bryn was regarding with interest.

Pouring the tea, she asked, 'how was your journey?'

'Really scenic, especially the last bit- what a beautiful village'

'Have you been here before?'

'Not since I was a child, we came here for family holidays.'

Rachel sipped her tea. 'So man of mystery, why do you want to rent the Lookout for a year? I'm intrigued, you mentioned a new start, are you on the run, a master criminal who needs to lie low?'

'I'm afraid it's not that exciting. I'm going to write a book'

'Sounds pretty exciting to me. An author in our midst. Are you famous? Can't say I've heard of you.'

'Actually, this is my first book'

'Okay, what's it about?'

'Not sure yet to be honest'

Rachel raised her eyebrows but declined to comment further. Instead she leapt to her feet, causing Stephen to slop his tea.

'Come on, you can tell me more later, let me take you up to your new home. I want you to see it properly before it gets dark, I went up earlier to light the wood burner and start the generator, so it should be nice and warm for you.'

She picked up Stephen's bag and headed for the door, whistling for Bryn. Stephen gulped down his tea and followed her. Outside was an old army soft top Land Rover. He winced as

21

Rachel hurled his bag into the back, closely followed by a leaping Bryn.

They drove noisily along the coast away from Aberdyssyni, jolting every time they hit a bump in the road, Rachel humming to herself, seemingly oblivious to the lack of suspension. The winter sun was already low in the sky, the sea glistening from its remaining rays. After barely half a mile they passed a large hotel then swept round a bend and Stephen caught sight of a small building above them perched precariously on the hill above the road. This must be the Lookout! They swung into a small parking area at the bottom of the hill and Rachel switched off the engine, the sudden silence deafening.

'Here we are! Welcome to your new home, I hope you like it.'

Stephen jumped out gazing up at the building. It occupied a commanding position overlooking the mouth of estuary and the sea beyond, protruding from the hillside. He imagined coastguards with telescopes scouring the horizon for smugglers, or vessels in distress. Stone steps wound their way up through the gorse to the building.

He jumped as Rachel's engine roared back into life. She threw him a bunch of keys. He'd been unaware she had already unloaded his bag.

'Go on in', she shouted above the engine, 'I hope you love it as much as I do.'

She began to pull away. Stephen had a dozen questions running through his head but no time to ask them.

'I've left you a bit of shopping, I'll see you in the morning'. Rachel's words were half lost in the noise and the wind, and then she was gone, her wheels skidding on the gravel and Bryn barking furiously.

Stephen waited until she had disappeared out of sight and then picked up his bag, opened the gate, bounding up the steps. He reached a wooden door on the ground floor of the building, through which he could hear the hum of a generator.

Dropping his bag he looked around, the views taking his breath away. Below, a panoramic view of the whole bay. Aberdyssyni nestled to his left and beyond the village he could just make out the railway line, snaking its way back up the estuary. Fishing boats bobbing in the harbour were pushed gently this way and that by the tide. The afternoon winter sun was already sinking into the water beyond lines of sand dunes and a long deserted beach. In the distance another village across the other side of the estuary.

A flight of steps on the corner of the Lookout led to a first floor narrow balcony. Leaving his bag by the front door Stephen climbed them. Another door appeared to lead directly into the main living area. He selected the biggest key on the ring, the lock was rusty but turned easily. Pushing the door open he stepped inside.

His first impression, warmth and brightness, as the last of the sun shone directly into the room through the large windows which dominated the front wall. He smelt polish, signs of recent cleaning. Beneath the window were fresh flowers on a rickety table.

On the side wall of the Lookout a gently glowing wood burning stove, on top of which stood an old cast iron kettle, beside it a basket piled with driftwood. In the corner a narrow staircase led back down to the floor below, along the back wall a small kitchen area with a sink, fridge and gas cooker powered by bottled gas.

The rest of the room was sparsely furnished. Next to the table were a couple of old wooden chairs and a striped deckchair. Slung across the corner of the room, suspended on two large hooks in the ceiling, a hammock. There was no other bed to be seen and Stephen regarded it with suspicion. Pulling himself gingerly up into it he stretched out. It was surprisingly comfortable and afforded a wonderful view of the sun sinking into a sea tinged with red. A fishing boat chugged back towards the harbour, racing the fading daylight. Stephen grinned, what on earth was he doing here? He examined the cupboards in the kitchen area, finding a pillow, quilt, a mixture of old crockery and glasses none of which matched. On top, covered in dust, he discovered what appeared to be old sea charts.

Deciding to explore the floor below, Stephen flicked on lights before descending cautiously down the narrow stairs. He found himself back at the first door, unbolting it he retrieved his bag. Inside were three more doors. First a small toilet and hand basin, next a store with wood in a variety of sizes piled around the room, together with lobster pots, fishing nets and an old bicycle. The third took him back outside to a covered area that housed the generator, vibrating and humming away, a sound Stephen found reassuring.

Re-climbing the stairs he noticed two shopping bags in the kitchen area, a long loaf protruding from the top. He realised how hungry he was, having not eaten all day since leaving his former home. 'Thank you Rachel' he said out loud, the sound of his voice startling him in the empty room. He emptied the contents onto the table; bacon, eggs, butter, orange juice, coffee, milk, a bottle of wine and, somewhat surprisingly, a can of WD40. Also in the bag, an envelope with his name on the front in a flowing script. Carefully opening it he pulled out a card the front of which was a drawing of the Lookout. Inside were the words *'to Stephen, good luck, Rachel.'* He smiled, standing the card next to the flowers.

The sun had disappeared, bringing with it the early darkness of a mid-winter day. Stephen flicked on more lights, wincing as a bright strip light burst into life. He made a mental note that this would be an early change to his home. He thought about unpacking but having nothing to unpack into reduced his options. He'd agreed with Rachel that he would make improvements to the Lookout in exchange for a low rent. Tomorrow he would begin his list.

Tonight though, he needed to eat and sleep. Although still early it had been a long day. He cooked himself a simple plate of food and ate hungrily. A frantic search revealed a corkscrew and he poured a glass of wine, silently toasting his arrival.

Later, after refilling his glass, he switched off the light and sank into the deckchair in front of the windows. The wood burning stove made the room deliciously warm. An equally warm feeling passed through him, an inner sense of contentment, helped by the wine. It was a still night, yet in the distance he could hear the steady roar of the waves crashing onto the beach. His eyes gradually became accustomed to the darkness. Looking up at the stars shining above he watched a fishing boat heading out to sea, it's navigation lights illuminating its path. A marker buoy flashed below him, sending a warning of the dangerous sand banks in the estuary. To his left he could see the twinkling lights of Aberdyssyni.

What struck him most of all was the silence, he had become used to quiet nights on his own since the divorce, but this was somehow more intense. Besides the breaking of the waves all he could hear was the ticking of a clock, the crackle of logs in the wood burner and the gentle hum of the generator. For someone who had spent most of his life surrounded by noise, the peace was wonderful. He closed his eyes and thought of the coastguards from years gone by sat in this very spot, keeping a watchful eye. With the food and wine lying warmly on his stomach Stephen slipped into a doze.

Waking with a start he looked at his watch. 9pm! He had been asleep almost two hours. He stood, stretching his stiff back. He washed, undressed and climbed into his hammock, pulling the quilt tightly around him. Laying in the darkness gazing out to sea, he drifted off to sleep, dreaming of a great sailing ship, on the deck of which stood Rachel and Bryn.

Chapter 4

Stephen drifted through the strange world that lies somewhere between asleep and awake, the semi consciousness of early morning. He felt a gently swaying sensation and for a few seconds was back on the deck of the galleon. Thinking he must be safely in bed in his Birmingham home, any second his alarm would shatter the peace at some unearthly hour, he would shower and leave Helen asleep as he headed off for another day of meetings and conference calls. Slowly reality returned, beds don't sway, and waves don't break on the shore in Birmingham, those things happen when you wake up in a hammock in an old coastguard lookout!

Opening his eyes a fraction he gazed out of the window. It was still dark. He fumbled for his phone. Not yet six o'clock. Closing his eyes tight once more he stretched out under the duvet enjoying the gentle sway of the hammock, the sense of wellbeing from last night enveloping him. He dozed for a short while then watched the day break slowly outside.

It was going to be another cold, bright winter's morning. From the warmth of his hammock Stephen could see frost on the ground. The sun was rising behind the Lookout, darting fingers of light playing off the sea. He saw a small fishing boat returning up the estuary towards the safety of the harbour, wondering if it was the same one he had watched go out the previous evening, shivering at the thought of spending the whole night out at sea on such a small boat.

Forcing himself to leave the comfort of his hammock, Stephen dropped to the ground. Shivering he looked longingly at the wood burner, but decided to light it later, instead pouring juice from the fridge. Picking up a book 'A Pictorial History of Aberdyssyni' he slipped comfortably back beneath the duvet and began to read about his new home. He was half way through a description of shipbuilding in the early 1800s when a loud hammering on the window inches from his head made him jump and tumble from the hammock jarring his knee as he landed in an unceremonial heap on the floor. Looking up he found Rachel in fits of laughter outside.

Protecting his modesty as best he could with his duvet Stephen tiptoed across the floor and opened the door.

'Morning Stephen' said Rachel looking him up and down, her mouth twitching at the corner, 'I didn't get you up did I?'

He couldn't help joining in with her laughter. Marching into the kitchen area Rachel deposited another bag of food, keeping her back turned as Stephen tried to quickly pull on a sweatshirt and jeans, his entangled feet causing him to hop around like a demented kangaroo.

Fastening his belt, he saw Rachel already preparing breakfast with items from her bag.

'Shouldn't I be doing that? By the way it's only just gone seven'

'Is it? I don't wear a watch; I've been up for hours. How was your supper?'

'Yeah good thanks, I wasn't sure if the WD40 was a sauce or a dressing.'

'It's for the generator,' laughed Rachel, 'I'll show you after breakfast.'

They sat at the table breakfasting and drinking coffee. Rachel lit the wood burner, the flames sending a warm glow across the room and slowly raising the temperature. Outside it grew fully light, revealing a crisp and beautiful winter morning.

'So when are you planning to start writing?' Rachel asked, pushing away her plate.

'Soon, but first I need to do some work on this place, I want...'

Stephen broke off as he caught a hurt expression on Rachel's face.

'Not of course that there's anything wrong with it, I didn't mean...'

Rachel's face broke into an already familiar grin, her grey eyes dancing.

'Sorry I couldn't resist it! So you still don't know what your book is going to be about?'

'No, that sounds ridiculous doesn't it? I'm hoping moving here will give me inspiration. But I need to be organised here first.'

'You should see the mess I work in.'

'Tell me about your work, did you say you have a shop in the village?'

'Yes, The Gallery, come down and have a look later, you can tell me your plans for this place, I know who can help you if you need it. First come outside and I'll show you the generator, bring your WD40 sauce.'

Over the next few minutes Rachel gave Stephen a brief lesson in the operation of the generator, showing him where to fill it with fuel from the line of cans on the floor, how to adjust the settings and what to do if it cut out. She liberally applied the WD40 to the plethora of working parts, finishing by deftly re-fixing the chain on the old bike and oiling the brakes.

'...Just in case you want to use it around the village.'

Rachel left, agreeing to meet him at the Gallery that afternoon. Stephen pottered around his new home, moving his few belongings here and there, deciding on the changes needed to make it even more bright and comfortable. A creature of habit from his old life, he began to compile a list of jobs, prioritising them as he did so. Things were going to be so different; he no longer had a PA and a host of staff to attend to his every need. He wandered around outside, braving the cold, passing the time of day with a sheep that stared quizzically at him from the other side of the fence.

Around midday pulling on his jacket he headed off on foot in the direction of the village. The bicycle would do another day. It was still icy as he walked briskly along the main road, his breath visible in the cold air. He first passed a boat yard, then the station and Rachel's cottage with smoke curling out of the chimney. Walking under a railway bridge he entered the village proper, past a row of terraced seaside properties resplendent in an array of pastel colours. A large car park stood between him and the sea, deserted save for maybe half a dozen vehicles.

Stephen imagined it full to bursting in the summer.

To his left was a small, attractive looking restaurant, and way above, high on the hill overlooking the village, a prominent white bandstand, glistening in the weak winter sun. There were very few people around, an elderly woman scrubbed the steps outside her front door, a middle aged couple nodded to him as they passed, walking a small dog. A post office bicycle was propped against the wall opposite, a woman in uniform emptying a post box. She smiled and waved cheerily.

Ahead of him, the harbour. Stephen walked towards it, distant memories of holidays with his parents returning. He passed the lifeboat station, above which was the blue building he had noticed on arriving yesterday, its prominent position dominating the harbour and jetty. A large, attractive balcony ran the length of the front of the building, overlooking the water. The entrance, on the ground floor, was next to the lifeboat station. It was closed, an empty menu holder next to it. A sign identified the building as 'The Lobster Pot Café'.

Next door another building with huge wooden doors. As Stephen watched they were heaved open and groups of people in life jackets emerged, struggling with two bulky canoes. Instructors yelled directions to lower the boats into the water. Stephen smiled as he watched the chaotic gaggle tackle an unfamiliar task, clearly more at home in suits, offices and Starbucks. He winced as he remembered similar corporate development programmes spent abseiling and raft building.

At the far end of the harbour, three fishing boats were out of the water, balanced precariously on blocks of wood, in various stages of renovation and repainting. A short, stocky figure in blue overalls scraped away at the hull of one of them. He straightened up as Stephen approached, revealing a weather beaten face and white beard.

Stephen smiled at him. 'Morning. Seems like a tough job.'

The fisherman nodded curtly, returning to his work.

Crossing to the harbour edge Stephen leaned over the fence, looking at the jetty, a wooden structure stretching out over the water. He walked along it passing piles of lobster pots and fishing nets. A father and his young son were leaning over the fence dangling a long line into the water. Stephen watched as the father began to haul up the line, his son hopping from one foot to another excitedly as a large crab emerged, clinging to the bait at the end of the line. To yells of encouragement the man dropped the struggling creature carefully into a bucket of water.

Stephen smiled, lost in memories. That could have been him, this was the very spot he and his own father had passed hours on seemingly endless, warm summer days crabbing. He gazed nostalgically towards the beach, remembering games of cricket, his mother unpacking picnics on a blanket, fighting a losing battle with the sand. Sitting down on a wooden crate he looked out over the estuary. Those days seemed so long ago, his parents were elderly now, the heart attack had reminded him of their vulnerability. Where had all the years gone?

On the other side of the estuary clouds hung low over the hills, giving a mysterious air. Stephen imagined a time when smugglers might have crossed the water at night, their boats weighed down with contraband. Maybe that would be a good plot for his book?

Retracing his steps along the jetty he passed the harbourmaster's office with tide times and positions of marker buoys neatly displayed on a large notice board. Stephen glanced at his watch. Time to visit the Gallery.

Crossing the main road he entered the village square, home to a number of businesses. A butcher was doing a steady trade, its proprietor deep in conversation with an elderly woman carefully examining her intended purchase with a prod or two. Next door, the fishmonger had a tempting display of local catch in its window. Walking round the square Stephen passed a chandler, with windows full of ropes, life jackets, clips, hooks of various sizes, floats and distress flares.

On the opposite side of the square a delicatessen with steamed up windows, ghostly figures sipping coffee, leaning forward in animated conversation. Next door, a bookshop. Crossing the road to take a closer look he was immediately attracted to the window displays. Outside a rickety table groaned under the weight of second hand paperbacks. Stephen loved bookshops spending many a pleasant hour browsing in them. Pressing his nose against the window he saw shelves overflowing with books of every shape and size, wondering if one day his own books would adorn those shelves. Maybe there would be a window display with his photograph, possibly a book signi...

A sudden movement brought his daydream to an abrupt end. A tall, elderly, distinguished looking figure in a bright bow tie stared back at him from the inside of the window, inches from his face. Stephen stepped back involuntarily, smiled sheepishly, and fled.

Rachel's gallery was on the other side of the road, a large double fronted building painted green and cream. Running the length of the windows a sign, *Water Colours by Rachel Saunders.* The window displays drew his eye, a seaside theme, with deckchair, lobster pot and fishing net flanking a large painting of the harbour and jetty proudly displayed on an easel. In the other window wooden carvings of boats in all shapes and sizes, beautiful for their simplicity. If they were Rachel's work, she really was a talented woman.

Stephen pushed open the door, a bell jangling as he entered. Rachel was nowhere to be seen. Pale colours gave the shop a light and airy feel, enhanced with fresh flowers, their scent and gentle classical music creating a feeling of tranquillity. Framed water colours covered one wall, in the same style as the one in the window, depicting a variety of local views, with the coastline and harbour prominent. Below them artists' materials, paints, brushes and sketch books, together with a rack of greetings cards with the same local themes. The other wall was given over to wood carvings, dolphins and lighthouses as well as the boats.

A counter ran across the middle of the room, the area behind it contrasting sharply with the neatness of the front of the shop. A bench and sink were stacked with paints, paper and sponges competing for space with part finished carvings, tools, sandpaper and varnish. Dirty coffee cups and a half full bottle of wine added to the chaos. In the middle was an easel with a part finished painting, next to a table strewn with invoices and account books.

An open door led to another room at the back of the shop, through which a voice shouted.

'Hang on, I'm coming.'

Moments later Rachel emerged, dressed in a man's shirt several sizes too big for her and shorts, her arms and legs splattered in paint.

'You made it, welcome, are you hungry?'

Before Stephen could answer she disappeared again returning with plates of sandwiches, a bottle of wine and two glasses. She set them on the table, several invoices falling to the floor as she made space, beckoning Stephen to join her, finding him a stool. Rachel poured the wine.

'I thought you might need some lunch.'

'Thanks, but you've got to stop doing every meal for me.'

'I will, you can have your turn when you're settled in.'

Rachel sipped her wine.

'How was your walk through the village?'

'Really interesting but very quiet, hardly anyone around.'

'It can be a ghost town at this time of year, but most of us locals quite like it this way, at least for a while. You wait until summer.'

'There was a guy working on his boat, white beard.'

'Sammy. He keeps himself to himself.'

'I noticed.'

Stephen allowed Rachel to top up his glass.

'How long have you owned this place? It's really impressive.'

'About four years, I rent it from a guy called Conrad, he runs the bookshop. He also lets out the holiday flat upstairs.'

'I met him as well, sort of. I guess this is your quiet time of year?'

'Very, it's not really worth opening, but I'm here anyway working. Sorry about the mess, I did warn you.'

'But it must be busy in summer?'

'Yeah, that's when I sell most of my paintings, I sometimes get commissions too.'

Stephen picked up a carving of a sailing ship.

'These are wonderful... and tasteful.'

'You weren't expecting 'welcome to Aberdyssyni' ash trays were you? So come on, your turn, tell me about you, I'm intrigued.'

'There's not that much to tell really, I've recently got divorc...'

The door swung open with a loud jangle as a tall man entered, needing to stoop to fit through the door. Rachel leapt to her feet.

'Nick you're back!'

She ran down the room and threw herself into the arms of the stranger. They embraced warmly, both talking and laughing at the same time.

Nick was big in stature and even bigger in presence, standing well over six feet tall. Stephen guessed he was around fifty, twinkling blue eyes, a wide smile, a receding hairline with bald patch, olive skinned. A brown leather jacket zipped to the neck, around which was a bright red scarf.

Rachel walked down the gallery arm in arm with the newcomer.

'Nick, meet Stephen, he's just moved into the old Lookout, he's an author.'

She winked at Stephen, who felt himself blush.

Nick shook his hand warmly.

'Welcome to Aberdyssyni, a real life author, are you famous?'

Stephen mumbled a reply and Rachel rushed to his rescue.

'How long have you been back?'

'We flew in last night, spent Christmas in Greece, Christ it's cold here!'

Nick spoke with a booming voice suiting his stature. Stephen immediately warmed to him.

'Did you say 'we' got back, who's 'we'?' demanded Rachel.

'Kelly, she's going to help me run the restaurant. I can't wait for you to meet her.'

'Kelly eh, you're a dark horse, I look forward to it.'

They sat and chatted as late afternoon turned to dusk.

'Nick owns the Lobster Pot Café,' Rachel explained, 'the restaurant on the harbour, he's our answer to Rick Stein.'

Stephen laughed as Nick pulled a face.

'It looks great, when do you re-open?'

'Easter, providing I can paint the inside, finalise the menu and hire some staff.'

'Staff are his biggest problem,' confided Rachel, 'they are for everyone around here, you should have seen the pair he ended up with last year.'

'Don't remind me,' groaned Nick, 'I must get back, I've left Kelly unpacking. Pop in for a coffee. You too Stephen.'

He leapt to his feet, grasped Stephen's hand, gave Rachel another massive hug and was gone, marching off in the direction of the harbour.

Stephen watched as Nick crossed the road.

'He seems a nice guy.'

'Nick's wonderful,' Rachel smiled warmly, 'moved to the village about the same time as me.'

'So who's Kelly?'

'Must be his new partner, he's never mentioned her before, he can be a man of mystery as well, our Nick, he never talks about his past. Anyway, what do you want to do to my lovely Lookout?'

They perused the notes Stephen had made earlier in the day. Despite Rachel's teasing they both knew a lot of work was required to bring it up to standard.

'I need to decorate and change the lighting upstairs, put a shower in below, some more power points and kitchen cupboards.'

'Curtains?'

'No, I don't want to spoil the view, providing I don't have too many early morning visitors.'

'So you need someone to do the work?'

'I can do some of it myself, but it looks like I need a decorator, plumber, joiner and electrician.'

Rachel smiled. 'Leave it with me, I'll have it sorted by tomorrow.'

A short while later Stephen was walking back towards the Lookout, having bought last minute provisions from the fishmonger and deli just as they were closing. He relit the wood burner, feeling tired but contented. He'd enjoyed his day, tomorrow he would start work on the Lookout, then it was time to begin writing. He listened to the waves crashing onto the beach and watched a lone figure below him walking their dog as he unpacked provisions and began to cook.

That night he slept soundly, without dreams, in his hammock suspended high above the water.

Chapter 5

Waking early Stephen felt rested, enjoying the soporific sensation that often follows a good night's sleep. He remembered it was Saturday, although which day of the week it was already seemed irrelevant.

As he finished breakfast he caught sight of a post woman on her bike, swaying erratically as she battled up the road, a bag of mail balanced precariously on the handlebars. She dismounted below him and began to climb the steps, clutching a small bundle of letters and a parcel, arriving huffing and puffing at his door. Stephen was greeted by a small, tubby, cheerful looking woman.

'I'm Glen...Glen...Glenda,' she panted, adding, somewhat unnecessarily, 'your postie. Those steps will be the death of me. Will you be getting much post?'

She took off her glasses and polished them vigorously on her regulation Post Office tie.

'So you're the author?'

'Gosh, news travels fast!'

'You'll have to get used to that here. Is the kettle on?'

Stephen barely had time to step to one side before Glenda had climbed the stairs in front of him. He surrendered himself to the inevitable, it looked like he would have to get used to early morning visitors. He made tea, 'two sugars please, I need the energy, have you got any biscuits? I know I shouldn't with my figure'.

He concentrated on trying to get a word in edgeways.

'Twenty years I've delivered the post. Not that they care how long these days. I remember when you got a gold watch if you did twenty years.'

'Twenty years, that's...'

'As for that Nick at the restaurant I've heard he's brought a woman back with him.'

'Really, I met...'

'We haven't had an author stay here before, had a naturist

once, always out with his binoculars, strange chap.'

'I think you mean a naturalis...'

'That's as maybe, I'm under the doctor you know.'

'I'm sorr...'

'It's riding that bike, it'll be the last thing I do, I should have a van. Mind you I can't drive.'

Eventually, with much smiles and persuasion, Stephen ushered Glenda back to the door, promising to ensure he had plenty of biscuits in for next time. She was halfway down the steps when he realised she still had his letters and parcel. To avoid any further medical mishaps he ran down to get them, chuckling to himself as he did.

He glanced quickly through his letters, a bank statement, and a couple of good luck cards from former colleagues, before opening his parcel and carefully pulling out his 'Writers Year Book.' He scanned the content, chapters on how to begin writing, pitch your novel and find a publisher. He began to read the section helpfully entitled *'Getting Started.'*

Stephen was so engrossed that he failed to hear a rusty old van pull up outside. A loud knock on the door startled him. Another visitor, it was as hectic as it used to be at work! Outside was a small, wiry man with white hair who could have been anything between sixty and late seventies. He was wearing old brown trousers which appeared to be held up with twine and a jacket several sizes too big.

'Morning,' his visitor had a strong Welsh accent, 'I understand you have a few jobs you want doing, I'm Evans.'

'Thanks for coming so quickly, are you the plumber, electrician, joiner or decorator?'

'That's me.' Evans took off his jacket, sat at the table and pulled out his old battered notebook, taking a pencil from behind his ear.

'So what needs doing?'

Stephen put the kettle back on. As it boiled they toured the Lookout outlining the changes he wanted to make. Evans made occasional notes, measuring this and tapping that with an air of authority. He asked more questions over tea and then closed his notebook.

'That's no problem, let's get started.'

'Hang on a minute, you mean you can do all the jobs yourself?'

'I'll need a labourer but Rachel said you might be able to manage that. Let's go.'

Stephen barely had time to grab his coat before they were heading for the van. He realised he had not asked Evans the cost of the work, but it seemed a bit late now.

He eyed the vehicle with some suspicion, it had definitely seen better days. Ladders were tied precariously to the roof, a Welsh flag fixed to the one that protruded the most. Along the side of the van, in fading letters, were the words *'Evans Property Services. All trades catered for.'*

Clambering into the passenger seat, he made room for himself amongst boxes of nails and screws, old newspapers, pens and pencils, a sandwich box and thermos. Behind him the van was piled with a plethora of plumbing and electrical items; boxes of tools, odd lengths of piping, coils of wire, taps, brackets and plugs.

Stephen was thrown back in his seat as Evans accelerated into the road with a squeal of tyres, causing a passing refuse truck to take evasive action, accompanied by a long blast on its horn. He held on tightly as the van sped up, swaying wildly, its contents rattling and bumping behind him, Evans gripping the steering wheel tightly, a picture of concentration. Heading away from Aberdssyni they soon arrived at the nearest town, careering through the streets, scattering unwary pedestrians before screeching to a halt in front of a builders' merchants.

A visibly pale Stephen emerged shakily from the van following Evans inside.

'Morning Evans', said the man behind the counter, 'I see you've terrorized someone else with your driving.'

For the next couple of hours they toured plumbing, electrical and hardware stores stocking up with supplies along the way.

Wherever they went, Evans knew everybody, stopping to chat and passing the time of day with fellow trades people. He seemed to have credit everywhere as no cash passed hands. They sped back to the Lookout, sheets of plasterboard flapping on the roof held on with old rope.

Making a mental note to check the local bus timetable as a preferable means of transport, Stephen helped unload, lugging their purchases up the steps. Evans walked around ticking items off his list, measuring this and that, before placing his pencil back behind his ear with a sigh of satisfaction.

'Got to go, the missus thinks I've popped down the bowls club, she don't like me working anymore. See you in the morning and we'll get started.'

Stephen found the next couple of weeks extremely satisfying. Evans would arrive promptly at eight, and after standing outside with coffee and a smoke of his pipe, work steadily until one. Afterwards he and Stephen would sit contentedly looking out over the water, enjoying a sandwich and an occasional bottle of beer.

Stephen worked hard in his role as labourer to the craftsman, holding wood while it was sawed and hammered into place, drilling holes and screwing up light sockets. He was also let loose with a paintbrush, pleased with his efforts, and the way light colours brightened up his main room. After so many years behind a desk and in countless meetings, it was a joy to be involved in something so practical. The business world and all its problems seemed light years away.

He found Evans easy company, most of the time they would work in silence, nails held firmly between Evans' teeth, a pencil always behind his ear, but increasingly he would chat with Stephen, about his 'missus', his children and his numerous grandchildren. He also spoke of the work he had done for Rachel, at the Gallery and Beach Cottage.

He always left promptly at four, Stephen could only imagine where his 'missus' thought he had been all day.

Little by little Evans began to tell Stephen more about himself as they talked together while engaged in a particularly time consuming task like wiring the light fittings or tiling the shower.

He learned that Evan Evans (he assured Stephen that really was his name) had been born in Swansea very soon after the outbreak of the Second World War. A quick calculation from Stephen placed Evans well into his seventies, much older than he looked. He was the only child of Dyfed and Mary Evans, his first home a two up, two down terrace with an outside toilet.

'I never knew my father', Evans confided, I never did get to thank him for his choice of name.'

'What happened to him?'

'He joined up just before I was born, killed at Dunkirk. Royal Welsh Regiment.'

'I'm so sorry.'

'I've still got his medal, and the telegram. My poor Mum never got over it, she used to work night and day to look after me and my sisters, I remember her always looking so frail.'

'You were too young to help out?'

'I was until I was thirteen, then I left school and got a job in a foundry, I lied about my age.'

Evans chuckled, a far off look in his eyes. 'That's the hardest I ever worked but we needed the money, they were a good bunch of boys, looked after me. The foreman called me 'Evans' and it just stuck, now everyone does.'

Stephen thought of his own comfortable upbringing.

'How long did you stay there?'

'When I was eighteen I moved to the local steel works. Better money, I needed it, Mum was really ill by this point and couldn't work, just used to lie in bed coughing and wheezing, gasping for breath. One day my foreman told me to go home quickly, as soon as I turned the corner and saw the ambulance I knew something had happened. I was too late, she'd been dead less that half an hour. They told me it was pneumonia, but I know it was a broken heart, she never got over Dad's death.'

'That's terrible, I'm so very sorry, what happened to your sisters?'

'They went to live with my aunt, just round the corner, I kept the house on and supported them, I was determined to after all my Mum had done. I decided to learn a proper trade, got a job as an apprentice electrician in the shipyard, best thing I ever did.'

'Did you stay at the ship yard?'

'For a while, then I did my National Service. When I came out I had all my qualifications, got a job in the maintenance team down at Butlins at Barry Island.'

Stephen smiled, visions of watching Ruth Madoc in *Hi de Hi* flooding through his mind. 'That must have been interesting.' Evans laughed, 'best job I ever had, lived in a chalet, learned other trades, ended up heading the maintenance team.'

'Not a bad social life either?'

The old man seemed lost in his memories. 'It was 1966 when I met Anne, you lot had just won the World Cup. She was a singer, I used to creep into the back of the ballroom to listen to her, finally plucked up the courage to speak to her, what a beautiful woman!'

Stephen put the kettle on, transfixed by the story. Work could wait.

'She was a couple of years younger than me, came from just up the road from here, I'd never even heard of Aberdyssyni back then. When we were courting she brought me up here, mind you she hated my driving!' Stephen winced in sympathy.

'I met her parents, her dad ran the local property business, we got engaged at Christmas and married the following summer.'

'Did you stay at Butlins?'

'No, Anne was ready to give up the singing by then, we moved back to Swansea, to my old house, I never did let it go, got a job as an electrician. Had our first child a year later, Anne was a wonderful mother, and she took the choir and dramatic society by storm.'

'How did you end up back here?'

'Don't rush me, all in good time,'

Evans took a sip of his tea, relishing the chance to tell his story.

'By the early seventies we had three girls, then Anne's old man announced he was planning to retire and asked me to take over the business. I finally sold the house and we bought a cottage here.'

'You settled in all right?'

'Yes, it's not easy here, but her dad had a first class local reputation and everyone loved Anne so I got accepted. Great place for the girls to grow up, I've got eight grandchildren now, I think it's eight, or it might be nine, or is it ten?'

Stephen laughed, 'any thoughts of retirement?'

Evans grimaced, 'you sound just like the missus. She pestered me for years but I kept putting it off, liked to keep busy, then I had my heart attack.'

'Goodness, what happened?'

'I was up a ladder down on the sea front, got pains, next thing I remember I woke up in hospital.'

'But you were okay?'

'Only just so they told me, I was lucky, Anne made me promise to retire there and then.'

The memory of his own father in the hospital bed shot through Stephen's mind. He studied the older man with his pencil still jammed behind his ear

'You've not made a good job of that, have you?'

'I've tried but I'd be bored stiff. I tell her I'm off to the bowls club but she knows, she's a smart one, I drive her dull, she keeps an eye on me. Anyway enough of this, we've got work to do.'

Stephen really enjoyed the next few days, it was such a contrast from his previous life of meetings, deadlines and constant pressure. Under Evans' direction he chiseled, laid pipes and learned the basics of electrics. He dug the old bicycle out of the basement, and with Evans' help fixed the brakes and gears, cycling into the village to buy provisions, exchanging nods with people he began to recognise.

He noticed a flurry of activity at the Lobster Pot Café. Various vans were parked outside, and he watched Nick unloading boxes from an old Jaguar, accompanied by an attractive young woman with long, dark hair. Evans disappeared a couple of times to help with electrical work at the restaurant.

On one visit Stephen popped into the Gallery to invite Rachel to dinner to inspect the Lookout once it was completed.

Finally the jobs were finished. Stephen and Evans toured the Lookout inspecting their handiwork- a new fitted kitchen, light fittings, renewed wiring, a shower room downstairs, light colours, stained floorboards. They sat and drank beer, toasting their achievements. After much cajoling Evans eventually produced a bill. Stephen studied it carefully, before doubling the small sum.

A couple of days later a removal van arrived with Stephen's furniture and belongings, blocking the road outside the Lookout. Evans directed traffic, significantly adding to the chaos. Stephen tried hard to stifle a laugh as the two men complained bitterly and variously about narrow roads, the climb up to the Lookout and the long journey home. In their broad West Midlands accents they expressed amazement that anyone could live in such a strange building, or Aberdyssyni, or Wales for that matter. Finally everyone was gone, leaving Stephen in peace to unpack his familiar possessions, delighting in arranging things, organising his new kitchen cupboards, setting up his writing table and filling the room with music.

The next evening he cooked dinner for Rachel. They toured the Lookout, he proud to show off his work, she loving his enthusiasm. As they ate they chatted like two old friends relaxed in each other's company, watching lights reflecting off the water below and the marker buoy at the head of the estuary sending out its own comforting light.

Chapter 6

Morning dawned with Stephen sat at his new table, gazing morosely at the shoreline. Strong gusts of wind were driving the rain into the windows, creating ever changing patterns. The wind rattled the glass and the Lookout seemed to shake in the storm. The shoreline was shrouded in mist, the sea choppy and threatening, waves driving powerfully onto the beach.

He watched Glenda wobbling along on her bicycle, struggling to maintain headway into the wind, a bag of letters swinging precariously from her handlebars. It was an uneven battle, and she was forced to dismount, battling against the elements. Stephen could almost hear her curses.

It was after eleven, and the weather matched Stephen's mood. His third cup of coffee lay next to him, untouched and cold. In front of him, neatly arranged, were the laptop, a large notebook and a selection of pencils.

The day had been full of much promise, laying in the hammock, with warm memories of his evening with Rachel, listening to the storm, looking forward to his first day of writing. By eight he was at his table, three hours later he was no further forward. The notebook was a mass of scribbled words. He had a vague idea for his book, based on his previous business life he could picture a thriller about international espionage, traded secrets, blackmail and intrigue but he could not even begin to pull the threads together. A want to be author experiencing writers block before he'd written a single word! He had no idea why he thought it would be so easy.

In frustration, banging the laptop shut, he stood up, despite the weather he needed a walk to clear his head. He decided to stroll down to the village and call and see Rachel.

Lacing up his boots and buttoning his coat tightly he set off, the strong westerly wind blowing him along. Black storm clouds scuttled across the sky, the strong wind and rain almost knocking him off his feet. It was good to be outside, he could already feel his head clearing.

Reaching the village, on impulse he decided not to visit the Gallery. He didn't want Rachel to tire of his company. Instead he headed for the harbour, standing holding tightly to the railings watching the fishing boats straining at their moorings, threatening to break free.

Continuing his walk and turning the corner by the Lobster Pot Café he almost collided with Nick, emptying large boxes from the boot of his car.

'Hi Stephen', Nick shouted above the noise of the wind, 'fancy a coffee?'

Stephen nodded and pulled another box from the boot, following Nick up the stairs into the restaurant. As the door closed behind them blocking out the storm, peace descended.

'That's some storm' said Stephen.
Nick laughed, 'this is nothing you should see it on a bad day, make yourself at home, I'll just grab the last box.'

Pulling off his wet coat Stephen looked around him. The room was large and inviting, primarily given over to restaurant tables, a bar along one wall with high stools in front of it. Behind the bar, wine racks, partly filled. Boxes of wine, spirits and glasses lay on the floor and bar counter. On the back bar a large coffee machine with a fascinating array of nozzles, pipes and levers. Double doors on the back wall of the room were propped open, leading to a modern looking kitchen.

The restaurant was bright and airy, full of tables of varying sizes, most of them laden with half full boxes of crockery and glasses. A wine rack ran most of the way around the walls. Blackboards promising daily specials were wiped clean. The whole of the front wall was made of glass with large doors that would slide back. Outside a balcony ran the length of the room, wide enough for tables to allow dining in fine weather, offering magnificent views of the estuary and sea beyond.

'Is a cappuccino okay?' Stephen jumped as Nick appeared behind him. He nodded and Nick busied himself with the coffee machine, steam gushing into the air accompanied by the hiss of frothing milk.

They sat at a table sipping their steaming coffees.

'What do you think?' Nick gesticulated around the room.

'It's wonderful, so you're going to reopen for Easter?'

'I hope so, although there's a lot to do.'

As Nick spoke about his plans Stephen warmed to him, becoming more aware of his engaging personality. He had a loud laugh, and just the faint hint of an accent Stephen couldn't place.

'You must have really good business over the summer, how long have you been here?'

'This is my fifth year, it was a seaside café when I bought it, run down to be honest.'

'What did you do before'?' Stephen was conscious of intruding but Nick fascinated him.

'I was head chef at a local hotel, I rented the flat above Rachel's gallery.'

Stephen smiled at the mention of Rachel's name.

Nick caught the smile. 'So you're falling for our Rachel's charms already?'

Stephen found himself blushing and stammering in reply.

'She's a wonderful person', Nick continued, 'always full of fun.'

Stephen was surprised at a sudden feeling of jealousy as Nick talked about Rachel. He tried to push it to the back of his mind.

'How does the Gallery do?'

'Very well, Rachel's a very talented artist, she gets a lot of commissions for her work, especially the local stuff. She eats here regularly, get her to bring you for dinner next time.'

Stephen nodded, but found himself anxious to move the conversation away from Rachel.

'Where do you live now?'

'In an old fisherman's cottage just down the road, one of those built over the water.'

'So what's on the menu?'

'Fish, mainly caught locally every day, or from the fish market in Aberystwyth Lobster's the specialty dish but you would have guessed that. Anyway enough about me, how's the book going?'

Stephen blushed once more.

It's early days, I haven't made a good start, I'm struggling for a story.'

'Maybe you should meet a friend of mine.' Nick did not elaborate.

The door opened and a young woman entered. She looked a little taken aback to see Stephen. Nick quickly crossed the room and embraced her.

'Stephen, this is Kelly.'

Kelly smiled shyly, shaking Stephen's hand a little awkwardly. In her mid twenties, about five feet eight inches tall, slim, with long dark hair cascading down her back, brown eyes, a dark complexion- she was strikingly attractive. Not for the first time that day Stephen found himself envying Nick, an emotion coupled with relief. He was also fascinated by the age difference between them.

Kelly sat at the table, pulling her chair close to Nick, seemed shy, more than once looked at Nick for reassurance before answering Stephen's questions. Her accent was similar to Nick's but much stronger, foreign sounding.

'If you've got a few minutes Stephen,' Nick asked, 'will you help me with one job, I want to get the balcony finished?'

They walked outside. The rain had stopped and the day was brightening up. On the floor was a big pile of sail cloth.

'It's a wind break, I just need some help fixing it.'

They unrolled it and Nick showed Stephen how to fasten it to the balcony rail using rope threaded through brass eyes. It was hard work but eventually it was done.

'Come on,' said Nick a little breathlessly, 'we need a drink after that.'

Kelly had disappeared and sitting on a stool at the bar was a newcomer. Stephen recognised the fisherman he had tried to pass the time of day with as he worked on his boat.

Nick shook the newcomer warmly by the hand. 'Stephen, meet Sammy.'

The man with the weather beaten face looked up and nodded. He did not leave his stool or attempt to shake hands, leaving

Stephen somewhat embarrassingly with a half extended arm which he quickly withdrew.

Sammy appeared to be in his mid fifties, although his ageless face made it difficult to be sure. Grey hair, longer at the back and a beard to match. Perhaps more than anything Stephen noticed his piercing blue eyes. He was stocky, strong looking, dressed in blue overalls, an old navy blue jumper and wellington boots.

Nick disappeared behind the bar and found a bottle of whisky. He poured three tumblers. Sammy took his and clinked glasses with Nick. He knocked back the whole glass and returned it to the counter with a bang. Then without a word he nodded to Nick glanced sideways at Stephen, slipped off his bar stool and left the restaurant.

'That was Sammy' said Nick with a smile, 'he's fine when you get to know him.'

They pulled up bar stools and sipped their drinks.

'Sammy's one of the local fishermen,' Nick continued, 'he supplies a lot of my needs, particularly lobster.'

They talked a little more about Stephen's writing.

'You said earlier you have a friend who might be able to help.'

'You just met him.'

'Sammy?'

'Yes, I'll tell you more about him another time.'

Eventually, with the whisky lying warmly on his stomach creating a convivial feeling, Stephen stood up to leave, promising to call in to eat as soon as Nick had reopened.

The day was drier now, although it was only mid afternoon it was already growing dusk. Stephen walked up the beach, the westerly wind whipping spray off the sea into his face. The sand was deserted apart from two figures in the distance heading in his direction. He walked with his head down, lost in thought. He had loved his visit to the Lobster Pot Café, but it had only acted as a brief respite from his earlier writing frustrations. What he was doing here? What had possessed him to give up a perfectly good job for some pipedream, and ended up in this isolated village miles from anywhere.

He failed to notice the two figures getting closer. Suddenly the smaller of the two, the one with four legs, came bounding towards him, barking madly and wagging his tail. Lost in thought Stephen looked up just in time as   Bryn launched himself at him, almost knocking him to the floor. Recovering from his shock Stephen stroked the Irish setter as Rachel ran up, breathless and laughing.

'Sorry about that, he likes you.'

'I wouldn't like to think what he would do if he didn't.'

Stephen turned and they walked together back along the beach, Bryn running ahead of them barking madly at the seagulls, who seemed to take delight at taking off seconds before Bryn reached them. As they walked Stephen told Rachel about his morning. She slipped her arm through his.

'Come on, you need a coffee.'

Back at Beach Cottage Rachel threw some logs on the fire and drew the curtains. Bryn settled down on the hearth rug with a contented sigh and promptly fell asleep. Rachel disappeared to the kitchen and Stephen relaxed on the sofa, enjoying the warmth and the cosy surroundings.

Relaxing in an armchair, hands cupped round her coffee mug, Rachel asked:

'Come on man of mystery, time to tell all, what are you really doing here? I still think you've robbed a bank, or maybe you're an international jewel thief.'

Stephen smiled. 'If only it was that exciting, it's quite boring really.'

'Let me be the judge of that, what were you doing before you came here?'

'I was with a big company, one of the directors, been there since university, worked my way up.'

'So why leave, was it them you robbed?'

Stephen smiled and sipped his coffee. 'You have a crazy imagination, I just got bored, disillusioned really'

'With what?'

'Big company politics, greed, lack of integrity, the usual stuff.'

'So you quit, just like that?'

'Kind of, it had been on my mind for a year, I just needed to be pushed to do it. The divorce saw to that.'

'Ah, the divorce, I thought there was more to it. How long were you married?'

Rachel noticed Stephen momentarily hesitate.

'I'm sorry, I'm being too nosey.'

'No it's fine, to be honest it's good to talk about it, I haven't been doing a lot of that.'

It was Rachel's turn to smile. 'I'm a good listener.'

'Helen and I had been married thirteen years, we met at university.'

'Children?'

'No, thank goodness.'

'Why thank goodness?'

'I don't know really, I'm just glad, it would make it all more messy.'

'So what happened?'

Stephen stared deeply into the fire, lost in his own thought. Rachel made no attempt to interrupt, watching him with a small smile on her face.

'She had an affair, someone at work.'

'Oh, okay. It happens'

'To be honest it wasn't a surprise, we had been drifting apart for years, in some ways it was a relief, brought things to a head, too much unsaid for too long.'

'Is she still with him?'

'Yes, she moved in with him, I really hope it works out, Helen deserves more than I could give her. Or her me.'

Stephen caught Rachel's eye. 'Do you believe in soul mates?'

'You mean that the right person's out there somewhere?'

'Yeah, I guess.'

'I don't know Stephen, I thought it happened to me once but maybe its just romantic twaddle. So why come here?'

'The divorce made leaving my job so much easier.'

'You must have had to give up a lot, like money I mean, status.'

'Maybe, but what's the point of any of that if you're not, I don't know, happy, fulfilled?'

'So you've come here to find happiness?' Rachel smiled.

'I know, it sounds ridiculous doesn't it? I think I just needed time away, a fresh start somewhere new, maybe to find myself. Christ, that's even more ridiculous! I also got myself into a bit of a mess before I left, had a few problems.'

Rachel raised an inquisitive eyebrow but didn't speak. She was a good listener.

'It's okay, just the usual stuff, drinking, late nights, women.'

'Really! I must tell the village to lock up their daughters!'

'Don't joke, that was never me.'

'I didn't think it was, you don't seem like a womaniser, I think you're quite shy.'

'It was never me.'

'Why then?'

'Everything, Helen, being lonely, working too hard, it just happened, but it's sorted now.'

Rachel looked at him with a new understanding. 'I'm glad.'

'Then there was my father's heart attack.'

Rachel winced, 'you have been through it, is he okay?'

'Yes, thank goodness, but it's what I needed to come to my senses.

'So what's this author idea about?'

'Don't think I haven't been asking myself that every day. I've been harboring an ambition to write for years, another thing I always put off. When I took the decision to leave it seemed the ideal opportunity to get away for a while, sort myself out and give it a go. So that's it really, no jewel thief or international espionage I'm afraid.'

They sat and finished their coffee in silence, staring deep into the fire, lost in their own thoughts, Stephen glad to have the chance to open up, Rachel feeling privileged he had shared it.

Eventually Stephen turned to Rachel. 'When we were in the Gallery you promised to tell me your story.'

Rachel smiled. 'Let me get more coffee, then I will if you're sure you won't be bored, I did promise.'

Chapter 7

Rachel settled back, sipped her coffee and began her story:

Ned Saunders was half way through his second pint of Guinness when next door neighbour Mary O'Driscoll burst through the door. He had called into O'Donnell's Bar on the way home from work and had taken his normal seat in the corner, dividing his time between the sports pages of the Irish Times and chatting to fellow regular customers.

'She's started', said Mary, trying to catch her breath, 'hurry up.'

Ned swore out loud, downed the remainder of his pint and followed Mary outside, acknowledging the good wishes and witty comments of his friends, promising to be back before closing time to wet the head of his first child.

The doctor's car was parked outside his neat, semi detached house, and the midwife's bicycle was leaning against the front wall. Mary disappeared upstairs to join his wife, doctor and midwife, leaving Ned pacing around downstairs. He offered a silent prayer, the baby was two weeks early. Other neighbours arrived and a large mug of tea fortified with whiskey was pushed into his hand. Minutes turned to hours and day to night. Occasionally Mary would emerge, a worried look on her face but assuring him all was well. He prayed that it would be, surely nothing could go wrong this time? He wished Phyllis had agreed to a hospital birth but she had been adamant, the baby must be born at home.

He passed the hours slumped in a chair in the sitting room or pacing up and down, trying to block out the increasingly loud screams. Finally, just before midnight, he heard his daughter's first cries. Mary led him to the bedroom, and there propped up on the pillows was his wife Phyllis, looking exhausted, tears in her eyes, gently cradling their baby daughter. Ned stepped forward and took his first look at Rachel Mary Saunders. He thanked the Almighty as his own tears flowed, gazing in wonder at his daughter's tiny features.

Ned and Phyllis had been born within a few days of each other and grew up together in a small village on the west coast of Ireland in the years during and immediately after the Second World War. Friends from the moment they could crawl they had graduated from playmates to childhood sweethearts. Leaving school at fourteen Ned served his apprenticeship as a carpenter, the sweethearts became engaged, and then married at the beginning of the sixties, aged just twenty.

The same year they moved to a village close to Cork, where Ned found work as a carpenter. Phyllis was pregnant almost immediately but their son was tragically still born. A miscarriage followed, and the couple despaired of ever having a child. Fifteen long years passed, happily enough but somehow unfulfilled, before, in early 1976, Phyllis discovered to her terror and delight that she was pregnant once more. The couple lived in dread of something going wrong again, but this time their prayers were answered.

As soon as she was old enough to walk Rachel's desire for adventure became a nightmare for her parents, always disappearing, to be found wandering local streets, or even venturing further afield into the countryside. She developed a love for animals, and these two passions combined into several hours of horror for Ned and Phyllis when the five year old vanished one day. As nightfall approached they commenced a frantic search with friends and neighbours, and eventually the police. Just before midnight, as Phyllis was becoming increasingly hysterical, Rachel was discovered, fast asleep in a neighbour's garden shed, cuddling a kitten with an injured leg.

When Rachel was six the family moved to Dublin, Ned's reputation as a craftsman was growing and he got a job helping to restore some of the city's most historical buildings. They bought a house on the coast, and Rachel added a love of the sea to her passion for adventure and animals, spending long days wandering along the beach, collecting shells and investigating rock pools.

Back then Dublin was not the bustling, cosmopolitan city it is today. Rachel fell in love with its gentle splendor and liked nothing better than exploring the city, its park and the zoo at weekends with her parents. She was conscientious at school, showing artistic flair. She also spent hours with her father, inheriting his skill with his hands, learning to carve simple shapes from wood, Phyllis cringing as she handled sharp tools with increasing confidence.

Just after her twelfth birthday Rachel's life took another turn. Ned's reputation as a craftsman was now much in demand and he was offered a renovation role across the sea in England. The opportunity was too good to refuse and the family moved to Shrewsbury, an attractive town nestling in the Shropshire countryside.

Unhappy at first to leave her old friends in Ireland behind, Rachel quickly settled in and made new friends. GCSEs were followed by a move to the local sixth form college, and her choice of art at A Level cemented her love for the subject. Her talent was obvious for all to see and the first exhibition of her work soon followed.

Now a tall, attractive young woman with long blonde hair and a cheerful personality she became a regular fixture of the local nightlife, dancing with friends in clubs and at parties. Boyfriends were plentiful, but Rachel did not allow any to become serious, her heart was set on an art degree at university.

Then, on a summer Saturday, just after completing her A Levels, her life took an unexpected turn. After shopping and on her way to the pub to meet friends, wandering through the town, she came across a crowd gathered around a street entertainer. She joined them and found herself looking at the most attractive man she had ever seen.

In his mid-twenties and a couple of inches taller than Rachel, his wavy auburn hair reached to his shoulders. Most of all she noticed his piercing blue eyes. He wore tight black jeans, a collarless white shirt with a red bandana tied round is neck. A top hat at his feet was already half full of coins and the odd banknote.

Rachel watched spellbound as his act moved towards its crescendo. Using a petrol soaked rag to light four clubs he began to juggle, throwing them high in the air, catching them effortlessly, skill and rhythm creating an illusion of a circle of fire surrounding him. With a flourish he caught the clubs and doused the flames with a fire eating act that had the crowd gasping. Bowing low to spontaneous applause, he passed round the hat, acknowledging the many donations. He paused in front of Rachel, smiling as she frantically searched for coins.

'You're very good,' she said, thrusting coins into the hat, and wishing she could think of something more original to say.

'Why thank you, stick around I'm starting again in a minute.' He had a pronounced American accent.

Friends and the pub forgotten, Rachel made sure she was in the front row for the next performance. Juggling balls were followed by a plate spinning act, bringing cheers from the growing crowd. People came and went but Rachel was transfixed. The entertainer noticed she was still there, catching her eye and giving her a smile that made her stomach turn somersaults. He finished this time with a series of magic tricks, signaling Rachel out, inviting her forward and producing a long line of brightly coloured handkerchiefs from her sleeve. With a final bow he took his hat round once more then started to pack away his equipment as the crowd dispersed.

Rachel waited, rooted to the spot, unsure what to do until the entertainer looked up, and wandered over.

'Did you enjoy that?'

'Yes, you were wonderful, really talented.'
The man bowed theatrically.

'Why thank you, I'm Luke, I don't suppose you fancy a coffee?'

They found a coffee shop and settled themselves at a corner table, piling the bags of equipment behind them. Rachel was sure Luke would be able to hear her heart thumping in her chest.

She discovered that Luke Van Buren (he insisted this was his real name and he was distantly related to the eighth President of the United States) was twenty six and had been born in Boston, Massachusetts to an American father and English mother. His father was an actor and the family had moved to London ten years ago, his father still performing on the west end stage.

'Is he famous?'

'No not really, he's been in a couple of films as well though.'

Rachel loved Luke's accent, she could have happily listened to him for the rest of the day.

'So what did you do after you came to London?'

'Picked up some work in the theatres, anything, stage-hand, selling tickets, but I spent most of my time learning magic and illusion. There were a lot of good teachers. I also travelled for a while.'

'Where did you go?'

'Asia, South America, the usual stuff.'

The usual stuff. Rachel felt a pang of having missed out on something. Her life in Shrewsbury suddenly seemed small and boring, why was she not travelling before university?

'What did you do after that?'

'Started performing, got on the bottom end of bills, tough but a great place to learn.'

'What are you doing in Shrewsbury?'

'In between shows. Decided it was time I discovered the country, had never made it out of London, got an old van and here I am. The street stuff is to pay for the trip, not a lot of money in the theatre.'

'How long are you staying here?' Rachel found herself crossing her fingers tightly under the table.

'Only a few days, until people get tired of me or the police move me on, I'm supposed to have a license, they get worried I'm going to burn someone.'

Rachel's heart sank.

Much later that afternoon, after talking for hours over cold coffee, they parted, agreeing to meet for a drink the next day. Rachel spent the evening and much of the next morning in a dream-like state, convinced she would never see him again.

Over the next couple of weeks they became inseparable. Luke spent part of each day performing his act, while Rachel watched. They walked and talked for hours by the river Severn, and spent evenings talking until late in pubs and cafes before Luke would walk Rachel home, with long kisses goodnight. Part of Rachel could not have been happier but that was tempered with dread about how long Luke would be around.

Then it happened, as they strolled hand in hand through a park by the river he let her know he would have to move on in a couple of days.
'I've overstayed my welcome, the police have told me to move on, it's what happens.'
Rachel felt the bottom drop out of her world.
'You can't go, I can't be without you.'
'Rachel you've got university, your whole life ahead of you.'
She burst into tears and clung to Luke
'I'm not going, none of that matters, I just want to be with you.'

Luke should have been firmer with her, told her this was ridiculous, she was throwing her life away, maybe disappearing in the middle of the night, it would not be the first time. But something inside stopped him, she intrigued him, he had always lived life on the edge, letting his heart rule his head, and he had fallen in love with Rachel.
For her part Rachel had never been so sure of anything in her life. She didn't think about the future and its implications, that would take care of itself. She had to be with Luke, he was everything she had ever wanted. The prospect of adventure together overwhelmed her.
They agreed Rachel would tell her parents Monday evening,

two days before she was due to go to university. She still clung to the hope they would understand.

It turned out to be the worst evening of Rachel's life. Ned and Phyllis were aghast, they simply couldn't comprehend what their daughter was telling them. Years later she could still remember the hateful words on both sides.

'You have to go to university, you can't throw all those years of studying away.'

'I can and I will, I love him.'

'Don't be so stupid you hardly know him, you don't love him, he's a drifter, a waster.'

'You can't stop me.'

'You're going to university, you'll have forgotten about him in a week.'

'If you stop me you'll never see me again.'

'Rachel...'

Rachel ran to her room in floods of tears, leaving her furious parents downstairs. When they knocked gently on her door at eight the next morning Rachel and Luke were already aboard the early morning ferry from Holyhead to Dublin. A short scribbled note told them she had to be with Luke and she hoped one day they would understand. Her room showed signs of frantic packing, clothes strewn everywhere. Her passport was gone as was the bank card for her savings account. In their eighteen year old daughter's bedroom, with early morning sunlight streaming in the window, Ned and Phyllis held each other and cried.

It would be three long years before they saw their Rachel again.

Luke and Rachel spent a month in Ireland travelling round in Luke's van. The start of university term came and went, there was no turning back. They visited Rachel's birthplace of Cork, and explored her haunts in Dublin where she grew up. They stayed in guest houses or occasionally slept in the van, and in each town or city they visited Luke would perform his street act, while Rachel collected the money, earning enough to get by before being moved on. Rachel was so happy, she felt she was living in a dream. At one point she tried calling her parents but put down the phone as soon as they answered. It was all still too raw.

At the end of the month they returned to England, crossing from Dublin to Liverpool. As they drove through the city past the university Rachel watched groups of students on their way to lectures. It was impossible to believe that only a few short weeks ago she would have been one of them.

They headed for London, Rachel spending the long journey south curled up in the passenger seat watching Luke as he drove. They arrived in Islington at Luke's parents home in the early evening and Rachel nervously approached the door clinging to Luke's hand. She need not have worried, Charlie and Kathleen Van Buren greeted her like their own daughter.

There began a way of life Rachel could never have dreamed of. Luke found work back on variety bills and magic shows. They moved around the country wherever the work took them, sometimes staying in B&Bs where they would linger in bed as long as they could in the morning long after they were supposed to have vacated the premises, talking, laughing, making love, but more often in the spare rooms or on the sofas of fellow performers, where they would talk long into the night over warm wine, cold takeaways and the occasional joint.

Their fellow performers made an eclectic mix; magicians and illusionists, acrobats and comedians, all young, all with dreams of making the big time. Some were in couples and others on their own, Rachel was well aware of how attractive some of the women found Luke, but he seemed to have eyes only for her.

Rachel watched every one of Luke's performances, usually from behind the scenes, marvelling at his growing confidence. At night she would often lay awake, watching him as he slept, his long wavy hair spread across the pillow. She could not imagine being happier, pushing to the back of her mind the guilty ache for her parents back in Shrewsbury and the worry about the future.

Within a few months they were married, diverting a journey back from Edinburgh to visit Gretna Green, the tackiness of the surroundings doing nothing to temper Rachel's joy as she became Mrs Van Buren.

Weeks later she discovered, with a mixture of elation and trepidation, that she was pregnant. She hardly dared tell Luke at first, scared by what his reaction would be, he was a free spirit, would he want the responsibility of a child? She needn't have worried, when she eventually broke the news he was delighted, hugging Rachel.

A month before the due date, as winter took hold, they returned to Luke's parents, and on Christmas Day twenty year old Rachel gave birth, with Luke at her side in the hospital delivery suite, crying tears of happiness and relief as she held her son Joshua for the first time, gazing in wonder at his tiny features and mass of auburn hair.

Days later Rachel plucked up the courage to call her parents and tell them the news. It was the first time she had spoken with them since that traumatic night over a year and a half previously, although she had sent the occasional postcard to let them know they were okay. The conversation was difficult at first, Ned and Phyllis sounded older and wary, but after the initial shock they were delighted with her news.

As soon as Josh, he was always Josh from day one never Joshua, was a few months old they started travelling again, trying to find longer bookings this time to allow them to rent rooms. Rachel was able to see Luke perform far less, her nightly battles to persuade Josh to sleep often exhausting her. She also began to notice changes in Luke, almost imperceptible at first, but he seemed to grow more distant, losing interest in Rachel and Josh, often arriving back in the early hours, preferring to spend time after the shows with his fellow performers. As the months turned into a year the distance between them grew, Rachel increasingly tired of travelling, Luke more restless. Rachel found herself more and more disillusioned with her way of life, and eventually, inevitably, with Luke himself.

The magician had lost his magic.

In the end the separation was almost amicable. Luke was offered work back in America, on the undercard of a Broadway show. For him the opportunity could not be passed by, it might be his breakthrough. He asked Rachel to go with him, but they both knew it was half-hearted. There were tears but no recriminations as they agreed to go their separate ways.

Swallowing her pride, Rachel returned to her family home, taking Josh with her. Once more she needn't have worried, Ned and Phyllis welcomed their daughter and grandson home with open arms. A lot of water had passed under the bridge in three years apart but Josh helped heal the wounds and Rachel slowly settled back in.

A day didn't go by without thinking of Luke. Sadness, regret and occasional tears balanced with a sense of inevitability. At first they spoke occasionally on the phone and e-mailed each other, the enthusiasm always there in Luke's voice as he told her of his latest shows, while Rachel updated him on Josh's antics as he learned to crawl.

Gradually, however, the contact from Luke dwindled, he seemed to lose interest in Rachel and Josh and no money was ever forthcoming to support them. Some months later Rachel caught a photo of Luke in the entertainment section of the Sunday papers, now headlining his own show, leaving a New York nightclub, a blonde girl on his arm. That night she cried herself to sleep, then in the early morning light resolved to do all she could to build a good life for Josh.

As Josh grew up, he attended the local primary school. Rachel let his wavy, auburn hair grow, already he was the image of his father. She took a series of part time jobs, but as her twenties slipped away she found her life increasingly dull and restrictive. She had few friends, there was the occasional boyfriend but her circumstances made relationships difficult. The only things that kept her sane, besides Josh, were her painting and wood caving.

Just before her thirtieth birthday her grandfather died in Ireland, leaving her fifty thousand pounds, a small fortune, together with ten thousand pounds in trust for Josh until he was 21. Rachel was overwhelmed, she knew this was the chance to change her life. She just had to decide how.

That autumn she and Josh decided to take a few days break over half term on the north wales coast. She travelled by train from Shrewsbury, and as Josh read Rachel gazed idly out of the window, enjoying her first view of the sea as the train manager announced they were approaching Aberdyssyni. She was transfixed by the village as the train clattered above it, and of the view of the beautiful harbour and boats, as Stephen would be years later. As they pulled into the station she noticed building work transforming the station building and a for sale sign. As the train pulled out of the station she looked back, intrigued.

Over the few days away she could not get the village out of her mind, and on the return journey, on impulse and much to Josh's consternation, she dragged him off the train at Aberdyssyni, and stood staring at the for sale sign as the train pulled away.

A conversation with the builder revealed that the old station building was being developed into four cottages, and over a cream tea in the village as they waited two hours for the next train, Rachel made her plans, her heart beating with excitement. Weeks later she was the proud owner of Beach Cottage.

They moved in soon after and Josh enrolled in the village primary school. A thoughtful and amiable child he made the transition easily, sensing his mother's growing happiness, although he found the compulsory Welsh language lessons challenging.

For her part Rachel experienced contentment and excitement in equal measure. She felt completely at home in her new surroundings and had already begun to make friends in the village. Some people were inevitably less welcoming to a single parent but Rachel found it easy to ignore such prejudices. She began painting more seriously, exhibiting her work in a local show, proudly selling her first paintings and earning a commission or two. As Josh moved to secondary school in the nearby town, Rachel would spend her days around the harbour, sketching and painting, increasingly a fixture in the community. She began to run small classes, especially attracting visitors during the summer months, and rented some space in a sea front gallery.

Josh would sometimes ask about his father, and Rachel would show him scrapbooks and photos, but they never heard from Luke and Josh never pursued the subject. Watching him some evenings in the cottage, engrossed in a book or his homework, Josh's looks and mannerisms reminded her so much of his father.

Rachel's business slowly expanded providing enough income for them to live fairly comfortably, but Rachel was anxious to expand her classes. She discovered from friends that the old, deserted coastguard lookout just outside the village was for sale. It was the perfect place for classes, with breath taking views of the sea. She dug into her savings and bought the property, once more allowing her impulse to guide her.

Over the next couple of years, as Josh completed his GCSEs and began his A Levels, (including art and music, which was no surprise to Rachel), her sales and commissions grew, and her next decision was to find a business premises of her own. She found the perfect place right in the centre of the village, an elderly couple running an antiques business were retiring. The shop was owned by Conrad Hamilton, a flamboyant character, who owned and ran a bookshop a few doors away. Within weeks she had taken a lease on the premises, and she opened her Gallery weeks later. It was a proud moment as she watched the new signs being fitted. 'Water Colours by Rachel Saunders'. With her divorce long since concluded it was not a hard decision to revert to her previous name.

Rachel felt completely settled in Aberdyssyni, and more contented than she had before in her life, she was popular with local traders and her reputation as an artist grew rapidly. She became particularly close to Nick Thorpe, who rented the rooms above the Gallery as he prepared to open a new restaurant by the harbour.

The only thing that affected her contentment was Josh's growing restlessness. He had inherited Luke's sense of adventure and found life in such a small community too restrictive. He had the urge to travel and Rachel knew she must not hold him back. He was now eighteen, in every way a man, A Levels complete, university beckoning. The mirroring of her own past was not lost on Rachel. They agreed he should take a gap year before university, and in no time Josh had secured his place on a sailing ship bound for the Caribbean. He had plans to then travel through South America before returning home.

One morning in September, not attempting to hide the tears, she waved goodbye to her son as he sailed from Portsmouth on the adventure of a lifetime.

At first Rachel found it strange being on her own. She threw herself into her work, her reputation growing with each new painting. She would often visit the Lookout and sit for hours gazing out to sea thinking of Josh and Luke. One night she even caught a glimpse of Luke on television, his hair still long but now flecked with grey.

She loved the Lookout but also knew it needed to earn her more money. She decided to try to let it out, even unmodernised.

As the months rolled by she heard from Josh regularly, by e mail and phone. He was captivated by South America, combining work on various NGO projects with travel and exploration. He was now travelling with a girl, a fellow back packer, and it was no surprise when he announced he would stay a second year. Although tinged with sadness Rachel was proud of her son and knew she would see him again when he was ready.

She felt completely settled in Aberdyssyni, it was without doubt now her home. She acquired an Irish Setter puppy from an animal shelter and every day they would walk for miles on the beach, regardless of the weather, Bryn madly circling her in a constant state of high excitement.

The two of them would spend winter evenings curled up in front of the fire, Rachel sketching or leafing through books and magazines. Late one January evening, as she watched the flames dancing in the hearth, the phone rang.

'My name's Stephen Blanchard, I'm sorry to bother you so late at night. I've just seen your advert for the property to rent in Aberdyssyni. Is it still available?'

Chapter 8

Next morning Stephen walked into Aberdyssyni, his head still filled with Rachel's life story. He felt a mix of emotions, privileged that she had shared it with him, sad for how much she missed Josh, in awe of all she had accomplished as an artist, and disconcertingly jealous of the mysterious Luke.

The beginning of spring was in the air. Blustery March was slowly giving way to the beginning of April. Strong breezes still blew in off the sea, causing small clouds to scuttle across the sky and white foam to create endless patterns as waves broke on the beach. Herring gulls screeched and swooped, their brown feathered young gawkily attempting to copy their parents.

Stephen could not believe he had only been in the village six weeks, already feeling so much at home, despite his frustrations with the book. The village was awakening from its winter slumber, and although it would be some weeks yet before the holiday season proper began one or two more shops were opening and guest house owners were busy painting doors and window frames.

He crossed the road by the harbour, exchanging shouted greetings with Evans who was deep in conversation with members of the outward bound team outside the boat store.

Making the most of the weather Stephen decided to explore the other end of the village. Passing the Lobster Pot Café he paused by the slipway at the far end of the harbour, watching a tractor haul a boat from the water, its engine roaring as it climbed the steep slope back to the road.

Continuing on his way he passed a cottage built out over the water, guessing that this may well be where Nick lived. Then the Literary Institute, which seemed like a throwback to times past. A grey haired woman smiled and nodded at him; Stephen unaware that it was Anne Evans.

At the far end of the village, where the road swept inland,

Stephen followed a path cut into the rocks just above the water. A couple of fishermen nodded a greeting. Walking a little further he turned a corner and settled on a rock looking back towards the harbour. His mind drifted over his first few weeks in Aberdyssyni, writing challenges dominating his thoughts and he searched once more for inspiration. He had the beginning of an idea, could he base his story right here in the village, even write about real lives? What he needed was a story line, something to get him started, a mysterious character, some adventure.

Apart from these frustrations Stephen could not have been happier. He knew the decision to leave his job had been the right one, those dreadful weeks of lost control seemed like another life. He loved the Lookout and felt he had been accepted in the village, at least by most people. He particularly valued the growing friendship with Rachel, her story had been fascinating, how much she must miss Josh. Her separation from her parents must have been difficult. He realised how little he saw his own parents and resolved to invite them to visit. The memory of those dreadful hours in A&E were still fresh in his mind. Maybe they could meet Rachel?

That thought intrigued him. Why did he want them to meet Rachel? Why the pangs of jealousy over Nick and Josh? He mulled his feelings over.

Lost in deep thought Stephen failed to notice the tide coming in until he felt cold water lapping round his feet. Jumping up in alarm he realised the path back was already well under water. In a moment of panic, he noticed the steep cliffs above him, his only route was back along the path. Pulling off his boots and socks, jeans rolled up as best he could, he waded back through the now knee high water, gasping at the cold, trying to keep his balance on the slippery rocks. He reached the road with some relief! He had a lot to learn about living by the sea!

Stephen made his way back into the village. Passing the Lobster Pot Café, he noticed it was open and on the spur of the moment decided to have lunch. Nick sat on a stool at the bar with Sammy and a couple of other locals.

'Stephen, it's great to see you.'

'And you, I thought I might have lunch, check out your great reputation for myself!'

'In that case you must have the best seat in the house, come with me.'

Stephen smiled and nodded at Sammy before following Nick. Sammy returned the nod. Progress indeed.

Nick led Stephen to a table for two in the middle of the room. He sat facing the sea and looked around him. The restaurant was predictably quiet so early in the year, just two other tables were occupied, an elderly couple tucking into their lunch while two women were deep in conversation, heads close together, sharing a bottle of wine.

The restaurant had a welcoming feel. Tables were laid with cloths, wine glasses and vases of daffodils. The balcony doors were shut, but outside a couple of tables were placed in readiness for fine spring weather.

Nick was soon back at Stephen's side handing over a menu, filling his water glass. He disappeared off to the kitchen, leaving Stephen perusing the choices on offer on the menu and also on the special's boards around the room. The emphasis was on local produce, not only fish, but Welsh lamb, beef and seasonal vegetables.

Stephen chose a steaming plate of mussels, washed down with a glass of white wine. Both were excellent. As he ate, he watched Nick and Sammy, now alone at the bar, sharing a bottle of red wine, deep in conversation, heads close together, Sammy occasionally casting what seemed to be furtive glances around him.

Nick was back at the table.

'How were the mussels?'

'Delightful, how's business?'

'It's early days, but we're about ready for the season. Coffee?'

Nick disappeared back to the kitchen and minutes later Kelly emerged carrying a cafetiere, setting it in front of Stephen.

'How's it going, are you settling in?'

Kelly answered shyly, in heavily accented English, hurrying back to the kitchen as Nick appeared with his own mug of coffee.

'Kelly seems shy.'

'She's settling in, it'll take a while.'

They carried on chatting until Stephen, glancing at his watch, was surprised to find it was already mid-afternoon. He paid the bill and wandered contentedly home along the beach.

Over the next few days Stephen began to sketch out some new ideas for his book, focusing on how he could combine fact with fiction, basing the story in Aberdyssini. It seemed a good idea to try to involve some of the local characters, especially if he could find out some local stories and intrigue. The whole project still seemed a mighty challenge though, he needed inspiration.

He took to walking early each morning to clear his head. He would see Sammy on the quayside unloading trays of freshly caught fish and lobster from his boat in the cold morning air. Nick would be there in jeans and sweatshirt taking the trays off Sammy. One day, as he watched from a distance, just out of sight, Sammy dragged a couple of sealed wooden crates onto the quayside, glancing around furtively before passing them quickly to Nick.

Stephen also took to popping into the Lobster Pot Café for a drink once his writing session (or too often his staring at a blank computer screen session) was over. The bar was a favourite haunt of local characters. Nick always made him very welcome, and Stephen, at first aware of intruding, quickly found himself accepted by the group.

In addition to Sammy, who appeared to fish all night, drink red wine or whisky all day and never sleep, there were four others who gathered on the stools round the bar on almost a daily basis.

Jimmy was in his mid-fifties, a hairdresser with a shop on the sea front. Just below average height he had grey hair and twinkling eyes. Although he had been in Aberdyssyni thirty years there were still traces of his Cornish roots in his accent. Jimmy had a gentle manner and a whimsical view of the world, sharing tales and anecdotes with the others of people he had known in the village over the years. He had a nervous affliction, which caused his hand to twitch. Stephen made a mental note not to ask for a shave.

Early each evening a regular on a stool at the end of the bar was Bob, landlord of the local pub. In his late forties, short and heavily built, he and his wife Sylvia had run pubs in the Midlands for many years. Sylvia's serious illness, from which she was thankfully now recovered, had made them rethink their futures. A dream of retiring to the village in which they took their annual holidays was brought forward and their life savings sunk into buying a local business. Bob was straight faced and initially came across as dour, but that belied a wicked sense of humour. He regarded Nick, a fellow publican, as a kindred spirit and would engage him in deep discussions of the relative qualities of various beers and wines. Like publicans the world over he liked nothing better than sitting on a stool in another bar deep in conversation before disappearing back to his own pub, no doubt to a similar stool and the same conversations.

Billy was a local decorator in his thirties who had lived all his life in Aberdyssyni. His father had been a fisherman and Billy had joined him at sea after leaving school at sixteen. It had been assumed he would take over the business continuing a family tradition spanning several generations, but on his father's retirement he had chosen not to, selling the boat and setting up a decorating business. He was small and wiry, appearing early most evenings in his paint splattered overalls, his van parked outside. There occasionally appeared to be some tension between Billy and Sammy, Stephen wondering if it was connected to the decision to quit fishing.

The final member of the four was a larger than life character in every way. At six feet three inches and eighteen stones, Gordon dwarfed the others. A farmer from the hills high above Aberdyssyni, he had a voice to match his size and a wicked sense of humour. A fanatical Manchester United supporter and season ticket holder, he made the lengthy round trip to every home game.

He would sit at the end of the bar holding court, musing on United's chances of winning a trophy or two, and regaling the others with a constant stream of funny stories. He had a nickname for everyone and would drop these liberally into conversation. From his vantage point at the bar he would watch for people coming up the stairs. 'Look out here's grumpy' he would announce as Bob appeared, and 'stand by your beds it's the captain' announced Sammy's arrival. Nick was 'the boss' while Jimmy, predictably, was 'pasty.' Billy was 'paint pot', Gordon often expressing to the boss his surprise that overalls were acceptable in such a fine establishment.

Gordon soon learned of Stephen's writing ambitions and became known as 'Shakespeare', his half-hearted objections belying his delight at being accepted into the group.
There was often banter between Gordon and Nick.

'Boss why do you bother selling all that fish here, you'd be much better off with my delicious Welsh lamb.'

'Maybe the restaurant name is a clue Gordon.'

He would also offer Nick cooking advice, although this was firmly tongue in cheek, Gordon's sole contribution in his farmhouse kitchen being to consume the large meals prepared for him by his long suffering wife.

Stephen felt more and more comfortable in the company of his new friends. He enjoyed the stories and the mickey taking and was content to sit back and observe the various characters. He also began to get on better with Sammy, who was noticeably less distant, and happy to engage in a quiet chat. Stephen quickly became aware of how intelligent and worldly wise Sammy was, conversing thoughtfully on a range of subjects. He spent long periods of the day sipping his red wine or whisky but never appeared drunk, often silent and distant for long periods at a time before interjecting with a sage comment.

Weeks went by, Easter came and went, and the restaurant became busier with diners. Nick would occasionally introduce some live music, usually a singer and guitarist. One night Stephen discovered Sammy's party piece. There was a break in the music as the singer took a drink at the bar. Sammy, who had been quiet all evening, suddenly began to sing, quietly at first, but then louder, although seemingly still to himself. Silence fell in the restaurant as the diners listened. Sammy had a deep, clear, melodic voice, perfectly suited to his sad lament about a young girl lost at sea. As suddenly as it started the song was over, Sammy not appearing to notice the loud applause around the room as he nursed his drink once more.

As the days went by Stephen felt more at home than he could previously remember. Accepted by his new friends, he was envious of their seemingly simple and uncomplicated lifestyles. He was also aware he was spending far too much time in the restaurant, and had virtually abandoned his writing, his laptop mocking him as it stood open but neglected.

The subject came up one evening as he sat at the bar talking to Nick.
'How's the book going?'
'Terrible now you mention it, I just can't get going, I'm still struggling for a storyline.'
He was unaware Sammy, at his most quiet and morose, was listening until he heard a voice to his left.
'Come out fishing with me and I'll show you what to write about.'
Stephen was momentarily taken aback.
'Are you serious?'
Sammy just nodded, head down again, and Stephen missed the broad grin spreading across Nick's face.

'Okay thank you, when?'

'Not tomorrow night, the night after, meet me here at 10pm, Nick will sort your gear.'

The next day, with a clear head, Stephen felt much more apprehensive about Sammy's offer. His experience of boats was limited to cruise liners and punting on the Avon, neither of which seemed to equip him for a night fishing at sea in a small boat.

He decided he needed to know more about Sammy and broached the subject with Glenda as she struggled up the steps with his post. She was delighted with the opportunity for tea and gossip.

'He's a rum one that Sammy, so many stories.'

'Go on.'

'Disappeared from the village one day, gone for years, then suddenly he's back, just like that.'

'Disappeared where?'

'No-one knew, and he never said, mighty strange I say.'

'How long ago?'

'Goodness, now you're asking, let me see, I reckon he came back twenty five years ago, and then there's the smuggling.'

'Smuggling?'

'It's only stories mind, but there's strange going on at night, and mark my words, there's no smoke without fire.'

After some persuasion Glenda was eventually on her way. Stephen would have discounted much of what she had said if he hadn't noticed the furtive exchange of boxes with Nick. A shiver passed through him, part excitement, part apprehension for the night ahead.

He sought out Rachel, who predictably had more balanced views, while expressing some hilarity at Stephen's night ahead.

'Are you going to be alright, you don't get seasick, do you?' Her voice displayed not an ounce of concern.

'I don't know, I survived my Mediterranean cruise.'

For a reason Stephen could not fathom Rachel seemed to find that even funnier.

'I don't know why you find it so funny; I was seasick on that cruise.'

'Seasick in the Med on a cruise ship?'

'Yes, well maybe, it might have been the oysters at dinner.'

Trying his best to ignore Rachel's hoots of laughter Stephen quickly changed the subject, even thinking about the night ahead made him feel queasy.

'Do you believe these smuggling stories?'

'Who knows, but it doesn't matter, Sammy's a good man, he doesn't make offers like this lightly, you should feel privileged. Just be careful.'

'Why careful?'

'No reason just don't want you falling overboard that's all. Come back tomorrow and tell me how it went, I'll have the brandy ready.'

The next morning Stephen woke early. A storm had blown up in the night and the wind was whistling around the Lookout. With a groan Stephen pulled the covers over his head, half wishing bad weather would postpone his trip. He sat up and watched the rain hammering against the windows. Below he watched Sammy's boat, battered by the waves, struggling up the estuary to the sanctuary of the harbour.

Chapter 9

The strong winds and rain of the early morning had abated by lunchtime, the late April day was clear and cheerful. Stephen did his best to keep himself busy but as he tidied his garden area and collected wood, he found himself glancing towards the sea in anticipation of the night ahead.

As he worked his mind drifted back over his life with the realisation that he had so rarely done anything that could be described as adventurous. If he ever wrote an autobiography of his life to date, he would entitle it 'An Uneventful Life', realising this would make it unlikely to be a best seller. He thought of Rachel and her flight to Ireland with Luke, and of Josh, currently somewhere in South America. He felt a sense of frustration that he was not living life to the full. Surely there was time to change all that, he was not yet forty. Where better to start than a night of lobster fishing?

He found his failure to write extremely frustrating. At work success had come so easily, and with it the accolades, promotions and financial rewards. He had assumed writing would come naturally as well. He realised until he found a story line that would not change. Sammy's words from last night played through his mind. Could he really help? What did he have in mind? Lost in thought he failed to notice the ominous dark clouds massing on the horizon.

Leaving the Lookout that evening, dressed warmly in jeans, sweatshirt and jacket, he walked quickly towards the village, rain clouds scuttling across the sky, the gusty wind and persistent drizzle making walking unpleasant. He turned up the collar of his jacket and hurried on. What on earth was he doing?

The Lobster Pot Café was quiet, only two tables occupied with diners, at the bar Sammy, Gordon and Billy were perched on their stools.

'Evening Shakespeare', Gordon greeted him, 'lovely night for fishing.'

Stephen smiled nervously and took his place at the bar. Sammy was at his most melancholy, staring down into his glass, giving the impression he had been there most of the day. Nick appeared at his side with a glass of brandy.

'Drink this, you're going to need it.'

Stephen sipped his drink and listened to Gordon's stories of disasters at sea over the years. Nick and Billy joined in with stories of their own, each more exaggerated than the last, until Stephen expected to hear of sea monsters gobbling up whole boats.

Suddenly Sammy, who had not said a word for almost an hour, slammed down his glass.

'Let's go.'

Nick produced oilskin trousers and top, and Stephen struggled quickly into them, hurrying after Sammy as he strode down the jetty, 'good luck' cries ringing in his ears. The rain was falling steadily, whipped around by the strong wind. He thought of his warm hammock and groaned.

The boat was tied up at the end of the jetty. Sammy deftly climbed down the ladder and jumped onto the deck. Stephen followed a lot more gingerly, feeling for each rung of the slippery ladder. He leapt from the bottom rung onto the deck, the sudden pitch of the boat causing him to stagger and almost fall. Sammy handed him a life jacket.

'Put this on, you might need it.'

As Sammy disappeared into the wheelhouse Stephen looked around him. The boat was painted blue and seemed ridiculously small. The wheelhouse offered the only protection against the elements, the rest of the deck was open. A lifebelt displayed the name 'Kerkira.' The choice of a Greek name triggered a thought pattern deep in Stephen's mind, but it was gone as quickly as it came.

The decks were covered in an untidy mess of fishing and other gear. Coils of rope lay everywhere, mixed with cans of diesel, buoys, buckets, nets and hooks. Nearby were containers filled with foul smelling bait, the stern piled high with lobster pots

The engine burst into life, vibrating under Stephen's feet. Sammy was back at his side, motioning him to go into the wheelhouse. He nimbly climbed the ladder to untie the ropes.

Then they were underway, the Kerkira butting out of the harbour into the estuary and towards the open sea. Stephen found the going easier, the boat making good progress as it rode the waves. Perhaps this wouldn't be so bad after all.

Stephen looked around. Sammy sat motionless at the wheel, staring straight ahead, almost trance-like, an impression accentuated by the omnipresent bleep of the radar and the whirr of the wiper blades as they fought a losing battle against the driving rain and spray. To the rear of the wheelhouse was a small table, two benches and an upturned crate on which a primus stove was balanced precariously.

Pulling his waterproof tightly around him Stephen edged past the table to the door. He was almost knocked over by the strength of the wind. He looked up at the coastline, watching the last lights of the village disappear and then catching a glimpse of another light ahead on the hill, which he was convinced was the Lookout.

As they left the estuary and entered the open sea the wind and waves increased in intensity, buffeting Kerkira and covering Stephen in spray, forcing him to withdraw quickly into the sanctuary of the wheelhouse, struggling to close the door behind him. A poem from schooldays by John Masefield drifted into his mind.

Dirty British coaster with a salt-caked smoke-stack
Butting through the Channel in the mad March days
With a cargo of Tyne coal,

Road-rail, pig-lead,
Firewood, iron-ware and cheap tin trays.

They struggled on for another half hour or so, following the coastline north, making slow progress through the swell. Stephen fought back nausea, more and more convinced he wasn't suited to a life at sea. He was sure it couldn't have been those oysters in the Med. Just when he was convinced he was going to be sick Sammy turned the wheel hard to starboard and headed for the shore. Stephen could see sand dunes ahead and felt they were getting dangerously close. He was just considering the merits of alerting Sammy to the danger when the engine was abruptly cut, and Sammy was squeezing past him. Moments later he heard the clatter of the anchor chain.

Sammy beckoned Stephen out onto the deck and motioned him to stay out of the way. Then he went to work, Stephen watching in admiration as Sammy deftly prepared his lobster pots. He attached a lead weight to a rope on a reel to the stern and let out the rope using a motor. As the lead weight reached the sea bed he attached an orange buoy which floated on the surface acting as a marker. He then attached each lobster pot to the rope, weighting them and adding bait. One by one ten lobster pots slipped to the seabed. Then Sammy raised the anchor and the Kerkira was moved a few hundred yards further north where he repeated the operation.

The lobster pots in place, Sammy raised the anchor once more and they headed out to sea. The wind and waves seemed to have dropped a little and the Kerkira made steady progress.

Stephen stood next to Sammy staring ahead. He broke a silence that had lasted since they left the harbour.
'What happens now?'
'We'll be back for the pots in five hours or so.'
'Are we going back to the harbour?'
A feeling of relief swept through Stephen, he could make an excuse to avoid the return journey, the warm lookout was very

inviting.

Sammy didn't reply but instead opened a flask and poured two still steaming hot cups of coffee, to which he added generous glugs of a dark, suspicious looking liquid from a bottle with no label. Stephen took a sip and almost choked as the alcohol hit the back of his throat.

'Christ, that's strong, what is it?'

'Just something to keep out the cold.'

Stephen groaned, realising they were going to spend the night at sea before retrieving the lobster pots, rather than returning to port. Sammy must do this every night. He sipped his coffee, becoming more accustomed to the warmness of the alcohol in his throat. It created a numbing which was far from unpleasant.

A while later they dropped anchor and Sammy joined him at the table, filling a tumbler each from the same bottle. He raised his glass, toasting Stephen in a language he did not recognise. They sat in silence, Sammy motionless, nursing his tumbler, staring down at the table. Stephen did not try to break the silence; he knew Sammy well enough by now to know he would speak only when he was ready. He glanced around him. The whole experience was surreal. What was he doing here at one in the morning in the middle of the Irish Sea? In fact, what was he doing in Aberdysynni? As much as he enjoyed time with Rachel and his new friends the idea that he could become an author was ludicrous. An image of his blank computer screen drifted through his mind, mocking him.

'So what's the problem with your writing?' It was if Sammy had read his thoughts.

'Just can't get started, it's as if....'

'What are you trying to write about?'

'That's it, I don't know, I had some ideas, maybe a local adventure story, spies or something, but I just can't get going.'

'Why write about stuff like that? You don't need made up stories, write about real life.'

'I don't understand.'

'That's the trouble, you haven't looked, but the stories are all around you, the village is full of people with much more interesting stories than some spy rubbish.'

'Who, what do you mean?'

'Start with Conrad.'

'The guy in the bookshop?'

Sammy nodded, and something about his manner warned Stephen that further questions would be futile. His mind drifted, what did he mean, what was it Conrad could tell him? He was so lost in his thoughts it took him a while to notice Sammy was now on deck. He was holding a flashlight. Was he signalling with it? Moments later he thought he saw a distant light flashing as well but he might have imagined it.

He must have drifted off for when he came to Sammy was back at the table, their tumblers refilled, singing one of his songs, almost to himself, in his low, melodic voice. It suddenly struck Stephen that if he was ever to learn Sammy's own story now was the time.

So he asked. At first Sammy was silent, as if he hadn't heard the question, staring into his drink, but slowly he began to speak in a low voice which Stephen at first struggled to hear above the noise of the wind and the rain.

Sammy was born in Aberdyssyni, in a small cottage in the centre of the village, the younger of two brothers. His father was a fisherman, who had lived in the village all his life, apart from when he served in the merchant navy during the war. On returning home he had gone into business with Jimmy Davies, an old school friend and together they had sunk their life savings into the Eleanor Grey, a fifty feet long fishing boat.

Once more Sammy was silent, lost in his memories. Stephen was cautious about interrupting, but anxious to hear more.

'It must have been a hard life.'

'As hard as they come. Out in all weathers, they needed the money, me and my brother spent hours in the harbour waiting for them.'

It was a constant struggle to make ends meet, there were loan repayments on the boat and two other crew members to pay as well as keeping a roof over the heads of two families. The necessity to earn money forced them to sea in even the roughest of weather, while other boats tied up safely in the harbour.

'Did you want to go to sea as well?'

'Of course, it was in my blood, but there was football too.'

Sammy had been a very promising footballer in his early teens, the star of his school and area teams, he had even attracted the attention of scouts from as far away as Cardiff and Wrexham.

His father promised that on his fourteenth birthday he would take him to sea for the first time, to join his seventeen year old brother who was already part of the crew, learning the trade in the harshest of conditions.

Two days before his birthday Sammy was playing for his school in a local cup final. His wing half released him with a pass and Sammy was bearing down on goal when the opposing centre half caught him with a scything tackle, Sammy rolling on the floor screaming in agony. He was taken by ambulance to hospital with a badly broken ankle.

Despite being on crutches there was no chance he could go to sea on his birthday. He was devastated. On a bitterly cold February afternoon with an icy wind howling off the sea he hobbled down to the harbour and watched as his father and brother, with Jimmy and two other crew members, hacked ice off the deck before casting off. As the boat nosed its way out of the harbour Sammy experienced a feeling of trepidation that would not go away. He was desperate to swim after the boat and beg them to return.

That night a giant storm blew up, the driving rain rattling their cottage windows. Sammy and his mother hugged each other, praying that husband and son, father and brother were safe somewhere out there on the wild sea.

The next day the storm had not abated. The boat was due back that afternoon. Sammy hobbled painfully down to the harbour on his crutches, braving the wind and rain staring at the mouth of the estuary, willing the Eleanor Grey to return. As it got dark the harbour master urged him to wait at home, radio contact with the boat had been lost during the day but this was not unusual in extreme weather conditions. The Eleanor Grey was strong and his father an experienced seaman. Their last reported position was close to the Irish coast and they may have run for cover for the safety of a harbour.

That night Sammy and his mother were woken from a fitful sleep in the early hours by the whoosh of a flare calling the lifeboat crew to action. They dressed and hurried as fast as Sammy's ankle would allow to the harbour. Most of the village was there as the lifeboat headed out through the storm. The minutes passed agonisingly, slowly turning into hours. Someone placed a blanket round Sammy's shoulders as he shivered in the cold. Moments later their worst fears were confirmed. Wreckage from the Eleanor Grey had been spotted only a few miles from Aberdyssyni. The next day bodies were washed up on a beach just up the coast. The boat had been lost with all hands; Sammy had lost two of the people he loved most.

The next few days were a blurred memory. There were funerals for all five who had been lost and a memorial service on the harbour attended by the whole village. There were hugs and tears wherever Sammy went. The village which earned its livelihood from the sea united together in shared grief.

Months later a Board of Trade enquiry concluded that the Eleanor Grey had been damaged in the storm close to the Irish coast and had lost radio contact. Rather than seek shelter in a harbour Sammy's father had taken the decision to head for home. Nobody in Aberdyssyni blamed him for that decision, they understood why. If the catch couldn't be landed no money would be earned and wages could not be paid. They had almost made it but just a few short miles from the safety of their harbour they must have been engulfed by a sudden rogue wave. Sammy paused and took a long drink. Stephen felt tears welling in his own eyes.

'Sammy I'm so sorry, that's awfu…'

Sammy's voice was barely audible.

'The sea gives and takes away.'

'But you were so young.'

'It was here.'

'What?'

'This is the spot it happened.'

Stephen gasped. Now he understood a little more why Sammy spent his nights at sea. He chose to anchor over the very spot the Eleanor Grey was believed to have been lost.

Slowly Sammy concluded his story. His mother had been helped by charitable funds and they had just enough money to survive. Sammy returned to playing football, but his heart was no longer in it. As soon as he was seventeen, he followed his father into the merchant navy. For the next three years he sailed the world growing from a heartbroken teenager into an accomplished sailor, visiting ports on every continent.

'When did you come back to the village?'

Sammy thought for a moment, 'must be almost thirty years ago, my mother died the following year, she never got over what happened.'

'You took up fishing after all that happened?'

'The sea is all I knew. It's all I've ever known.'

Sammy lapsed into silence once more. Stephen was deeply moved by the story, he sensed he was one of the privileged few it had been shared with. The effect of the alcohol and the late hour made him more and more drowsy, his eyes closing and he began to drift off, leaning his head on his elbows on the table. His last thought before he fell asleep was that the time Sammy had spent away from the village didn't add up, there were a few years missing.

As he dozed fitfully, he thought he heard Sammy on the radio talking urgently in a strange language, then out on deck signalling with a large lamp. He came momentarily to. Sammy was nowhere to be seen. It must have been a dream.

Later he gave up trying to work out if he was awake or dreaming. At one point he was sure he heard voices. Peering through the rain splattered window he thought he saw Sammy leaning over the side of the boat, shouting to two figures dressed in oilskins in another smaller boat alongside, as they struggled to pass wooden crates up to Sammy.

He slipped into a deeper sleep before the noise of the engine forced him awake, every bone in his body aching. They were underway, Sammy motionless at the wheel. Stephen glanced at his watch, five thirty in the morning. Sammy nodded for him to pour coffee from the last remaining flask. His head was throbbing, and he sipped the still hot liquid gratefully.

Within half an hour they were back over the lobster pots. Stephen watched fascinated as Sammy hauled them one by one to the surface. Each pot contained lobsters, Sammy emptying them into containers of sea water. Once they had raised the second batch of pots Sammy counted his catch. Eighty lobster. A good night's fishing.

They made their way steadily up the estuary as it got light, the sun showing signs of breaking through after all the rain. Stephen stood on deck, tired and stiff, but enjoying the wind clearing his head, his eyes drawn to his home high above him. He felt almost serene, the long night increasingly a blur. There had been very strange dreams, and what was it he needed to remember about those missing years?

Moments later they were safely moored up in the harbour and there was Nick, Rachel and Bryn to meet them. Over breakfast in the Lobster Pot Café Stephen tried to explain to Rachel the events of the night. He shared Sammy's comments on the man from the bookshop. Was this Conrad the key to his writing ambitions?

Below them, just out of sight, Sammy unloaded his catch and passed two wooden crates up to Nick who swiftly carried them to his nearby storeroom.

Chapter 10

A few days later Stephen stood outside Aberdyssyni Books examining the second hand offerings on the trestle table. They made an eclectic mix; best sellers fought for space with classics by Charles Dickens and Jane Austen, while 'The Complete Works of Shakespeare' was sandwiched next to 'The Penguin Book of Quotations' and slightly less popular texts including 'The Accountants' Year Book' and 'One Hundred Favourite Crochet Patterns.'

Cautiously Stephen gazed into the window, checking carefully that Conrad wasn't looking out this time. Once he was sure it was safe, he examined the displays. To one side sports books were presented around a plethora of sporting equipment, including cricket bats, fishing nets and golf clubs, while the opposite side of the entrance door travel and cookery were featured, a globe and assorted pots and pans framed travel guides, maps and cookery books.

Taking a deep breath Stephen plucked up the courage to enter the shop. Parts of his night at sea already felt like a distant dream, but Sammy's words kept coming back to him. 'Go find the man in the bookshop. His name's Conrad, find his story. This is where I found her.'

An old brass bell rang loudly as he pushed open the door, making Stephen jump. He steadied his nerves and looked around what appeared to be an empty store, the smell of polish and old books mingling pleasantly. Shelves groaned under the weight of books of every description, divided somewhat randomly into subject areas including history, politics, economics, business, travel, sports, classics and art. Every shelf seemed to overflow, and where there was no space, books were piled on the floor.

He moved around admiring the packed shelves, occasionally

pulling a book out to examine it more closely. Several armchairs invited browsers to sink into them and read, an old leather desk to the rear was stacked with books and paperwork, next to which a spiral staircase led up to a mezzanine level with more book shelves. Framed photographs lined the stairs, each featuring a distinguished gentleman instantly recognisable as the bookshop proprietor next to a familiar face. Stephen moved closer to examine the dinner suited characters in the photos. Roger Moore with Conrad, with an inscription that read *'it's supposed to be me who gets the girls'*, followed by Moore's flowing signature. Next to it Conrad was featured with Oliver Reed *'here's to the next million'*, Brian Johnston, *'keep bowling those maidens over'*, Peter O'Toole, Peter Stringfellow and Leslie Phillips. This was indeed a well-connected man.

'Hello there, can I help you?'

Stephen jumped as the voice boomed out behind him, dropping the book he had been holding. Conrad Hamilton cut an impressive figure. Aged around seventy and six feet tall he exuded a distinguished air, with perfectly groomed grey hair and an upright posture. He sported a Harris Tweed jacket, perfectly creased trousers and highly polished brown shoes. A yellow silk bow tie completed his elegant outfit.

Flummoxed, Stephen dropped to his knees to recover the book, mumbling an apology as he did so. As he struggled back to his feet Conrad held out his hand, a smile on his face and a twinkle in his eyes.

'Conrad Hamilton, it's a pleasure to meet you at last Mr Blanchard.'

His cultured voice portrayed no accent.

'I thought you might call. How can I help you- or are you just browsing?'

Stephen felt his face redden and was once more lost for words. An all too familiar embarrassed feeling engulfed him along with the need to escape, emotions unrecognisable from his previous life. He mumbled an apology and fled from the shop. He was halfway to the Gallery when he realised, he was still carrying the book. Now they could add book thief to his charge sheet. It was not proving to be a good morning.

He did not stop hurrying until he was safely inside the Gallery, bursting through the door startling a couple who had been examining one of the paintings. They left in a hurry, casting Stephen a bemused glance.

'That's quite an entrance, I almost sold that painting, is there a fire or is this part of your fitness regime?'

'Yes, no, neither, I was in the bookshop and...'

'I see you bought a book'

'I didn't, I stole it,'

'You did what?'

'No I don't mean I stole it, I just forgot to, what I mean is...'

'Stephen sit down for goodness sake and have some coffee.'

As Stephen slowly recovered his breath and composure, he looked around the Gallery. Rachel was gearing up for summer, paintings covered the walls, and carvings the shelves. Classical music flowed from the speakers, helping Stephen relax a little.

Sipping coffee, he explained somewhat sheepishly his visit to the bookshop and his hasty departure.

'It was like he had been expecting me.'

'What do you mean expecting you?'

'He appeared from nowhere, he knew my name.'

'Well you are somewhat of a local celebrity. Or at least you will be following your court case for shoplifting.'

'Rachel, stop it, it's not funny.'

'Believe me, it's hilarious. What did you find out?'

'I didn't have time to find out anything.'

'I've been thinking back,' Rachel continued more seriously, 'there were stories about Conrad when I first arrived here.'

'What sort of stories?'

'All sorts of things, womanising, casinos, famous people he knew, I thought it was just gossip, but there was something else, a scandal.'

'Go on', Stephen sat bolt upright.

'Something about a woman drowning, a tragedy, a court case.'

Stephen put down his cup with a clatter, 'we have to find out more, do you know when this all happened?'

'Not exactly but I remember the late 1980s being mentioned.' Stephen thoughtfully sipped coffee before continuing.

'There's more. Sammy's up to something as well. Those voices at sea, and the boxes.'

'One thing at a time', Rachel smiled, 'let's focus on Conrad first.'

Over the next few days Stephen and Rachel began their investigation into Conrad's past. Stephen felt good to be involved in a meaningful endeavour at last and enjoyed having an excuse to spend more time with Rachel. He adopted what he believed was the manner and cunning of a secret agent, creeping past the bookshop on the way to the gallery. One morning as he walked by the harbour, he spotted Sammy and Conrad deep in conversation outside the Lobster Pot Café. He quickly crossed the road pulling up the collar of his jacket, failing to notice them watching him with amused interest.

They searched online for any leads or clues as to Conrad's past and news of a drowning or court case without success. They broke off for coffee and to consider other options when Rachel's lap-top pinged. As she read the e-mail Stephen noticed the sad look in her eyes, she sniffled on a tissue.

'Are you okay?'

'Yes, I'm sorry, I didn't mean to get upset, it was Josh.'

'A problem?'

'Not really, he's told me he's now travelling in Bolivia with his new girlfriend so won't be home anytime soon.'

'You must miss him.'

'Desperately but I'm the one who encouraged him to travel so I've only got myself to blame.'

'Did he say when he might be home?'

'No, and I don't want to be seen to be pushing him, but I so hope he'll be back for Christmas, he's twenty one on Christmas Day. Where does the time go?'

With a quick change of subject from Rachel they reviewed

next steps. There must be detail of what happened somewhere. They decided a search of back copies of the Western Mail might provide some answers. Further research revealed that those from around the time were not available online yet but could be viewed at the National Library of Wales in Aberystwyth. A visit there seemed the logical next step.

Stephen planned to make the journey by train, but Rachel insisted he should borrow her Land Rover for the day. He was not enthusiastic, already viewing her vehicle with suspicion, but Rachel was adamant. A couple of days later, on a bright morning in mid-May, Stephen climbed warily into the driver's seat, turned the key and the engine burst noisily into life.

He selected first gear with a jarring crunch and pulled away from the kerb. As he did so he heard Rachel shout 'don't forget to...' but the rest of the sentence was lost in the roar of the engine.

Stephen drove slowly out of Aberdyssyni. He was used to the comfort and refinement of an executive company car and this was an altogether different and more challenging experience. The noise of the engine made it almost impossible to think, there was no radio, not that he could have heard it anyway, and the vibration and wind noise when he reached forty miles per hour was disconcerting in the extreme! In addition, whenever he changed into third gear it jumped back to neutral causing even more shudders and shakes and the heater blasted out hot air constantly defying his attempts to switch it off.

Two hours later, extremely relieved, he pulled into the car park of the National Library. As he turned off the engine the silence was deafening. He carefully climbed out, every bone in his body aching.

Explaining the purpose of his visit to the bored looking woman at the enquiries counter he was directed to a reading room on the second floor. There he struck lucky. An earnest young man who introduced himself as Peter was intrigued by Stephen's story and only too willing to help. He explained that he was a student from the nearby university who volunteered at the library.

They began by examining microfiche records of the Western Mail from 1987 onwards. Stephen hoped Rachel had been right about the dates. It was painstaking work but Stephen loved having a purpose to focus on again. He realised there were things about his previous life he missed, especially immersing himself in a project.

It took him more than two hours to do the first two years, and he was beginning to despair when he reached an edition from the middle of 1989. Gasping with excitement he grabbed Peter's arm. There it was, a page three story with a picture of a much younger but instantly recognisable Sammy staring out at him under the headline *'Fisherman finds body in Irish Sea.'*

Stephen studied the photo. Sammy was standing next to his boat, stacked with lobster pots, on what was without question the jetty at Aberdyssyni. He read on. Below the headline was a further one in smaller font, *'Playboy arrested in Aberdyssyni, murder charges likely,'* followed by the article.

'Police are beginning a murder investigation in the Aberdyssyni area after local fisherman Sammy Owen (27) found the body of a woman in the Irish Sea. The body, which became tangled in the fishing nets overnight, has been identified as Tania Phillips, 37, from Surrey who had recently arrived in Aberdyssyni by yacht with her husband Dominic Phillips, 55. Mr Phillips had reported his wife missing the previous day.
Following a tip off Conrad Hamilton, 42, a renowned playboy and gambler who recently moved to the village, is helping police with their enquiries. DCI Lewis Hughes told our reporter 'enquiries are at an early stage but I can confirm that a 42 year old man is in custody.'

Stephen read and re-read the article several times, his palms sweaty with excitement. At last he was on to something. But what had happened next? Did they have a murderer in their midst? Had Conrad served his time in prison and returned to Aberdyssyni? So many unanswered questions. He thought about continuing his search for newspaper articles, but that might take several more hours and he needed to get back. He thanked Peter profusely and left clutching a copy of the article.

Stephen drove back deep in thought, hardly noticing the roars and bangs which accompanied every gear change. In the middle of a quiet stretch of road the Land Rover suddenly lost power, jerking and jumping before the engine cut out completely forcing him to coast to a stop on the grass verge. He desperately tried to start the engine again but with no success. Checking the fuel gauge, it showed three quarters full, Stephen climbed wearily out and opened the bonnet, staring at the engine in the hope of inspiration. Vehicle maintenance had never been his thing.

He pulled his mobile from his pocket, but had no signal, no doubt due to his remote location surrounded by hills. Cursing the gods that seemed to be conspiring against him he began to trudge towards some distant buildings ahead in search of a telephone. Ten minutes later he arrived to find one was a pub, a ramshackle old inn called The Farmers Arms. He glanced at his watch, already three in the afternoon, then pushed open the door. The landlord, a large balding man, was behind the bar, deep in conversation with four customers also standing at the bar. Conversation ceased abruptly as he entered, as five faces glared suspiciously at him. Stephen assumed that strangers were not regular of welcome visitors to this particular hostelry.

He was naturally uncomfortable in these situations and took a deep breath.
'Good afternoon, I've broken down up the road, do you have a telephone I could borrow?'
Maintaining absolute silence, and under the watchful eyes of his customers, the landlord reached below the counter and pulled out an ancient coin operated telephone which he set

down on the bar. With a sigh Stephen realised he would have to make the call in front of his audience, who were regarding him as if he had just arrived from some distant planet. Stephen reckoned that this was just about as exciting as it gets in this village.

Trying to pretend they were not there he inserted some coins and dialled the number of the Gallery. Rachel answered almost immediately.

'Rachel, it's Stephen, I've broken down'. 'What? What do you mean I need a doctor?' 'No I mean your old Land Rover has broken down, not me, stop trying to be funny'. 'What?' 'Okay I'm sorry your Land Rover isn't old'. 'What's wrong with it?' 'I've no idea, I wouldn't be ringing you if I knew, would I? No I'm not losing my temper, I'm very calm. Where am I? I'm in a pub. I know it's too early to drink, I needed the telephone, will you be serious for just one moment?'

Stephen glanced round and his companions, who had been staring at him, clinging to every word, immediately looked down at their glasses. He began to speak in an exaggerated whisper.

'No I haven't run out of fuel. I'm not that stupid. What do you mean stop whispering? I said I'm not stupid, the gauge is showing three quarters full. What do you mean it doesn't work? Why didn't you tell me? No you didn't. Don't shout I'm not deaf. When did you tell me? Hang on.'

He glanced round the room again and this time his audience did not look away but stared at him, willing him to continue the call. It must be a long time since they had entertainment like this! He felt uncomfortably like the village idiot, although looking around he reasoned he had competition for that particular title.

Continuing even more furtively, his hand over his mouth-

'You said something as I drove away but I couldn't hear you. I didn't know I needed to buy fuel. Okay, of course I will, I'm not stupid.'

A few minutes later he was trudging down the road, laughter still ringing in his ears, aware that the landlord and his customers would be dining out on this story for weeks to come. After a mile or so he spotted an ancient petrol pump up ahead and soon arrived at a small garage which seemed to have been lost in time since the 1960s. The owner, who belonged to the same era, extracted himself from underneath an old car and stood up, wiping his grease covered hands on equally covered overalls. He began his story but the owner just nodded and ferreted around for a can. Jungle drums beat fast in this village.

Twenty minutes later Stephen was on his way having filled up with fuel and returned the can. The rest of the journey passed without mishap and by early evening he was nosing along the main street in Aberdyssyni, achy and tired but also exhilarated with the progress he had made. He looked forward to sharing his findings with Rachel. He noticed how many people were now around enjoying the last of the sun. Summer had crept up unnoticed. It was time to get on with writing and mystery solving.

Chapter 11

'Go on, tell me once more what happened when you got to the pub'

Stephen groaned. This was the third time Rachel had asked him to recount the story, she seemed to find it even more hilarious each time.

'Leave it now, it's embarrassing.'

'You embarrassed Stephen? Never!'

Stephen cringed once more at the memories of the previous day then turned his attention back to the article spread out on the Lookout table. They had been pouring over it for half an hour already.

'Tell me again about the stories you heard about Conrad.'

Rachel frowned, trying to remember.

'It's what I told you before, it's all a bit hazy, it was over ten years ago, I remember when I first moved here there were stories about a drowning and a court case, even then it was ancient history though.'

'What else?'

'Nothing I remember, it's funny though, I have a vague memory of something local in the news when we first moved to Shrewsbury, a court case.'

'What was it?'

'I can't remember, why don't you just ask Conrad?'

Stephen felt himself reddening up again.

'I can't, not after what happened last time, and I've still got the book.'

'Ah yes, the master criminal, the Ronnie Biggs of Aberdyssyni, I forgot.'

'it's not like...'

Too late he caught the grin on Rachel's face. 'Stop it, what do we do next.'

'Why don't you talk to Sammy again?'

Later that day Stephen went in search of Sammy. He was not on his usual stool in the Lobster Pot Café, and Nick had not seen

94

him all day. He suggested Stephen try Sammy's cottage.

Stephen walked back across the square, hurrying past the bookshop with his head down before giving Rachel a conspiratol thumbs up as he passed the gallery. Feeling every inch an agent on a mission he crossed the road and climbed the hill towards the bandstand, remembering the directions Nick had given him. Near the top of the hill a lane on his left led to three small white cottages. To the left of the blue front door was its name 'Ipsos'. Another Greek connection.

Sammy did not seem surprised to see him. He led Stephen into a small and snug front room, muttered something about coffee and disappeared. Stephen looked around him, taken by surprise. He had expected a typical fisherman's cottage, plain and old fashioned, instead he stood in a tastefully decorated room, painted terracotta and cream, furnished elegantly with antique chairs and cabinets. Classical music filled the air, a bookcase overflowed with books on art and wine. Paintings on the walls depicted Mediterranean scenes, white cottages against a background of blue sea and azure sky.

Sammy returned with coffee accompanied by tumblers of brandy. The warm taste in his throat reminded Stephen of his night at sea. Connections ran round his head but he just couldn't piece them together.

Stephen recounted the story of his visit to the National Library, carefully omitting any mention of the fuel incident. With a flourish he pulled out the copy of the Western Mail article. Sammy studied it carefully, a smile on his face as he examined the photograph.

'I haven't seen this in years. So long ago, almost thirty years.' For a moment he was lost in memories before handing back the article.

'That's a good start, but what else do you know, who was Tania Phillips, why was she here, how was Conrad involved?' The look on Stephen's face confirmed these were exactly the questions he had been asking himself.

'Remember what I said,' Sammy continued, 'you can't be given the answers, you need to find them out for yourself.'

Early that evening Stephen sat on his stool at the Lobster Pot Café staring morosely into his drink having spent a fruitless afternoon trying to work out what to do next. Even a long walk to clear his head hadn't helped. He considered how he would have approached the challenge in his previous life, no doubt he would have delegated it to his team, expecting the solution on his desk within a couple of days.

Sammy and Nick joined him, and he shared his frustrations.
'So that's where I am, I still don't know why he did it or how to find out more about...'

He jumped out of his skin as a hand was placed on shoulder.
'Well dear boy,' said a familiar cultured voice, 'you could always try asking me!'
Stephen swung round to find Conrad facing him. He opened and closed his mouth like a goldfish, unable to summon up any words beyond 'it's you...'
'It certainly is,' replied Conrad, trying to keep a straight face, 'I understand you've been doing a little detective work behind my back.'
'No, I mean yes, no, sorry...'
He broke off as he noticed Conrad wink at Nick and Sammy, all three of them trying unsuccessfully to suppress laughter. Stephen realised he had been set up.
Trying to keep a straight face Conrad put him out of his misery.
'Well dear boy why don't I fill in the gaps, but it's going to cost you dinner tonight, and a bottle of Nick's best wine. See you at 8pm sharp, and I think you might have something to return to me.'

Stephen was back in the Lobster Pot Café in good time, he'd even put on a tie for the occasion. Under his arm he clutched the book, still cringing with embarrassment. He had called in quickly at Beach Cottage to update Rachel, who hadn't seemed at all surprised, she was no doubt also in on the act.

Nick showed him to a reserved table in the corner and five minutes later Conrad joined him, impeccably dressed as ever in a dark blazer and yellow and blue bow tie, every inch the archetypal country gentleman. They drank to each other's health and Stephen launched into the opening speech he had been rehearsing earlier.

'Mr Hamilton, I'm really sorry about snooping, let me expl...' He was cut off with a wave of the hand.

'Dear boy, please call me Conrad, there's nothing to apologise for, it's a long time since I had so much fun. Sammy, Nick and Rachel have a lot to answer for. You have good friends there. Sammy's told me I'm going to feature in your book and I'm about to enjoy an excellent dinner. Talking of books have you got something for me?'

'I'm so sorry, I don't know what came over me.'

'Don't worry old boy, I'll tell the police they can call off the investigation. No need to involve Interpol after all, now shall we order, that's the important business.'

Nick appeared carrying a bottle of red wine, which he and Conrad studied reverentially. He poured a small taste for Conrad who nodded appreciatively.

'Excellent, simply divine.'

As they ate Conrad asked Stephen about his past. He was a first class listener and genuinely interested in his decision to move to Aberdyssyni to write. Main course plates were cleared away and Conrad sank back in his seat with a deep sigh of satisfaction, cradling his glass.

'Well dear boy, you've been very patient, let me tell you my story.'

Cheese arrived, accompanied by glasses of vintage port. Stephen relaxed and listened attentively, trying not to interrupt the flow.

Conrad Cecil Augustus Hamilton was born soon after the Second World War. There is an old story about being born with a silver spoon in your mouth, and this was certainly the case for Conrad, the second son of Major General Cecil Herbert Hamilton and his wife Primrose. His father, already fifty, had enjoyed a distinguished military career, which included medals for bravery won as a young officer in the First World War. He was now Lord Lieutenant of Hertfordshire, and home was a magnificent stately residence set in acres of parkland. The young Conrad was looked after by a succession of nannies as his parents focused on their official duties in the austere post war years. He would spend days on end exploring the house and grounds with Richard, his elder brother by three years, who possessed the ability to cause constant mischief and then ensure Conrad took the blame.

Sculleries, cellars, the kitchen garden, greenhouses, orchard and even a lake with a boathouse made a fine playground, but Conrad was most fascinated with the library, covered from floor to ceiling in dusty old volumes. He discovered an early love of books and would spend hours gazing at the shelves and leafing through volumes, much to his brother's disgust.

When he was seven, Conrad was sent away to join his brother at boarding school. He grew distant from his father, a strict disciplinarian still living in Victorian times. Even then he realised Richard was the favourite, already excelling academically and at sport, Conrad showing no interest or application for either.

As time went by the gap widened between father and younger son, and between the achievements of the siblings. Richard gained a place at Eton, his father's Alma Mater, while Conrad was sent to a minor public school. Richard excelled at Eton, winning prizes for classics and mathematics, representing the college at rugby and cricket. Conrad struggled in comparison, school reports depicting him as a loner prone to day dreaming, possessing little aptitude for Latin, Greek and the Classics or enthusiasm for sport, always with his nose in a book.

He rarely saw his father, who had no desire to discover or support his interests, preferring to cheer on Richard's tries and runs. He was closer to his mother who, overshadowed by her domineering husband, was too often distant.

In the early 1960s Richard went up to Cambridge to read Classics and win sporting blues. In comparison Conrad drifted through the last of his school years feeling increasingly alone, deeply saddened by the death of his mother after a short illness. He struggled through his exams, scraping a place at University College London to read English Literature.

Two months after starting at university Conrad's life took a new turn with the sudden death of his father from a heart attack.

A few weeks later Conrad sat with Richard in the family solicitor's office, surrounded by relatives, some of whom he had never met. It certainly proved the old saying 'where there's a will there's a crowd.' An hour later he understood fully the gulf in his father's feelings for him and his brother. Richard inherited the family estate, various other properties, shooting rights in the Scottish highlands and close on a million pounds. Some relatives received bequeaths leaving others indignant. A terse final paragraph left Conrad fifty thousand pounds and the contents of the library, together with an instruction that money and books would be placed in trust and only released if he achieved a first class honours degree. Anything else and they would pass to Richard.
Conrad paused to empty his glass. Stephen, listening intently and immersed in the story, leaned forward.
'That was so unfair.'
'Yes well there's my father for you.'
'What happened, did you get the first clas...'
'Slow down, all in good time.' Conrad motioned to Nick to refill their glasses before continuing.

Over the next three years Conrad worked to prove his father wrong. He had a genuine interest in his study of literature, for the first time enjoying his studies. In the summer of 1968 he emerged with a first class honours degree, followed a fortnight later by a letter from the family solicitor confirming the money and books were now his.

Conrad and Richard had not spoken for almost three years. Richard was now combining a career in the law with first class cricket for Middlesex, where a century against the Australian tourists had marked the trainee barrister down as a potential future England captain. In truth Richard's progress was of little interest to Conrad, he had his own life now, with money aplenty and his book collection safely placed in a secure vault. He was ready to live life to the full.

Although it was almost the end of the 'swinging sixties' there was still no better place to be living than London. Conrad broke into his savings to buy a flat in Chelsea and spent his evenings in clubs throughout the West End, gaining a reputation as a young man with money who knew how to enjoy himself, never short of friends or an attractive woman on his arm, cruising the streets in his open top MG.

His first forays into the business world were less successful. Taken on as a junior manager in the textile trade he found the work tedious and walked out after a month. Similar experiences followed, he had a low boredom threshold and struggled to arrive on time in the mornings.

Worse was to come, Conrad was a trusting person who made friends easily, and it was not long before that trust was exploited. One night Tommy Martin, a small time criminal with convictions for fraud, got talking to him in a dark Soho nightclub. Over bottles of champagne he convinced Conrad to invest in a music business. A week later Conrad was several thousand pounds poorer and a little wiser.

It was not all bad news, Conrad found a job with a publishing house and at last a job he loved. His knowledge and enthusiasm impressed his bosses and he was highly regarded, settling into a life of hard work and partying, the difficult economic times of the 1970s passing him by unnoticed.

All this changed on his thirtieth birthday. After an evening of free flowing champagne and dancing, his friends drove him to a

Mayfair casino. Within minutes of entering this new world Conrad was hooked, staring in awe at the tables, men in dinner jackets with beautiful women at their sides, the mixture of nationalities, the croupiers, the spinning roulette wheels. He stood and watched as piles of chips were lost and won, waiters passing unobtrusively between the tables dispensing champagne and caviar.

He joined a roulette table, transfixed with the spinning wheel. Nervously he placed his first bet, an hour later he was £500 richer. He had found a new love.

Conrad took to visiting casinos several nights a week, returning home at dawn. Inevitably his work suffered and within months his position at the publishing house was no longer tenable. His employers were more sad than he was, he already saw himself as a professional gambler, playing the Monte Carlo tables with a glamorous woman on each arm.

He took his new profession seriously, reading as much as he could on the art of gambling, studying the varying approaches of different players, separating the professional gambler from the amateur, noticing how they moved table as the odds moved against them. Slowly he developed systems of his own as he played more seriously, becoming a member of several casinos. At first his bets were small, but gradually he increased the size of his stakes, a sense of exhilaration accompanying every win. He developed a gambler's ability to forget the losing nights, when he would return home penniless, before visiting the bank the next day to cash another cheque.

The thrill of gambling became a drug for him, and he noticed how many doors it opened with members of the opposite sex. Alluring women would arrive on their own during the evening, seeking out unattached men at the tables. Conrad would regularly leave at the end of winning evenings with a different woman, returning to his flat, and make love as the morning rush hour traffic passed below them.

Becoming aware that there was more to the world of gambling than London, Conrad visited Cannes, Monte Carlo and Paris, running up huge bills in five star hotels, keeping up a lavish image with a lifestyle to match. He met famous people, and became recognised wherever he went, treated with deference by casino and hotel managers. He became more and more of a womanizer, often seeing married women while their husbands were on business trips.

It was inevitable the house of cards would come crashing down. He was not winning enough to fund his lifestyle. He began to get letters from his bank manager, polite at first, then more formal. Conrad ignored them, refusing to believe he had tapped far into his vast inheritance, putting it down to the cautious nature of the banking profession.

It all changed when he tried to check in to a hotel in Nice. The manager discreetly advised him that the cheque had not been honored for his previous stay. A few days later he sat in front of his bank manager and learned the shocking truth, his fifty thousand pounds inheritance was spent. Conrad was at first distraught, deciding he would have to sell his flat and find a job. He briefly thought of seeking help from his brother Richard, but dismissed the idea immediately, they had not spoken in fifteen years, his only contact being via the sports pages and society columns.

Then he remembered his book collection, almost forgotten over the years. He arranged for it to be valued. A few days later he was incredulous to be informed it was likely to fetch a quarter of a million pounds at auction. With some misgivings he agreed to the sale. Two months later his inheritance was on its way to America and Conrad was a wealthy man again.

He intended to mend his ways but soon returned to his old life with gusto, growing his reputation as an international playboy, courted by casino owners, recognised by celebrities, targeted by women. As he approached his fortieth birthday he seemed to have the world at his feet.

Conrad paused the story as the cheese arrived selecting some Stilton with an approving nod. Stephen leaned back in his seat.

'What an amazing story.'

Conrad smiled, a far off look in his eyes, lost in a distant memory.

'The best is yet to come dear boy, or the worst,'

Selecting a little more cheese he continued.

One evening over dinner in Monaco, attended by Prince Rainier no less, Conrad found himself sitting next to the most beautiful woman he had ever met. Tania Phillips was in her mid-thirties, tall and slim, with blonde hair to her shoulders, combining a sophisticated air with enchanting looks and a wicked sense of humour. They hit it off the moment they started talking, the one dark cloud being Dominic Phillips, her millionaire husband, sat on his wife's other side and clearly irritated by the attention they were giving each other. Unimportant details like jealous husbands had not deterred Conrad before, by the end of the meal phone numbers had been exchanged.

He called the next day, and within a week they had arranged to meet. Her husband's frequent business trips made liaisons in discreet country hotels across the south of England much easier. They both believed their relationship had stayed secret but by chance a business associate of Dominic's was staying in the same hotel one night and spotted them. Word soon got back.

Dominic was a jealous man, well aware of his wife's good looks and tendancy to stray. He employed the services of a private detective, his suspicions soon confirmed, backed by a dossier and photographic evidence. Rather than confronting his wife Dominic bided his time.

When he wasn't making a fortune on the property market, Dominic's great passion was for sailing. He owned an impressive motor yacht, spending weeks on end along the coast of Britain, Ireland and France with his reluctant wife. He announced to a horrified Tania that they would be cruising for several weeks that summer, visiting ports either side of the Irish Sea. He waved away her objections, expecting her to accompany him for the entire voyage.

Conrad was equally horrified. Neither he nor Tania regarded their relationship as simply an affair any longer, their feelings had grown much deeper, they were already discussing ways in which Tania could leave her husband so they could start a new life together. It was unthinkable that they could be parted for even a few weeks.

A week into the voyage they moored in the harbour of a small Welsh village. Tania managed to slip away to a phone box under the pretext of stretching her legs ashore, conscious of how close an eye Dominic was keeping on her and increasingly wondered if he suspected something. Struggling with the pronunciation, she told Conrad they had arrived in Aberdysynni and were likely to be there a week.

It was time to act. Conrad drove through the night to Aberdyssyni and checked into rooms above the local pub, overlooking the harbour. Next evening Tania slipped ashore again, calling Conrad, arranging to meet at the bandstand on the hill above the village. They held each other as they watched the sun sink over the water, the sky an intoxicating mix of red and orange. They were determined to be together, whatever the cost. Tania would return to the yacht to tell her husband she was leaving him, then meet Conrad at the pub. They embraced and Conrad watched Tania as she walked back down the hill, his head full of plans for their future together.

He had reckoned without Dominic. She had hardly begun to announce her intentions when he exploded in a fit of anger. He pushed Tania down into the cabin locking the door. As she battered the door furiously with her fists he set sail, taking the yacht out into the Irish Sea. Twenty minutes later he dropped anchor, unlocked the door and a furious row developed. Tania told him of her intentions, letting him know that Conrad was waiting ashore for her. What happened next was never proven but at some point during the argument a struggle ensued and

Tania fell off the deck into the cold water.

Next morning, back in Aberdyssyni, Dominic phoned the police to report his wife had gone missing, claiming he had not seen her since she went ashore the previous day. A few hours later news came through that a local fisherman had recovered the body of a woman in his nets. Dominic immediately pointed the finger of suspicion at Conrad, citing the affair, his reputation for womanizing and his presence in the village. Shortly after, as Conrad waited at the pub, the police burst in and arrested him. Such a major incident in such a quiet community made for a big story, featuring in the national press.

Conrad was refused bail and held in the cells as the investigation got under way. DCI Lewis Hughes, a thorough if somewhat pedestrian detective, began to painstakingly piece together the facts. He interviewed Conrad at length and could find no motive for murder. Delving into the background of Dominic Phillips he found evidence of shady property dealing and a charge of actual bodily harm against him relating to a previous marriage, one which had carried a suspended prison sentence. The clinching evidence came when eye-witnesses confirmed the yacht's hasty departure from port the previous evening, and the commotion on board at the time. Conrad was released without charge and Dominic arrested.

The trial took place six months later at Shrewsbury Crown Court. Conrad appeared as a key witness for the prosecution, baring all in the witness box. Cross examination by Dominic's expensively hired defense barrister proved difficult as every aspect of his life was exposed, much to the delight of the watching press.

From the dock Dominic gave his version of events, carefully led by defense counsel. He told of his distress at discovering his wife's unfaithfulness, and that the voyage was an attempt at a new start, painting Conrad as an adulterer and philanderer. He admitted to locking Tania in the cabin and setting sail in a fit of anger, and that he had dropped anchor to allow them to talk. He spoke of Tania becoming hysterical and attacking him. As he tried to calm her increasing agitation she had slipped and accidentally fallen over the rail, describing his desperate but fruitless attempts to save her.

He returned to port and raised the alarm, admitting to lying about the circumstances of her disappearance because he was terrified the police would think he was involved and also because he saw a chance to gain revenge on Conrad.

The prosecution's case floundered in the face of the highly skilled defense team. One vital fact was missing, there had been no witnesses to confirm exactly what had happened. After two hours of deliberation the jury, under the judge's guidance of innocent until proven guilty, returned a verdict of not guilty, and Dominic left the courtroom a free man. Some time later the coroner recorded a verdict of death by misadventure and the case was closed.

As Conrad paused, lost in thought, Stephen gave an audible gasp.

'He can't have been found not guilty, he murdered her didn't he?'

'Dear boy, we'll never know, but if I was a betting man...'

'But it could have been you in court, he tried to frame you. What happened afterwards?'

Conrad drained the last of his coffee.

The whole incident had a profound effect on Conrad's life. Next day he drove back to Aberdyssyni, returning alone to the bandstand. He had loved Tania deeply and remained convinced she had been murdered. Reflecting on his life he realised how much of it had been wasted. It was not too late to change, he was still in his early forties with half a lifetime still ahead of him. Now was the time for redemption.

The village seemed as good a place as any to make that new start, he had no wish to return to London, let alone Cannes or Nice, this was the place he felt most connections with Tania. He spent many hours that day staring out to sea, imagining Tania slipping to an early grave, planning the future. In the days that followed he found a cottage to rent, and discovered to his delight that a small bookshop in the main square was up for sale. Within a month he had bought the business, reunited with the other love of his life.

It took Conrad many years to be fully accepted in Aberdyssyni, a small community, prone to being insular, many fingers were pointed and accusations whispered behind his back. Time moved on, he contributed as much as he could to village life and, having sold his Mayfair flat for an obscene profit, expanded his property ownership in the village, buying the shop premises that would later become Rachel's gallery, and settling on a delightful property above the village as his home, with magnificent views of the coastline.

There were one or two liaisons with local women, but never married ones, and none too serious. Over time he became a respected and popular pillar of the community, quite the country gentleman, chairing the parish council and Chamber of Commerce for many years. The events of that night almost thirty years ago had been forgotten by many people, but not by Conrad and Sammy, who had developed an unbreakable bond.

'That dear boy is that, my story, as much as it is.'
Stephen realised he had been listening engrossed for over an hour, they were now the only remaining customers.

'Conrad, I don't know what to say, it's an extraordinary story. Thank you for sharing it.'

'It's my pleasure, and please feel free to include it in your book if that's what you decide.'

'Do you still think of Tania?'

'Those who say time heals are mistaken dear boy, yes, every day.' Conrad raised the remains of his glass. 'To special memories, and what might have been.'

Stephen walked slowly up the beach towards the Lookout. It was a beautiful May evening, darkness only just falling. He wondered if he would ever find love as deep as Conrad's. He felt humbled that Conrad had shared his story, but also liberated. He was ready to write, to move forward, to fulfill his own dreams.

Chapter 12

It is generally accepted that the late spring bank holiday marks the beginning of summer in Aberdyssyni. Although the number of visitors begin to grow from Easter, it is over this weekend, and the half term week that follows, that the real influx begins.

Over the years as traditional industries, including fishing, have declined, tourism has become the lifeblood of the village. Many properties are now holiday homes, available to rent for the weekend or longer, or second homes, and over the summer the population of the village swells to almost twice its winter number.

With an economy so dependent on tourism local traders know they have barely four months to earn an income to see them through the winter. The beginning of summer results in a hive of activity as final preparation takes place for the season. Evans has been hard at work painting and decorating and as an air of expectancy grows, traders look nervously to the sky, ice cream sellers agonizing over how much stock to order. On street corners locals gather to discuss the prospect of a record hot summer, expressing concern at the chaos the traffic will cause, while secretly praying for sunshine.

The last remaining pleasure boats are lowered back into the water, gleaming with fresh coats of paint, while day trippers begin to arrive towing speedboats and jet skis, causing gridlock on the single slipway. The harbour master busies himself ensuring newcomers are aware of rules, regulations and tide times.

Shops burst back into life, with displays of buckets, spades, flags, footballs and crabbing lines on the pavement, while cafes and pubs update their menus in an attempt to entice customers. Families gather outside, perusing the offers, conscious of their budget.

The village comes alive, once more open for business.

On the Saturday of the Bank Holiday weekend Stephen awoke early, stretching out in his hammock. It was barely 5am, but already getting light. Away to the east the sun was an orange ball peeping over the horizon. Gulls swooped low over the water, in search of a tasty breakfast, then soared upwards into a cloudless sky, it was going to be a beautiful day. Below him the Kerkira gave two blasts of its horn as it returned up the estuary from a night's fishing.

Stephen turned his head and gazed around the room, even after several months he still took great pleasure from his new home. He marvelled at its individuality and character, proud of the further improvements he had made. Bright cushions and pictures created a homely feel, while in the corner a bookcase had been fashioned from an old rowing boat Stephen had discovered early one morning while walking on the beach. They had borrowed a trailer to salvage it, and Sammy, Evans and an ever complaining and breathless Gordon had manhandled it up the steps to the Lookout, where Evans, ably assisted by Stephen, had stripped, varnished and repainted it, adding shelves cut from driftwood. It now took pride of place in the room.

The biggest breakthrough for Stephen had been his writing. Dinner with Conrad had proved a liberating experience, not only did he now have the beginning of a structure for his book but it was as if the conversation had given him permission to write. Gone were vague ideas of fictional adventures, now he knew Sammy had been right, stories were all around him. His book would focus on those real life stories.

He had met Conrad for coffee, scribbling furiously in his notebook, filling in the gaps. Conrad was happy for his story to be told providing he could approve the drafts. Sammy had also agreed, although Stephen was conscious of gaps still to explore.

Stephen lowered himself from his hammock, dressed and made coffee. This time of day was his best time to write. Feeling alive and refreshed he flicked on his laptop, still engrossed two hours later as Glenda struggled up the steps with the post.

It was late morning when Stephen stopped, stretching his aching back. He decided to take a walk into the village, the day bright and warm, hardly a cloud blemishing a perfect blue sky, the biting winds of February a distant memory. Across the estuary the hills shimmered, out on the water pleasure craft and sailing boats weaved this way and that, their wakes creating ever-changing patterns.

The car park was filling quickly, parents and grandparents unloading buckets, spades, rugs and picnic baskets while excited children rushed ahead to the beach. As he reached the jetty he glanced upwards to the balcony of the Lobster Pot Café, where early lunches were being served under brightly coloured umbrellas. He passed families leaning over the jetty edge dropping crabbing lines into the water, parents holding tightly onto excited children, pausing by the harbour master's office where Sammy and Jimmy were deep in conversation, the three of them exchanging pleasantries. Across the road Bob stood outside his pub supervising a beer delivery. Judging by the number of barrels, he was expecting a busy weekend. He hardly looked excited at the prospect.

Crossing the road to the square Stephen pushed open the door of the bookshop to greet Conrad before popping into the gallery. He realised lately that he was coming up with excuses to see Rachel as often as he could.

'How's business?' he asked, helping himself to coffee.

'Getting better every day, how's writing, should J K Rowling start worrying?'

Stephen brought her up to date with progress, breaking off from time to time as customers came and went, most to browse, some to buy greetings cards, one or two more carefully examining the paintings and carving. Most were appreciative but one or two could be overheard commenting on the prices.

For her part Rachel was delighted with the progress Stephen had made. The role she had played behind the scenes with Sammy and Conrad had helped although that was best kept secret. She also enjoyed Stephen's visits far more than she let on. He was different from men she had met over the years, she found his lack of ego refreshing and his low embarrassment threshold hilarious, he represented a stability missing from her life for too long. She had taken to wondering how he felt about her. Only one thing continued to blight her inner happiness.

'Penny for your thoughts?'

'Sorry I was daydreaming.'

'You looked sad, are you okay?'

Rachel nodded, forcing a smile. 'I'm fine, just missing Josh.'

'Have you heard from him?'

'Not for a couple of weeks, I expect he's well off the beaten track.'

'Don't worry, he'll be fine.'

'I know, but mums always worry.'

As the gallery filled up, Stephen quietly slipped away, edging past a young boy who seemed intent on testing the durability of a carving of a sailing ship. He headed for the Lobster Pot Café promising himself a relaxing lunch as reward for his writing progress. It was just after 1pm and the restaurant was already three quarters full, a noisy chatter filling the room as families studied the menus and blackboards. A harassed looking Nick passed him in his chef's whites, shouting a greeting, carrying plates of cod, scampi and steaming mussels.

Stephen bought a glass of wine from an equally harassed Kelly and found a small table by the window. Five minutes later Nick appeared briefly at his side.

'How's it going Stephen? Sorry I'm in such a rush, I'm having to do the cooking and half the serving, you should see the staff I've ended up with.'

'What's happened?'

My regular staff let me down at the last minute, exam

commitments, I had to get a couple from the agency, what a disaster!'

As if on cue the kitchen door opened and a mousey girl emerged, looking terrified, precariously balancing plates on her arms. She was followed by a young lad who looked about fifteen, who called her back into the kitchen, shouting about a wrong order.

'Meet Gary and Dawn,' Nick groaned, 'otherwise known as Gormless and Dozy.'

'Which one's which?'

'Take your pick!' Nick ran back to the kitchen.

Settling down to enjoy his lunch, Stephen watched proceedings with amusement. Gary and Dawn would appear and just as quickly disappear in varying states of confusion. Through it all Nick remained calm, greeting new and returning customers with a smile and cheery word, seemingly able to give each of them time. Kelly never seemed to stop, dashing from table to table taking orders, clearing plates, a smile always on her face.

As he tucked into his lemon sole Stephen noticed a family across the room, a harassed overweight man and his wife were trying to keep their young children quiet as they waited for their food. His back was to Stephen but there was something familiar. He realised with a start it was Larry Middleton, a former colleague. Stephen watched in fascination. Although an intelligent and likeable man Larry spent his days at work lurching from crisis to crisis brought about entirely by his complete lack of organisation. It was clearly an outside work trait as well, he was dressed somewhat incongruously in a formal work shirt with shorts, socks and sandals, clutching his mobile phone which suddenly rang loudly, much to the obvious annoyance of his wife, and glares from neighbouring tables. An animated conversation followed during which Larry managed to knock his cutlery onto the floor.

Stephen continued to watch as the family ate their lunch, interrupted by two more calls. When they had finished eating

Stephen slipped across the room and placed his arm round Larry's shoulder, his former colleague swinging round in surprise, knocking over his glass of wine.

'Stephen Blanchard, how the devil are you, you look so well, I hardly recognised you.'

He shook Stephen warmly by the hand, turning to his wife.

'Louise, it's Stephen, you remember him from the Christmas party, he's the one who threw it all...'

He broke off sheepishly.

'...I mean it's great to see you.'

Larry's embarrassment was spared by his phone ringing again.

'Sorry, bit of a crisis at the office, you know how it is,' he explained before launching into a conversation about a missing order.

Lunch finished, Louise and the children disappeared off to the beach while Stephen and Larry found a table on the balcony, catching up on the latest news and gossip back in Stephen's old company.

'You know everyone was shocked when you left,' confided Larry, 'there was even talk of a breakdown. Not that I thought that, obviously,' he added quickly.

Stephen smiled, this did not surprise him, it would be a lot more plausible explanation for several former colleagues than there being more to life than big cars and corporate politics.

For his part Larry was shocked with the change in Stephen's appearance, he looked so tanned and relaxed.

Draining the last of their coffee they shook hands again and Larry disappeared down the stairs, Stephen watching in amusement as he marched across the beach, shirt tails flapping, narrowly missing demolishing a child's sandcastle, mobile pressed firmly to his ear. He reflected once more that he had definitely made the right decision.

Through the rest of the weekend and into June the sun continued to shine, enticing hordes of holiday makers to

Aberdyssyni for day trips and longer breaks. Car parks overflowing, guest houses posted their no vacancies signs, the constant ring of cash registers bringing smiles to traders faces, even though they continued their normal complaints about crowded pavements and the lack of parking. Beaches were rammed with a colourful display of deckchairs and windbreaks while kite flyers competed for space with beach cricket played with the intensity of a Lords test match. Stephen would rise early, write for the morning, followed by a long walk and an afternoon at the gallery or in the Lobster Pot Café watching with amusement as Nick and Kelly dashed here and there yelling instructions to their hapless staff.

Early one morning Stephen joined Nick on his twice-weekly visit to the fish market an hour down the coast. They met at 5am, a bleary-eyed Stephen dozing fitfully as they drove down in a van Nick kept especially for this purpose and which, predictably, smelled strongly of fish. They arrived at a large warehouse on the quayside, even at this early hour teeming with life. Fishing boats unloaded their catch, large trays of fish filling the various stalls. Stephen wandered round the stalls, intoxicated by the noise, sights and smells. Restauranteurs, hoteliers and wholesalers exchanged greetings as they moved from stall to stall inspecting mussels, sea bass, sea bream, flounder and skate, there were even tanks of live lobster.

Half an hour later, purchasing complete and the van loaded, the fish packed in trays full of ice, Nick led Stephen to a pub a short way down the quayside. As they pushed open the door it was already half full, loud chatter filling the air, and Stephen noticed pints of beer and glasses of whisky already being consumed despite the early hour. They found a table in the corner and Nick exchanged pleasantries with the waitress while ordering cooked breakfasts and mugs of tea.

'My secret haunt,' Nick confided, 'don't tell Kelly she worries about my health. It's open at six every morning, special license because of the market.'

The food was delicious, with local sausage and bacon. They chatted as they ate.

'How's the writing going?'

'Very well,' Stephen broke off to sip his tea, 'much better than I imagined, I've almost finished Conrad's story, you were a devious lot by the way.'

Nick laughed. 'We enjoyed it! We love a bit of mystery and intrigue, and we wanted to help, people have warmed to you which can be unusual around here. Have you interested anyone in the book?'

'It's early days but I've sent the synopsis to a couple of publishers, I just need some more stories now.'

'You know what Sammy would tell you to do.'

'Now there's an interesting character, you two are very close.'

Nick laid down his knife and fork with a satisfied sigh. 'We go back a long way.'

'How long have you known Kelly?'

Nick smiled. 'A long time, but she's only just agreed to move here with me.'

'She seems happy to be here.'

'Yeah well, we've got a lot of catching up to do, anyway enough about me, have you settled in?'

'More every day. I love it.'

'You and Rachel are getting on well.'

Stephen found himself blushing.

'Do you think so?'

'Well you never seem to be apart, you're just what Rachel needed.'

'How do you mean?'

'Rachel's good at putting on an act and hiding her emotions but I've known her a long time. She's lonely, she's needed a close friend.'

Stephen felt a tinge of disappointment.

'Just a friend?'

'Who knows, maybe more but give her time. Come on, we need to get back.'

An hour later they were back at the Lobster Pot Café

unloading the crates. Having bagged and labelled part of the catch Stephen was dispatched to the storeroom to stow it in the freezer. He looked round the carefully ordered room full of two large freezers and storage shelves piled high with dried goods and table linen. Then in one corner, part covered with a tarpaulin, he noticed a stack of wooden crates. He was certain these were what he'd seen being hauled onto Sammy's boat that night. Glancing furtively around he examined them more closely, they were nailed down and had writing on the side in a foreign language. Reluctantly Stephen pulled the tarpaulin back over them and climbed up the stairs, he was no closer to solving that particular mystery.

One June Saturday Nick held a special Greek night at the Lobster Pot Café. Tickets sold out quickly and when Stephen and Rachel arrived the room was already almost full with a mixture of visitors and locals. Greek music competed with animated chatter, a large Greek flag was hung on one wall, the tables were decorated with blue and white cloths, and earthenware jugs full of wine. A very busy Nick appeared, closely followed by Kelly and Dawn in simple peasant blouses, Kelly looking beautiful.

Food was served, a constant colourful array of dishes arriving at each table. Mezethes of baked olives, spinach parcels and stuffed filo pastries followed by lobster and red mullet, then baked figs and honey cakes.

As Greek brandy and ouzo were served Nick stood on a chair clutching a microphone to rapturous applause from appreciative guests.

'Ladies and gentlemen, some traditional entertainment for you.'

There was more clapping, accompanied by whistles and whoops no doubt fuelled by generous amounts of wine as Sammy and Kelly, both dressed in traditional Greek costumes, walked to the microphone. Sammy sat on a high stool tuning a bouzouki, beginning to play a slow, melodic tune. Then Kelly, in a soft haunting voice, sang of a young girl's love for a soldier who had gone to war and would never return. Then it was Sammy's turn to sing, another of his sea shanties in the same clear voice, this time in Greek. They finished with a duet, the whole room rising as one as the last notes drifted away,

Nick returned to the microphone announcing it was time for dancing, leading Sammy and Kelly to the front where the three of them performed a traditional dance arms interlinked. Nick and Kelly moved amongst the tables encouraging a dozen people to join them at the front. With a grin he arrived at their table and with Rachel's help they dragged a protesting Stephen to the front. They joined a long line and as Zorba the Greek began to play, a wild dance began, high on effort and low on finesse, Rachel's performance badly hampered by a staggering Gordon clinging to her arm.

The evening concluded with a demonstration of plate spinning by Nick, placing them on canes, running from one to the other, keeping them turning, before just after midnight people staggered from the restaurant into the warm midsummer night.

Stephen and Rachel, both somewhat the worse for wear, made their way slowly back along the beach. Stephen, warm and fuzzy from too much ouzo, tried to focus without success on walking in a straight line. He slipped his arm through Rachel's.
'That was a good, good night, a verrrry good night.'
'Stephen, you're drunk.'
'Me no, I'm never drunk, well maybe a little.'
He staggered and Rachel tightened her grip on his arm.
'Rachel, I've something to tell you.'
'Is this a good time?'
'It's a very good time.'
'Go on then.'
'You're nice Rachel, verrrry nice.'
'Thank you, so are you.'
'I mean very nice, verrry...special.'
'You're a good friend too Stephen.'

They arrived at Beach Cottage and stood unsteadily outside the door.

'Goodnight Stephen.'

Stephen was suddenly overcome by an overwhelming desire to kiss Rachel, he leaned forward, lost his balance, tumbling clumsily to the ground.

Rachel sighed. 'You'll never make it home, you'd better come in, I'll make up a bed on the sofa.'

Ten minutes later Stephen was curled up under a duvet listening to Rachel moving around upstairs. Through his fuddled brain he tried to remember their conversation. He had a feeling that being a good friend might not be enough for him. With that final thought playing through his head he sank into a deep sleep.

Chapter 13

It was Gordon who spotted the boat first. Perched on his normal bar stool one lunchtime, in animated conversation with Nick on the relative nutritional value of Welsh lamb and seafood, he suddenly broke off mid-sentence.

'Bloody hell,' he exclaimed, 'what's the lunatic doing? He's going to hit something!'

Nick, Stephen, Sammy and Jimmy span round and followed Gordon's outstretched arm as he pointed up the estuary. The subject of his concern was immediately apparent. A sleek white motor launch was approaching the jetty at far too high a speed, zig-zagging in alarming manner. As they watched open mouthed it narrowly missed a dinghy from the outdoor activities centre, which was forced to take evasive action, and headed straight for an anchored fishing boat.

'Good grief, it's going to hit that old boat,' shouted Gordon.

'That's not an old boat, that's my boat,' yelled Sammy, leaping from his stool and heading for the stairs.

The others followed, arriving breathless at the jetty edge, where Sammy, the harbour master and a growing crowd of onlookers were gazing in horror at the approaching launch. At the last moment it moved to starboard, missing the Kekira by inches, showing no sign of slowing down. The low tide meant running aground was now a distinct possibility.

Sammy and the harbour master pushed themselves to the front and began to wave and shout, urging the launch to stop. Not only were their actions to no avail, a woman on the forward deck waved back with equal enthusiasm, as if assuming the swelling crowd was a welcome party.

Showing agility and a turn of speed few thought him capable of, the harbour master sprinted to his office, returning moments later with a megaphone.

'Heave to,' he bellowed, his amplified voice deafening those close to him, 'heave to, you're going to run aground.'

His words seemed to provoke a heated debate between the

woman and a man at the wheel, then they heard the roar of the reverse thrust and the launch slowed to a halt and dropped anchor. A collective sigh of relief ran through the onlookers as they gradually dispersed, excitement over, leaving Sammy and the harbour master shaking their heads in disbelief.

Back in the restaurant Stephen, Gordon and Sammy took coffee onto the balcony to watch developments. A small dinghy had been lowered into the water as the couple prepared to disembark, the rather well-proportioned lady climbed precariously down a short metal ladder fastened to the stern of the launch, her progress hampered by a voluminous blue dress, handbag and what appeared to be high heels, while below, the hapless man, smartly attired in navy blazer and nautical cap, did his best to assist her. With a final ungainly step, she landed heavily in the dinghy, causing it to rock precariously. They rowed unsteadily towards the harbour, the woman issuing advice on rowing techniques as they did so.

Having secured the dinghy below the jetty, the man waited below while the woman hauled herself up the ladder, threatening to lose her balance at any moment, eventually reaching the safety of dry land where she straightened her dress and hair. Sammy and the harbour master had disappeared (Stephen later concluded on purpose) and, before they had a chance to duck out of sight, the woman spotted the friends above.

'I say,' she yelled up to them, 'I need a word, we'll come up.'
A few moments after they arrived on the balcony, where the friends had been joined by Nick, Kelly and a gawping Gary and Dawn.

'Good day,' she intoned, recovering her breath, 'my name is Rosemary Dutton- Greene, that's Greene with an 'e', and this is my husband William, we need your help.'

They made such an unusual couple the assembled group could barely stop themselves smiling. Mrs Dutton-Greene (with an 'e') was a formidable lady in her mid-fifties, towering above her husband, who regarded her with an air of resignation, a sentiment Stephen could understand.

'Can you please confirm to us,' she continued, eyeing the group disapprovingly, 'that this is Porthmadog?'

Stephen could keep himself in check no longer. He let out a loud guffaw. desperately trying to disguise it with a coughing fit. It was too much for Dawn, who fled back to the kitchen snorting, closely pursued by Gary.

Stephen did his best to recover his composure.

'Porthmadog?'

Behind him Gordon was murmuring 'Porthmadog, Porthmadog.'

'Yes, Porthmadog,' replied Mrs Dutton-Greene, regarding Stephen as if she had discovered the village idiot.

It was Nick who came to Stephen's rescue. 'Err no, this is Aberdyssyni, Porthmadog is about forty miles north of here.'

The woman turned to her husband triumphantly, 'you fool William, I told you you'd missed Porthmadog.'

Her husband spoke for the first time, his Essex accent contrasting with Rosemary's more refined tone, which Stephen surmised was well practised.

'It's not my fault dear, it looked like Porthmadog on the map.' From under his arm he produced his map of the coast, which he opened carefully.

'Look dear, here's Anglesey where we started, and there's Porthmadog, I can't understand how we missed it.'

Rosemary shouldered her husband out of the way and studied the map herself.

'Where's this Aberthingy place?' she demanded, fixing Stephen with a glare that made him wonder if it was all his fault and shoving the map into his face.

He pointed to Aberdyssyni.

'There you are William, I knew you were to blame, you turned right when I distinctly told you to turn left.'

'Starboard dear, and port, and it was you who said turn right.'

'Don't be so impertinent William.'

Her husband rolled his eyes with the look of a man who knows he can't win.

'Yes dear, whatever you say.'

Mrs Dutton-Greene straightened her dress and addressed the

group once more.

'We must go,' she announced, 'time for lunch on our yacht, we'll be back tomorrow for coffee at eleven.'

They were off, Rosemary setting a good pace up the jetty, Richard scurrying after her, the map once more tucked under his arm, returning precariously to the dinghy, leaving the friends watching in silence, incapable of speech.

They were indeed back the next morning at eleven sharp, Rosemary dressed in a vast white sailor suit that Stephen suspected would offer camping facilities to a whole troop of sea scouts. Stephen was at the bar with Sammy, Gordon and Jimmy, anxious not to miss a single moment, already sniggering like schoolboys. Nick glared at them as he approached the table with trepidation.

'A cappuccino for me, my man, and a coffee for my husband, a little milk, no cream, it plays havoc with his bowels. And scones for both of us strawberry jam, no cream.'

Nick opened his mouth to explain that he did not have scones on his menu but thought better of it, dispatching Dawn to the village bakery. Mrs Dutton-Greene surveyed the sparsely populated room, her eyes settling on the group at the bar, who suddenly seemed to take a great interest in their coffee dregs.

'That's our yacht in the bay you know,' she announced to them, waving her hand regally in its general direction, 'the large white one, it has a jacuzzi you know. We always have cocktails at six, you must join us.'

For the rest of the week the Dutton-Greene's were regular visitors to the café. Each morning Gordon would be on watch.

'Stand by your beds, here come Cocktails and Jacuzzi.'

Nick had been waiting to pay the group back for their obvious delight as they observed the morning ritual, and let it be known that Stephen was an author of some renown. Rosemary, never one to miss an opportunity to enhance her social standing, summoned Stephen to her table, much to the delight of his friends. She confided loudly that she had also dabbled in literature, having two poems published in her church magazine.

Ignoring his filthy and increasingly desperate looks, Nick informed her that Stephen would be delighted to offer her some tips.

'Excellent, you must join us for dinner tonight, cocktails at six o'clock sharp, I will have been shopping, you can row me across.' She waved away Stephen's protests imperiously, 'I'll be ready at five, we'll use your boat.

Any chance Stephen thought he had of an unobtrusive departure were dashed as he made his way to the quayside, dressed self-consciously in a jacket and tie. His friends were out in force on the balcony, full of words of encouragement and helpful advice. Foiling his only remaining get out clause, Sammy had lent Stephen his rowing boat, and Stephen climbed down gingerly into it, laden with shopping bags. Rosemary followed, with no more finesse than before, almost knocking Stephen overboard. Not having rowed since a sedate day on the river many years before, progress was haphazard to say the least, his friends watching the spectacle with growing hilarity while Rosemary issued instructions.

On the yacht, over cocktails and dinner, Rosemary insisted on telling Stephen her story. Stephen was at least an avid listener, his book never far from his mind.

The Dutton-Greene's lived just outside Southend on Sea, William having been employed for many years in a local bank, where he performed his clerical duties with diligence. Rosemary was the social climber, always out to impress with her dinner parties and membership of the WI and church committee. In contrast William, devoid of airs and graces, craved the quiet life, he was never happier than when pottering in his greenhouse, or enjoying an occasional round of golf with friends. After thirty years of marriage he had given up many years ago trying to influence his wife's behaviour, settling instead for amused acquiescence.

Never content to play second fiddle, Rosemary was particularly irked when Daphne, a friend from the WI, let it slip that she and her husband were now the proud owners of a yacht. She regarded her friend as a social inferior, her husband worked in a factory for goodness sake, and their home didn't even boast a jacuzzi. She imagined William and herself with a yacht of their own, popping over to France for the afternoon, inviting friends on board and watching as they turned green with envy. Her mind was made up, a yacht it must be.

William was aghast when he heard the idea, he had no interest in boats of any kind. Rosemary was determined, waving away his protests. She calculated that a combination of an inheritance and her husband's generous share options would be enough to cover the purchase price. William reminded her of the importance of financial prudence, something he had preached to bank customers for thirty years, but once Rosemary's mind was made up it was like trying to turn an oil tanker.

Enlisting the help of another friend's reluctant husband, ('he used to be in the navy William, an officer, probably almost an Admiral, he knows what he's talking about'), a suitable vessel was identified, moored in a marina on the Menai Straits in North Wales. Rosemary declared that she and William must travel there immediately.

She was delighted with the sight that awaited her. 'Fair Lady', a thirty-seven feet offshore cruiser, was perfect, boasting two cabins, a sun deck and even a jacuzzi. A guided tour was all she needed. The vendor was surprised at the ease of the sale, but that was nothing compared to the shock when he discovered that the couple had absolutely no sailing experience.

The deal completed Rosemary and William returned home, a subdued William shaking his head with a combination of disbelief and despair. For her part Rosemary was already busy on the phone spreading the news.

She waved away her husband's concern at their complete lack of knowledge of all things nautical, enrolling him on a local day skipper's course. Despite his initial trepidation William found he enjoyed the experience, gaining basic sailing, navigation and safety knowledge and skills, although he knew it would be some time before he felt confident enough to take the 'Fair Lady' to sea.

Once more Rosemary would hear none of it, she wanted to sail her purchase back to a local marina as soon as possible, she had already fixed a date for the first viewings from jealous friends. She declared that sailing couldn't be that hard, after all William was a good and careful driver. They must return the very next weekend so he could get some practice in. William must book a week's holiday to hone his skills.

A reluctant vendor handed over the keys to the vessel making William promise to stay within the Menai Straits until his confidence improved. Once more that was not enough for Rosemary. She announced they would take their first trip down the coast, staying a few days. She pointed to Porthmadog on the map. Only a short distance, what could be easier?

A couple of days later Rosemary announced it would be their last in Aberdyssyni, they must 'cruise the coast back to Anglesey, the bank are anxious for William to return, they rely on him you know.'

Stephen was the most delighted. Since dinner Rosemary had all but adopted him, demanding he accompany her on a latest shopping trip, hailing him in a loud voice every time she caught him scurrying up the road.

As they set sail the next morning a large crowd gathered on the harbour side to see them off. A collective cheer went up as they weighed anchor and got underway with Rosemary waving farewell. Leaving the harbour was much easier than their arrival, word had spread fast and boat owners had moved their craft well out of harm's way, affording the Dutton-Greene's a clear passage back out to sea.

Chapter 14

The blue skies and warm sun of June gave way to an equally glorious July, day after day of fine weather bringing comparisons from older residents to the sun scorched summer of 1976. As schools broke up for their summer holidays the number of visitors increased to almost breaking point, car parks overflowing, vehicles parked on the grass verges leading into the village, on the busiest days stretching almost as far as the Lookout. Families laden with picnics, buckets and spades headed for the beach, excited children running ahead across the dunes.

As cash registers jangled even the more cynical traders had smiles on their faces, counting their takings as they planned winter breaks to exotic locations.

Aberdyssyni was content, doing what it did best, basking under warm sunshine, displaying its many attractions. It knew these few short weeks of summer were the lifeblood of the community.

For his part Stephen preferred to avoid the village when it was at its busiest. His friends were fully occupied anyway, Rachel opening into the evening, while any spare space at the Lobster Pot Café was at a premium. Nick and Kelly worked flat out from dawn to dusk serving drinks, lunch and dinner. Even Gary and Dawn had stepped up to the mark under Nick's training and encouragement. Sammy was also busy during the day, running pleasure trips on the Kerkira to view the dolphins that could often be spotted out in the bay.

Even though it was only just outside the village, Stephen loved the peaceful solitude the Lookout provided. His writing kept him fully occupied each morning as he worked on re-drafts of Conrad's story. He was anxious to ensure accuracy, devoting a significant amount of time to researching online, including exploring background on Dominic and Tania Phillips. This could be painstaking work, but Stephen enjoyed employing the disciplines well practiced in his former life.

As he worked his mind wandered, still amazed at how much

he had changed. He felt more relaxed, developing an inner peace missing for far too many years. It had taken time to adjust to the change, there had been too many years of working every hour under the sun and he no longer had a team of people at his beck and call.

In so many ways his success at work had masked some of the wider issues he struggled with. He had always had a low embarrassment threshold, maybe that explained his hapless behaviour at the bookshop.

The one cloud on the horizon was his confused feelings for Rachel. He cringed was he remembered his clumsy attempts to kiss her after the Greek night. What had he been thinking of? Maybe it was fine, Rachel had behaved perfectly normally the next morning, or as normally as she was capable of, bringing him coffee, averting her eyes from his pile of clothes scattered across the floor.

For several days since, he had been trying to work out how he felt. On one hand his feelings had intensified in a way he had not known since those early days with Helen. He was attracted to Rachel in many ways, she had an intoxicating joie de vivre and was great company. On the other hand, he was desperate to do nothing to ruin a blossoming and special friendship, which he really valued. Was he ready for a new relationship? Was it too soon? How did Rachel feel, was he no more to her than a friend? In the odd flight of fantasy he imagined he and Rachel together, building a life in the village. He needed to talk to her, preferably when sober.

Consumed by his thoughts it was only when he rose and stretched that he noticed a new addition outside. A brightly coloured gypsy caravan had arrived in the night, and was parked on the grass next to the boat yard opposite. A tethered horse grazed nearby, next to him a dog lay asleep. The remains of a camp fire smoldered. There was no other sign of life.

Stephen tried to refocus on his writing but found himself frequently looking up, intrigued. It was just after midday when a figure emerged, stretched and began to rebuild the camp fire. Once it was ablaze he hung a kettle above it then poured the boiling water into a mug before settling on his caravan steps sipping contentedly. It was difficult to pull out every feature of the visitor from a distance away but he appeared to be in his sixties with long grey hair and a wiry build.

Stephen continued to watch as his new neighbour disappeared into the sand dunes, the dog at his heel, returning with a pile of driftwood adding it to the fire. Fetching an easel and paints from the caravan he settled on a low stool and began to sketch.

Realising he was spending more time watching developments than writing, Stephen closed his laptop and wandered across the road. The dog, raised from his slumbers, wandered across wagging its tail in greeting.

'Good day to you sir,' the visitor greeted Stephen in a pronounced Irish accent, 'and what a beautiful day it is.'

'It certainly is,' Stephen replied, 'I live across the road, up there in the Lookout.'

'I know that', the older man continued, setting down his brushes and moving his easel, 'how are you Mr Blanchard, I've heard a lot about you?'

Stephen was momentarily taken back.

'How do you know my name?'

'Well there I have an advantage on you sir, my name's Alfred.'

So saying he jumped to his feet, with movement quick and agile for a man who Stephen now realised must be at least seventy if not older, and shook Stephen's hand warmly.

'Would you join me for a mug of tea sir?'

He disappeared into the caravan returning with a stool for Stephen and threw more wood onto the still smoldering fire. As the heat increased, he hung his kettle once more and spooned a generous quantity of tea leaves into a large battered metal teapot. Handing Stephen a steaming mug he lit a pipe, sank back onto the caravan steps and puffed away contentedly.

Stephen did not rush the conversation, one of the lessons he had learned from Sammy was the value of silence. Instead he studied Alfred as they sat. Barely five and a half feet tall and dressed in frayed clothes, his ruddy complexion suggested many years of living in the open air. His hands were noticeably slim and smooth.

It was Alfred who broke the silence.

'It's been a grand summer so far, how do you like Aberdyssyni?'

They chatted amiably about the weather, the village and the Lookout. Disconcertingly Alfred always seemed to be one step ahead of Stephen. He was mystified as to how the visitor could know so much about him and the village.

Eventually Stephen stood to go.

'It's a pleasure to meet you, but how do you know so much about me?'

'Why not join me for supper tonight?' replied Alfred.

'That would be great, somewhere in the village?'

'How about right here, in my famous restaurant under the stars?' Alfred chuckled, a twinkle in his eyes.

That evening a still intrigued Stephen wandered back to the caravan. It was a wonderfully clear fine night. A table and two chairs had been set up next to the caravan, laid with plates and glasses. Alfred was busy inside, delicious smells of cooking wafting from the metal chimney.

He petted the dog, which he now knew was called Charlie, as Alfred appeared proffering a bottle of red wine. He poured two glasses before reappearing with simmering bowls of stew.

'Rabbit', he announced, 'Aberdyssyni's finest, caught this afternoon.'

Stephen dug into the sweet and tender dish, flavoured with herbs. It was delicious. Alfred cleared the plates and poured more wine. The sun set, a red ball on the horizon before slipping into the sea, and the first stars appeared.   This truly was a restaurant under the stars.

Utilising his newly found listening skills, Stephen encouraged Alfred to tell him something about his past. The old man smiled and relit his pipe.

Alfred had been born seventy two years ago into a travelling community in the very south of Ireland, his early life spent on the move from village to village. He had no formal schooling but was an inquisitive child, anxious to learn and explore, at one with the natural world. At ten he might not be able to read and write, but knew the name of every plant, could trap and skin any number of animals and was adept at knowing which berries and mushrooms were safe and which poisonous. He spent hours on end listening to the tales of the older members of his extended family, learning of the myths and legends of Ireland.

Thirsting for adventures of his own, he left the travelling community when he was just seventeen, travelling to Cork where he found work in the docks unloading container ships. He slept wherever he could find shelter, usually in the open air. But others resented a traveller amongst them, and soon he was out of work, penniless and starving.

He decided to try his luck in Dublin, his only option being to walk there. He slept in barns and under hedges at night, foraging for food or calling at farmhouses in hope of picking up some scraps.

It was difficult to imagine how Alfred's life might have ended up if fate hadn't dealt a hand. Rounding a bend on a country road he noticed a bridge ahead crossing a fast flowing river, swollen by heavy rain. There was a commotion, a woman distraught and screaming.

She caught sight of Alfred.

'Help us, my husband and daughter, they're drowning.'
Alfred sprinted to the bridge. In the turbulent water below a man was desperately hanging on to a young child. They were both in imminent danger of being swept away. Alfred pulled off his shoes and coat and without a thought for his own safety dived into the water. He was a strong swimmer but even he found the conditions difficult. Struggling against the current he

managed to reach the child, gesticulating wildly for the father to let go before pulling her to the shore into the arms of her sobbing mother. Then he struck out for the man who was clinging to a tree root, pulling him to the water's edge with the last of his energy, before collapsing exhausted on the river bank.

As they recovered from their ordeal he discovered that the couple and their daughter lived nearby. Ignoring warnings, the child had slipped while climbing onto the bridge to get a better view of the river. Sobbing with relief they thanked Alfred for saving their lives.

Alfred insisted he was fine to continue his journey but the couple would not hear of it. They insisted he return with them to their home for a hot bath and some food. He was in for a huge shock. Prominent and successful in the Irish business community, they lived in no ordinary house but something more resembling a cross between a stately home and a castle, set in acres of gardens. There was even a butler to greet them at the door. He was shown to a guest bedroom where a hot bath was run for him, the first he could ever remember, with dry clothes laid out in the guest bedroom.

The couple insisted he stay for dinner and also spend the night under their roof. Alfred found it impossible to settle in the soft bed, eventually sleeping on the floor covered in a single blanket.

Over breakfast next morning they insisted he share his story. The couple were so moved by his circumstances and indebted to him for saving their daughter's life, that they made a proposition to him. Would he stay for just a short while, they had a vacancy for an assistant gamekeeper, a job that came with a small cottage on the estate? Alfred was reluctant at first but the couple were insistent, and eventually he agreed, but only for a few weeks.

He was shocked at how quickly he settled in, getting on well with Fergus, the elderly head gamekeeper, learning much from him, while Fergus was the first to admit he learned even more in return. He also loved the simple cottage, the first time he had ever been anywhere he could call home. He also developed a warm and friendly relationship with Sally, the couple's daughter, a devoted nine year old who would follow him everywhere, silently acknowledging her debt to him. Weeks turned into months and months to two years, during which Sally and her governess had helped him learn to read and write.

Fergus was due to retire that year and the couple offered him the job of head gamekeeper. After some thought Alfred agreed provided he could stay in his small cottage rather than move to the bigger property that came with the job.

He stayed in the role twenty years, the poacher turned gamekeeper, becoming almost part of the family, watching as Sally grew into a beautiful young woman, leaving for Dublin to pursue a career in the law. He adored the solitude the job offered him, walking for hours alone around the estate. He would often gaze at the distant hills, however, remembering his days on the road.

He also became a self-taught but accomplished artist, spending many hours at his easel capturing the beauty of the estate.

Then tragedy struck, the couple were killed when the light aircraft they were travelling in came down off the west coast of Ireland as they returned from a business trip. Alfred was distraught, he regarded the couple as much parents as friends. Sally returned from Dublin, assuring him his job was secure and the cottage he had lived in for so long now his. She also revealed that Alfred had been left one hundred thousand Irish pounds in her parents' wills.

As tempting as it was to spend the rest of his days in a place and job he loved, he decided it was time to move on. He was not yet forty, still a young man, and he knew so little of the world. The money he had been left gave him security but beyond that he had little interest in it, his needs were simple. He would travel again, starting by crossing the sea to explore Britain. His sole purchases were a beautiful gypsy caravan and a horse. The open road and adventures awaited him once more.

That was over thirty years ago. Since then Alfred's life had slipped into a comfortable routine of travelling, following an established route around the country each year. He had few needs, his inheritance lay almost forgotten, gaining interest in an Irish bank account. He would fund his few needs through selling his paintings or taking odd jobs wherever he stayed for a few weeks before moving on. Each summer he would visit Aberdyssyni for two, maybe three weeks, returning to the same spot opposite the Lookout.

Alfred sat back with a contented sigh, relighting his pipe. Stephen realised he had been listening engrossed for almost an hour. It was now completely dark, the sky above a myriad of stars, the flickering flames from the camp fire sending dancing images in all directions.

'That's an amazing story, you're a hero.'

'No hero, anyone would have done it, it was a long time ago.'

'Thirty years on the road, don't you ever tire of it?'

'Never, how could I? They can carry me out of my caravan in a box.'

'What happened to Sally, did you stay in touch?'

'She's back on the family estate now, just retired from a top law firm, grandchildren of her own. She always kept the cottage for me if I wanted to go back. We keep in touch, she sends letters sometimes to Miss Rachel and she passes them on.'

'Miss Rachel, that's how you know my name, I should have guessed.'

'She looks after me every summer when I visit, sells my paintings, we swap memories of Irish childhood, she's a very special person.

As Stephen climbed wearily back up the Lookout steps he paused for a moment, peering back down to the caravan. In the fire's dying embers he could just make out the shadowy figure of Alfred, pipe in mouth, back on his caravan steps. An old man at peace with the world. Stephen envied his simple life.

Next morning Stephen was woken by a knock on the Lookout door. Slipping out of his hammock he glanced at his watch, after eight, the latest he had slept in months. All that fresh air and red wine were the perfect tonic for a long sleep.

Outside was a postman, clearly in a hurry. He thrust a handful of envelopes at Stephen with a quick 'good morning' and turned to leave.

'Thank you, where's Glenda, on holiday?'

'No', the postman called back briefly, 'she was taken to hospital yesterday, someone back at the office mentioned a heart attack.'

Leaving the letters unopened on the table Stephen pulled on some clothes and headed for Beach Cottage. She may be a gossip but he had a soft spot for Glenda and was shocked by the news. He felt guilty for not taking her breathlessness and tales of medical ailments seriously.

He found Rachel in one of her perpetual states of chaos. Since getting up she had managed to fuse the kettle, break the washing machine, lose the keys to the gallery and drop a full pack of museli over Bryn. As he opened the door the dog ran past him depositing a shower of raisins onto the floor.

As Rachel mended the kettle fuse they talked about Glenda. They searched for the telephone number of the nearest hospital and rang for news. Glenda was indeed there, and yes they could visit briefly.

An hour later a busy but helpful nurse ushered them into a side room off the main ward. They found Glenda sitting up in bed, propped up by pillows. A short, overweight man, who could have been her twin, sat by the bed.

'We heard the news, are you okay?'

Glenda polished her glasses and introduced Martin, her husband. Despite feeling poorly the heart attack had been a mild one and she was already on the road to recovery. She was touched that Stephen and Rachel had visited so quickly, and anxious not to miss the opportunity this audience offered her.

'It's the weight of that post bag you know, I've been telling them for years.'

'Twenty minutes I had to wait for an ambulance, twenty minutes, can you believe it, I could have got here quicker on my bicycle.'

She glared at her husband, who had not yet said a word.

'I blame him, cares more about his tomatoes than me.'

It was a relieved Stephen and Rachel who left the hospital half an hour later, delighted that Glenda was on the road to recovery but also glad to have escaped a monologue that had also encompassed the NHS, privatisation of the Post Office and the price of stamps. They felt sorry for her long suffering husband and also for the Post Office management once she got hold of them.

As they drove back Stephen told Rachel about his dinner with Alfred.

Rachel smiled, 'he's a wonderful man, been coming here each summer for years.'

'You sell his paintings.'

'Maybe half a dozen each year, he's very talented.'

'He certainly seems to live the simple life.'

Rachel smiled again, 'he's got all he needs, nothing more, we could all learn a lot from him.'

At the end of July Stephen awoke to find the gypsy caravan gone. Alfred had moved on to pastures new and fresh adventures. He lay there remembering Rachel's words, she was so right, Alfred's needs were so simple. He thought about the change to his own life over the last few months, never particularly materialistic, he had still enjoyed the trappings a high salary brought him; a smart house, an expensive car, the latest technology. He realised how little he missed all that, looking round the Lookout and thinking of his friends, he realised how little he really needed.

He'd also miss the time he spent chatting with Alfred. In his previous life, time had always been at a premium, dashing from meeting to meeting, but over the last few weeks he enjoyed nothing better than chatting over countless mugs of tea with Alfred. He gazed out to sea, overcome with a deep sense of peace with the world.

Later that morning, wandering into the village for some shopping, he noticed a sleek, dark Mercedes parked outside the

Lobster Pot Café. A man in a grey suit was polishing the windscreen, looking every inch a chauffeur. Intrigued, Stephen climbed the stairs to find out more.

Nick was seated at a table at the far end of the restaurant, Sammy by his side, deep in conversation with two visitors. Although Stephen could only see them side on, they had a Mediterranean appearance, given all the recent connections he assumed they were Greek. The man was in his late fifties, distinguished with grey hair, wearing an expensive looking dark blue suit. Open on the table in front of him a briefcase was overflowing with official looking documents. A large gold chain flashed on his wrist as he waved his arms to emphasise a point he was making.

The woman was a little younger, maybe in her late forties, attractive with long dark hair, wearing a blue skirt and white top. She reminded Stephen of someone but he was momentarily unable to make the connection.

Then Kelly appeared, looking anxious, carrying four small cups of espresso on a tray. She hardly seemed to notice Stephen as she scurried across the room, setting the cups down nervously. As she paused next to the woman the penny dropped, he could have been seeing double, they were almost identical in appearance. They could be sisters, despite the age difference.

Kelly appeared behind the bar, distracted as she made Stephen his cappuccino, casting worried glances across the room, where the four participants were locked in animated conversation in low voices, as if aware of Stephen's presence, heads close together. Voices were raised, as the interaction became more heated it was clear all was not well.

Kelly pushed Stephen's drink in front of him and he caught her eye, mouthing if she was okay. She nodded her head in a distracted way that did nothing to convince him.

Eventually the man pushed the documents back into the briefcase and snapped it shut, clearly frustrated. He spoke loudly in a foreign tongue to Nick and Sammy. Nick shook his head vigorously, and it was Sammy who replied, in the same language. The man said something to the woman, picked up his briefcase and headed for the door. The woman hung back and touched Nick's arm, speaking earnestly to him in a low voice, as if pleading with him to do something. Even from a distance the touch seemed gentle and caring. As she moved towards the door Kelly came from behind the bar to meet her, they embraced warmly if seemingly sadly. They exchanged whispered words as she too disappeared down the stairs, moments later they heard the purr of the Mercedes as it departed.

Nick and Sammy continued to converse earnestly at the table, Stephen, who felt he had intruded on private family business, slipping away quietly.

The following day, when he called at the restaurant, Nick was not around. Kelly, still looking fraught, explained he had been called away on business. Through the open kitchen door Stephen could see Sammy, dressed in chef's whites, issuing instructions to Gary and Dawn.

It was a week before Nick returned. When he did, despite his attempts at bon homie, it was obvious he had much on his mind.

Chapter 15

On the first Sunday in August, Gordon invited Stephen and Rachel for lunch at his farm, high in the hills above Aberdyssyni. On hearing the news Nick warned Stephen not to eat for at least three days beforehand, a Gordon lunch was not for the faint hearted. It was therefore with some trepidation that Stephen waited to be picked up by Rachel, a bottle of wine under his arm. It had taken a while to decide what to wear, before eventually deciding on a jacket and tie, he didn't know how formal the occasion would be.

Rachel arrived wearing a shirt and jeans. She shook her head as she took in Stephen's tie, enquiring if he was expecting royalty. They drove through the village, edging up narrow streets rammed with holidaymakers, joining a country road snaking upward into the hills. Cottages soon gave way to green fields, then to vast expanses of hillside, dotted with sheep, occasionally interspersed with dry stone walling. They twice crossed cattle grids and encountered large gates, Stephen climbing from the vehicle to open and close them.

As they drove, Rachel, competing with the roar of the engine, described some of the local legends, pointing out a lake below them where a Celtic warrior was reputed to lie in a watery grave, allegedly rising from the water on one night each year. Stephen shivered, preferring the view behind them where the sea provided a stunning vista.

At last Rachel swung off the road onto a farm track, following it even further uphill before steering carefully through a gate and pulling into a large courtyard. Two black Labradors trotted over to them, barking madly.

'Are those dogs okay?' Stephen asked suspiciously.

'Of course, come on we're here.'

Stephen climbed gingerly down, still clutching the wine, the dogs continuing to bark at him.

'Why do dogs never like me?'

'Cos you don't like dogs, they know, they're not stupid,' Rachel smiled making it clear that she thought that distinction was reserved for certain humans.

In front of them was an imposing stone farmhouse, three floors high, over a hundred years old. The oak front door was huge, leading off a small, carefully maintained garden. Around the courtyard were farm buildings of all shapes and sizes; barns, a huge lambing shed and out houses. Two large tractors were parked next to the barn, while a random array of machinery was scattered everywhere. A 4x4 truck stood next to a smart Mercedes, belying Gordon's claims of poverty.

With the dogs running around them, seemingly intent on tripping Stephen, they made their way round the side of the farmhouse. Wellingtons and a boot scraper stood next to a further door, suggesting this was the one in everyday use. A cat lay asleep in the late morning sun, unperturbed by the dogs. Pots of flowers and hanging baskets brought a dash of colour to the outside of the farmhouse.

Gordon appeared in the doorway, larger than life as ever.

'Shakespeare, good day to you,' he boomed, 'and to you Rachel, welcome to my humble abode.'

He grabbed Stephen's hand, shaking it vigorously, taking the proffered wine before kissing Rachel.

'Come in, come in, Stephen why the tie, it's not a job interview!'

He led the way into a large farmhouse kitchen, immediately cheery, warm and welcoming. A huge wooden table, easily able to seat a dozen people, stood in the middle of the room, a large range radiated heat, hosting bubbling pots and pans. Generous work surfaces were stacked with piles of vegetables, freshly baked bread and cheeses, a pot of coffee simmered on the range. An intoxicating aroma filled the air.

A woman joined them. She and Rachel exchanged hugs.

'Margaret, meet Shakespeare,' Gordon boomed once more, seemingly incapable of moderating his voice, 'he's the author.'

Margaret was petite, the absolute opposite of Gordon, they made an extraordinary contrast as they stood together. She was in her late forties, and smartly dressed.

'It's good to meet you at last Stephen,' Margaret came across and reached up to kiss him, 'I've heard a lot about you. Lunch will be an hour yet Gordon, why not take Stephen on a tour of the farm, Rachel and I have a lot to catch up on.'

Ignoring Gordon's protests that he couldn't wait a whole hour before eating she shooed him fondly out the door. They climbed into the truck, the dogs leaping into the back still barking madly.

'Right then Shakespeare, let's show you what farming is really about.'

They drove back out of the courtyard and picked up another track heading across a large field. Above them the hillside was dotted with sheep. Gordon steered through a gate, engaged the four wheel drive, and then Stephen was hanging on for dear life as the truck bounced and juddered, traversing a steep slope. Twice he closed his eyes, convinced the truck would slip, but Gordon was an accomplished driver.

'How many sheep do you have?'

'Just over a thousand, the finest Welsh lamb you'll find anywhere.'

'How do you cope with that number?'

'I have some help, especially for lambing, but they mainly look after themselves.'

Stephen looked around him as the midday sun beamed down.

'It'd beautiful today but how do you cope in winter?'

'It's bad, especially in snow, it's what we do.'

For the next half hour, they toured the vast expanse of the hillside, climbing higher and higher, Gordon describing the many challenges of hill farming, Stephen's respect for his friend growing all the time.

They arrived back to the farmhouse and its mouth-watering aroma. Margaret was stirring a large pan of gravy while Rachel sipped a schooner of sherry. Gordon poured beers for the men.

Shooed from the kitchen once more for trying to taste the gravy, Gordon took Stephen on a tour of the farmhouse. Each room had high, imposing ceilings but a variety of touches with decorations, cushions and throws had left them warm and cosy. The farmhouse was clearly Margaret's domain, a large sitting room, off which was a study, dominated by a grand desk and leather chair. On the wall hung a Manchester United signed shirt in a frame, next to which was an aerial photograph of Old Trafford. Gordon pointed out the signatures on the shirt and the various parts of the ground with reverence.

Margaret poked her head round the door, rolling her eyes at Stephen.

'I might have guessed he'd be showing you that, he's obsessed. Gordon will you carve the meat?'

Gordon disappeared with the look of a man about to perform the most important task of the week while Margaret led Stephen and Rachel to the dining room. Stephen gaped at the large table sagging under the weight of a banquet fit for a whole host of royalty let alone a single king. Steaming plates of roasted, mashed and new potatoes, at least five other different vegetables, a precarious tower of Yorkshire puddings, a large jug of gravy, mustard, horseradish and mint sauce.

Gordon stood at the head of the table carving from large joints of beef, lamb and gammon with the precision of a surgeon, his face a picture of concentration. In front of each of them was a dinner plate the size of a dustbin lid. Stephen loosened his tie wishing he had dressed more comfortably, Nick had been right, this was not going to be for the fainthearted. He already felt full just looking at the food.

Gordon filled his and Stephen's wine glasses with generous measures. Margaret contented herself with a glass of water, while Rachel put her hand over her glass, reminding them that she was driving.

Gordon raised his glass, proposing a toast, before getting down to the serious business of the day. He took his own plate and proceeded to pile it high with all three meats, mounds of vegetables, and several Yorkshire puddings, a mountain range, before pouring gravy onto the summit creating the impression of a volcano erupting.

Stephen shook his head in disbelief.

'You'll never eat all that Gordon.'

'This is yours Shakespeare,' Gordon laid the plate down in front of Stephen and taking his in return, 'it'll get you started anyway.' He waved away Stephen's protestations, much to the merriment of Rachel and Margaret, then proceeded to pile his own plate with even a bigger serving while Margaret busied herself with much smaller portions for Rachel and herself.

All conversation ceased as Gordon started to attack his plateful with gusto, demonstrating the logistical planning skills of a military commander, a large napkin tucked into his shirt front. Gravy dribbling down his chin was dabbed, to be replaced moments later by trickles of red wine. Each time he topped up his wine glass he would do the same with Stephen's, ignoring his refusals.

Stephen, for his part, made a valiant effort with his meal. The food was delicious, warm and satisfying, but the sheer quantity was overwhelming. Two or three times he placed his knife and fork together to indicate he had finished before wilting under Gordon's glare and picking them up again. He carried on gamely, each mouthful becoming more of a challenge. Eventually, with a supreme final effort he cleared the last of his plate.

Gordon wiped his mouth, took a deep draught of wine, and let out a contented sigh.

'Now that, Shakespeare, is what I call proper food, none of that pretentious seafood stuff that friend of ours served up in the restaurant. Seconds?'

Stephen let out a groan, waving his napkin in mock surrender, while Gordon filled his own plate with more food, returning to his mission. Then plates were cleared by Margaret and Rachel, allowing Stephen to let out a sigh of relief. Despite his aching stomach it looked like he had survived the ordeal.

He spoke too soon. The door swung open and Margaret and Rachel reappeared, each bearing a large tray piled high with dessert, bread and butter pudding, treacle sponge, jam roly poly, and apple pie, accompanied by jugs of custard and fresh cream. Margaret took a bowl and turned to Stephen.

'What do you fancy,' she asked, adding somewhat ominously, 'to start with.'

At least Margaret was a little more understanding than her husband, cutting Stephen a small slice of apple pie, while Gordon opted instead to try to fit a generous portion of each pudding into a single large bowl, smothering them in both custard and cream.

Finally, a cheeseboard appeared, with an impressive array of Welsh cheeses, accompanied by glasses of port.

Eventually Gordon untucked his napkin with a deep and contented sigh and poured Stephen and himself one more glass of port. The serious business of Sunday lunch over he was now able to address his other favourite topic, talking about himself! For the next hour or so he waxed lyrical about farming, Welsh lamb, tractors, the Welsh Assembly and Manchester United, while an increasingly drowsy Stephen tried to stop his eyes from closing.

It was Rachel who came to the rescue. As Gordon paused for breath, she pointed to a photo of two young men on the dresser.

'How are the boys?'

Margaret was grateful for the interruption.

'They're good thank you, they came up last month for my birthday.'

'What are they doing now?'

'William's in London, at drama school, he wants...'

Gordon interrupted.

'An actor, he wants to be an actor.'

He shook his head in disbelief.

'What about David?' Rachel asked.

'At agricultural college.'

This time Gordon smiled. 'Cirencester, then coming back to help run the farm. He's engaged to the daughter of a farmer just up the road.'

It was clear which he regarded as the more important

profession.

Eventually it was time to leave. Stephen rose from the table in some discomfort still, reflecting on a wonderful afternoon despite the challenges of the food. He had warmed to Margaret, loving how devoted she and Gordon clearly were to each other.

After a round of thank yous and goodbyes with much kissing and handshaking Stephen settled himself into the passenger seat. He still felt far too full and was forced to undo the top button of his trousers, which made opening and closing the gates on the return journey a hazardous exercise.

They drove back down the hill towards the village in contented silence. Ahead of them the sea shimmered in the afternoon sun, the combined effects of food and drink making Stephen drowsy. He concentrated on keeping his eyes open.

'What a great lunch, Gordon certainly knows how to entertain.'

'He loves it,' Rachel smiled, 'he's in his element.'

'It's Margaret I feel sorry for, she seems really nice.'

'Don't be fooled, Gordon knows what he can get away with and nothing more, she rules the roost, Gordon wouldn't have it any other way.'

'They do seem devoted to each other.'

'They are, and don't be fooled by his appetite either, it's just an act for you, Margaret watches what he eats.'

They drove in silence once more, enjoying the view.

'Mind you, she's not right about everything,' Rachel continued.

'How do you mean?'

'Before we left, she told me you and me would make a lovely couple. Foolish woman.'

Rachel noticed the pained expression on Stephen's face, and pulled into the village, doing her best to supress a smile.

Over the next couple of weeks Stephen returned to his writing. He had managed to track down Lewis Hughes, the detective who had investigated Tania's death. Now retired, he was surprised to receive Stephen's call, after initial hesitation he agreed to meet. Stephen took the train up the coast to Harlech. As they strolled across the dunes under the shadow of the imposing castle, the ex-Inspector's trained mind recalled details of the case with remarkable clarity, filling in some gaps in the story. He confided that he had never believed Conrad had committed the crime, and to this day was convinced Dominic was the guilty party despite his inability to secure a conviction.

Stephen also persuaded Conrad, over another bottle of fine wine in the Lobster Pot Café, to help him find a possible publisher for his book. He was well aware of the challenges of becoming first time published. Over many years Conrad had built up an impressive list of contacts in the literary world and a few phone calls had lined up a promising lead.

Later in August Stephen's parents came to visit for the weekend. He booked them a room in a nearby hotel, and together they spent their time exploring the area, reminiscing about family holidays. They loved the Lookout for its charm and panoramic views, even though they found the hammock a perplexing choice of a bed. His father looked so well; his mother assured Stephen she was keeping a close eye on him.

On their final evening Stephen booked a table at the Lobster Pot Café, inviting Rachel to join them. It was a great success, his parents warmed to Rachel immediately and Nick went out of his way to make the evening special. Rachel especially delighted in seeking out stories of Stephen as a child, much to his mother's delight and his embarrassment.

Next morning Stephen and Rachel stood on the platform as his parents boarded the train for their return trip. Just before the doors closed his mother hugged Stephen and as he turned away shouted after him.

'She's lovely Stephen, perfect for you, we're so pleased for both of you.'

Then the train was on its way, his parents smiling and waving fondly, Stephen opening and closing his mouth like a goldfish with Rachel struggling hard to contain her mirth.

Chapter 16

The Bank Holiday weekend in late August is widely acknowledged as the busiest few days of the year in Aberdyssyni. Summer reaches a crescendo as day trippers mingle with those staying longer and the village fills to bursting point. A large marquee is erected on the quayside providing entertainment for children including face painting and a circus workshop, a welcome distraction for parents. On the beach the donkey rides do a roaring trade while jet skis, yachts and pleasure boats compete for space on the water.

Next to the jetty stalls have been erected beneath brightly coloured gazebos as the annual food and drink festival takes place. A queue forms in front of the Lobster Pot Café stall where Nick and Sammy are hard at work cooking seafood paella in a giant pan, the delicious smells tempting holiday makers and stall holders alike. Next door Bob morosely serves pints to thirsty customers.

The events of the weekend culminate with a magnificent firework display, multi-coloured flashes of light illuminating the night sky with classical music providing a fitting backdrop.

Anxious to avoid the weekend crowds, and conscious of how busy his friends would be, Stephen preferred to focus on his writing, glancing up from time to time to watch a never ending stream of traffic heading for the village. Engrossed in his endeavours, he was interrupted by what at first appeared to be gunshots. It took a few seconds to realise the Lookout was not under attack, it was the sound of a vehicle backfiring.

An old, bright orange VW camper van rounded the bend heading towards Aberdyssyni, travelling at a snail's pace, jerking movements accompanying the backfiring, causing a logjam in its wake. Two large surfboards were tied to the roof. As it approached the Lookout it slowed even further and, with a final hiss and bang, limped onto the grass verge opposite, expiring in a cloud of smoke.

Stephen watched fascinated as two young men climbed from

the van and opened the bonnet, scratching their heads as they peered inside. After a little fiddling, their investigations ceased. Untying their surfboards, they headed for the beach.

An hour or so later they were back, laughing and joking. The taller of the two climbed into the driver's seat somewhat optimistically trying the engine. After a brief council of war, they crossed the road to the Lookout and climbed the steps.

Stephen opened the door to the two friendly looking men in their mid-twenties, dressed almost identically in long shorts, surfing t shirts and sandals. The taller of the two had bleached blond hair, his friend an unruly mass of dark curls, both were well tanned.

Bleached blond spoke first.

'Oh hi, sorry to bother you, we seem to have broken down. Would you have some water for our radiator?'

Stephen smiled. 'Of course, come on in. Cup of coffee? I was just making some.'

'Well yeah, sure, if that's no trouble,' dark hair spoke this time, 'hey do you really live here? So cool! Sorry I'm Tommy, this is Jed.'

Stephen busied himself in the kitchen while Tommy and Jed wandered around the Lookout, exploring the unusual building and taking in the views.

'Wow, you actually sleep in a hammock?'

As they drank their coffee the boys asked Stephen questions about the Lookout, fascinated by its history.

'So what's wrong with your van?'

'Radiator's bust, we've been topping it up for days but we need to get it repaired.'

'Where are you headed to?'

'Just on down the coast, been up in Snowdonia, beautiful area.'

'Why not get it repaired here in the village, there's a good garage, it'll be no problem you camping over there for a couple of days.'

The boys thought this was an excellent idea and disappeared back across the road. Stephen returned to his writing, glancing up from time to time as Jed and Tommy pitched a small two person tent before climbing into the van and with a plethora of bangs and wheezes headed for the village.

That evening Stephen and Rachel took Bryn for a long walk along the now quiet, sandy beach, enjoying a spectacular setting sun. As they returned across the sand dunes they stopped to watch as Jed and Tommy emerged from the sea in their wetsuits clutching their surfboards. They walked up the beach and clambered over the dunes, stopping to stroke Bryn, who leapt around the boys, barking excitedly.
'How did you get on with the van?'

'All good, going to be done in a couple of days, thanks for your help, we've got some beer if you fancy one.'
They walked back to the tent and sat down by a campfire, still smouldering, which Tommy built back up with wood from the beach. Jed passed round bottles of beer, and, much to Bryn's delight, began to cook sausages on the fire.
'So what are you doing here?' Rachel asked as she sipped her beer, 'is this a holiday?'
'Kind of,' Jed replied, we've got this idea of travelling round the coast of the whole country, to be honest it's just an excuse to put off finding a job.'
'And growing up,' Tommy added, 'or so our parents keep telling us.'
Rachel smiled, 'you want to put that off as long as possible, I did.'
'We are, we've strung it out for a couple of years already, been a bit of an adventure.'
Stephen was never one to miss the chance of a story. 'Sounds fascinating, tell us.'
Jed found some more beers and settled back down by the fire, feeding a sausage to Bryn.

Jed and Tommy had met at university, drawn together by their mutual interest in surfing, music and girls. They developed a close friendship, combining just enough studying with parties, gigs, surfing trips and countless liaisons with fellow students. They scraped through their degrees, rather more by luck than endeavour, and having no idea of what to do next, hatched plans to go travelling. They found a series of jobs in bars and hotels for a few months and managed to save up enough money, before setting off on their adventure, planning to be away for maybe two years.

First stop was South America where they spent some time in the Amazon rain forest before heading for Peru and the obligatory hike along the Inca trail to Machu Picchu, then flew to New Zealand exploring both the North and South Islands, enjoying the Bay of Islands, Rotorua, glaciers and mountains.

Next they headed for Australia, where they stayed for the full six months of their tourist visas. They began in Melbourne, enjoying the bustle of the cosmopolitan city, finding work in bars to fund the next part of their adventure. The city was full of young people with many opportunities to enjoy time with the opposite sex, but eventually they dragged themselves away and headed for Uluru, and spent time exploring the Gold Coast and Sydney.

They decided to complete their travels having up to three months in south-east Asia, flying in high spirits to Bangkok. Here they intended to spend a couple of weeks before heading south to the islands and then on to Cambodia, Laos and Vietnam. They had the prospect of a few more weeks of adventure in such an intoxicating part of the world before returning to the reality of finding jobs at home. Little did they know it was about to go terribly wrong.

From the islands, with their beautiful white sandy beaches, they headed inland to a town close to the Cambodian border and booked into a hostel. Part of the back packing experience was meeting new people from around the world, and a group of them were soon heading out to a local bar in high spirits. Predictably it did not take long for Jed to move in on the most attractive girl in the group, an Australian called Sarah with long blonde hair. Unfortunately, a Canadian guy, who had spent the entire previous evening pursuing Sarah, took exception to the newcomer.   An inevitable altercation developed, Tommy dragging Jed away before it could turn violent. A few drinks calmed Jed down, and they returned to their hostel the worse for wear.   As they walked to their room, they passed the Canadian coming in the opposite direction.   He cast a threatening glance at Jed before disappearing around the corner.

The next morning, shaking off hangovers, the previous evening's altercation forgotten, they headed on a bus to the Cambodian border.   Tommy was first through the customs checks, looking forward to his experience of a new country, when a commotion broke out behind him. The customs official was shouting at a bewildered Jed, while two border guards were quickly on the scene, automatic weapons drawn.   Tommy started back to see what was going on but another border guard quickly intervened, no longer giving any pretence of being friendly, pushing Tommy away out of the customs building. His last view of his friend was of him being manhandled roughly into a room.

Shaken almost to the point of panic, and unsure what to do next Tommy hung around a while, then approached an official next to the checkpoint, desperate to glean information. None was forthcoming beyond learning that his friend was under arrest. At his wits end and with no real plan, Tommy grabbed his backpack and headed by bus for the nearby town. He found the hostel they had booked and anxious to do something walked out in search of a police station. Initially rebuffed by the desk officer he was persistent, he had to find out what happened to Jed. Clearly upset, eventually a more senior officer took pity on him and showed him into a side room. An hour went by, Tommy staring helplessly at the empty coffee cup in front of him, before the officer returned, a serious look on his face. He addressed Tommy in broken English.

'Your friend in big trouble.'

'Why, what's happened?'

'He tried to smuggle drugs into our country.'

'No, not Jed.'

'They were found in his backpack. Stupid man, big penalty for smuggling drugs.'

'He'd never do this, where is he?'

'We take him to prison. He been charged.'

Despite his increasingly desperate protestations of his friend's innocence Tommy found himself back on the street. His head was spinning but he had to remain calm, he must do something, he needed help.

Somewhere through his muddled thoughts he realised he must find a British embassy, he needed to talk to someone. He returned to the hostel explaining his plight to fellow travellers, together they discovered there was a British Counsel in the nearest city. That afternoon Tommy travelled by bus, eventually locating the Counsel building. He was shown into a room and eventually an earnest young man appeared, hardly older than Tommy, who introduced himself as Peter Smithson, Assistant Attaché.

Tommy told his story, the young man taking notes. When it was finished, he leaned back in his chair.

'You know how serious smuggling drugs is, especially in Cambodia?'

'I know, but Jed doesn't do drugs, there's no way he'd do it.'

'Are you sure?'

'I'd stake my life on it. What can we do?'

'First thing is we visit him in prison, let's find out what's going on.'

A couple of hours later Tommy sat beside Peter in an Embassy car as they nosed through the gates of the prison, an ugly building on the outskirts of the city. Peter displayed a persistence and presence which belied his age, he was clearly cut out for a career in the diplomatic service and within half an hour they were led through locked doors into a scary, squalid world. They were shown into a room with a counter and glass screen. On the other side of the screen was Jed, dressed in a prison regulation orange jumpsuit. A look of terror and helplessness on his face was replaced with relief at seeing his friend. He was deeply distressed and close to tears.

'Are you okay Jed?' Tommy leaned towards the glass in concern.

'I guess, but I can't believe this is happening.'

Peter took over, introducing himself with reassuring calmness.

'Tell me what happened.'

'I was coming through the border, this sniffer dog was all over my backpack, there was a parcel in the bottom, I swear I've never seen it before.'

'You're sure. You must understand how serious this is."

'I do, it wasn't mine, I'm so scared.'

A guard entered the room indicating their time was up.

'We've got to go mate.' Tommy touched his friend's hand through the screen, 'but we'll be back, we're going to get you out.'

Tommy and Peter made the first part of the journey back in silence.

'What do you think?' Tommy asked.

'I believe your friend; I've come across enough people who do try and smuggle their drugs in to this country to know when someone's lying.'

'What can we do?'

'If the drugs aren't your friend's someone must have put them in his bag. Think back, did anyone ask you to take anything through the border for them, did you leave your bags somewhere, have you fallen out with anyone?'

'No...hang on!' A thought struck Tommy, 'there was one guy...'

Peter listened intently while Tommy told the story of the altercation with the Canadian, recalling seeing him later near their room. He had thought nothing of it at the time, but now the possible implications were clear.

Peter sighed, 'it's a long shot but it's the best we've got.'

Next day Tommy passed through the border in the opposite direction. He had no clear plan but at least felt he was doing something. Back in the town he returned to the hostel. The chances of finding the Canadian or anyone else for that matter was slim but he had to do something. He was in luck, entering the hostel dining room he found Sarah, the Australian girl, clearing plates with a couple of friends he also remembered.

He explained their predicament and Sarah nodded her head vigorously.

'It was him; I should have done something.'

'Tell me.'

'The Canadian, creepy guy, he's moved on now but he told me the next day that he'd taught your friend a lesson, he said something about a surprise he wouldn't forget.'

'The bastard, he must have planted them when we saw him near our room, where is he now?'

'Gone, he was heading for Bangkok.'

Tommy sighed; he'd never find him now. Sarah was his only chance.

'I need you to do something for me...'

Next day Sarah and Tommy sat with Peter in the Counsel building, as she told the story again, upset she had not acted at the time. Desperate now to help she agreed to go with Peter to the local police chief and sign a statement. Once more Tommy watched as a helpless bystander, his respect for Peter and the diplomatic service growing in leaps and bounds. It took another week, and the involvement of the British Ambassador himself, but their intervention literally opened doors. It was a greatly relieved Tommy who made one final visit to the prison with Peter, hugging his friend as he walked through the gates, a free man once more.

Their desire to continue their trip was now nil and days later they flew back home, a chastened Jed realising how lucky he had been. Their friendship had been strengthened by the experience into an unshakable bond, Jed would always be in debt to his friend. What could have happened to him was the stuff of worst nightmares. Neither could settle into jobs and the following summer they were ready to travel again but opted for the coast of Britain this time instead of venturing further afield. They needed tamer adventures for a while!

Stephen lay back by the campfire and emptied his bottle of beer.

'You were very lucky Jed.'

'Don't I know it man, and I've got this guy to thank,' he punched Tommy playfully.

'Story of my life, that is,' Tommy smiled, 'he gets the girls and I clear up the mess!'

Next morning Rachel called at the Lookout for coffee, watching Jed and Tommy as they disappeared to the beach with their surfboards.

'I really envy those two,' Stephen sighed.

'Why?' Rachel smiled, 'did you fancy a week in a foreign jail, that's the going rate for book thieves?'

'For once and for all I was not a book thief! It's just they're so chilled out about life, taking it as it comes, I always seemed to have a plan, up to now anyway.'

Rachel considered for a minute, 'I know what you mean, I've never had a plan, always acted on impulse, like with Luke, but it can mean you drift.'

'It's the travelling as well, I never did it, school, university, job.'

'It's never too late.'

'Maybe, you know I envy you lot as well, you, Nick, Sammy, Conrad.'

'Why?'

'None of you have settled for conventional lives.'

'Look at you now, the writer in the Lookout, very conventional!'

'Yeah but I'm thirty nine next week, I'll be forty next year, that's so depressing.'

'So you're written off at forty are you? I'd better get my bath chair and shawl ready.'

'Stop it, it's just...' Stephen drifted into silence, deep in thought.

Over the next few days Stephen watched the boys as they surfed or disappeared to the village. He would miss them when they left. The only person who had a downer on them was

Glenda, now recovered and back at work.

'Lock your doors,' she warned him, adding ominously, 'hippies they are, shouldn't be surprised if there's a whole commune on the way.'

Conscious that they were surviving on a constant diet of burgers and sausages, Stephen and Rachel took the boys for lunch at the Lobster Pot Café. As ever recently, Stephen had an ulterior motive, their story was too good not to include in his book.

Somewhat amused that Jed and Tommy both ordered the house burger, they chatted as they waited for the food to arrive. Both boys were intrigued with Stephen's book, Jed able to fill in graphic details of his Cambodian jail experience. Kelly appeared with the food, dressed in a white shirt and tight denim jeans, looking her most attractive.

Jed's eyes did not leave her until she was back through the kitchen door. 'Wow, just wow, who is that?'

Tommy rolled his eyes, 'man you are so predictable!'

'Sorry Jed,' Stephen smiled, 'she's taken, she's with Nick, who owns this place, anyway I'd be in front of you in the queue.'

Stephen could not help noticing Rachel's wounded look, and quickly changed the subject to pudding choices.

Over the next couple days Stephen noticed that Tommy seemed to be on his own at the camper van. On a trip into the village he noticed Jed by the harbour wall deep in conversation with Kelly, their heads close together, laughing as they chatted.

A few days before his birthday, Rachel took Stephen for dinner to celebrate. They drove to a restaurant in a village a few miles from Aberdyssyni. Comfortable in each other's company they chatted convivially as they enjoyed the local lamb, Stephen reflecting on how much time they now spent together, and how close they had become. Once more he thought about mentioning his growing feelings for her but again something held him back, he was scared of spoiling what they had.

As their dinner plates were cleared Stephen looked round the crowded restaurant noticing a couple at a far corner table immersed in each other's company, heads close together. There was something familiar about the boy's bleached blond hair, the girl's long and dark, cascading to her shoulders. Stephen's heart missed a beat.

'Rachel,' he lapsed into a stage whisper, 'over there, in the corner, it's....'

'Are you okay, why are you whispering like that?'

Stephen's mouth opened and closed in a passable impression of a goldfish.

'It's them, Kelly and Jed, they're...together.'

Stephen sank lower in his chair, desperate not to be spotted. He felt sick, what were they doing together? Rachel glanced over her shoulder in the direction Stephen had been staring.

'What on earth are they doing together?' she snorted angrily, 'I can't believe Kelly would do this to Nick.'

'Shhh, they'll hear us,' Stephen sank even lower as he watched Jed lean across and kiss Kelly, 'what are we going to do?'

'Nothing,' Rachel replied after a moment's thought, 'it's none of our business, come on let's leave.'

Stephen nodded, and attempted to signal to the waiter to bring the bill, frantically waving an arm in his general direction while retaining his low seating position. If she hadn't been so angry Rachel would have found the spectacle hilarious. Once it was paid, they headed as stealthily as possible for the exit, although Jed and Kelly were so engrossed in each other it was unlikely they'd have noticed a herd of elephants.

As they pulled out of the car park they noticed Nick's Jaguar.

'They're even using Nick's car,' Rachel exploded, 'I can't believe it.'

'Are you going to tell him you saw them?'

'I don't know, I need to think about it, it's not our business but Nick's a good friend.'

'There could be an innocent explanation.'

'Like what?'

'I don't know, maybe Jed had some problem he needed to share.'

'That doesn't normally involve kissing, Stephen.'

A couple of days later Jed and Tommy climbed up to the Lookout to say goodbye. Their van repaired; they were heading off down the coast. They were surprised at how cold Stephen was, especially with Jed. Stephen watched as they drove away, still seething at the betrayal of his friend.

The first day of September was Stephen's birthday. He had decided to celebrate the occasion with a BBQ, a chance to thank his friends for everything they had done for him over the last few months. Rachel had helped with arrangements and his fridge was bursting with food and drink. Nick was lending him the BBQ and with the weather set fair the whole event would be in the small garden area below the Lookout.

On his birthday morning he woke early and lay in his hammock watching the sun come up. He could already see the blue sky, it promised to be a good day. Stretching out, comfortable and contented, his mind drifted over how much had changed in his life since his last birthday.

Today he was thirty-nine, in just one year he would reach forty. He wondered where he would be on that day, his intention had been to spend just one year in Aberdyssyni, but already he could not imagine leaving. The village and its characters had crept up on him, enveloping him in a cloak of familiarity and warmth.

He was woken from his daydreaming by Glenda arriving with the post, at least a dozen envelopes containing cards and two parcels. Setting them on the table he made coffee then settled down to open them. There were cards from his parents, a couple of aunts, friends and ex colleagues. Some contained brief notes with snippets of news. He realised how quickly and willingly he had lost touch with his previous life.

Now for the two parcels! The first contained a jumper knitted by his mother. He examined it with some trepidation, knitting was not her strong point despite her enthusiasm. This year's offering was bright blue with a lighthouse pattern on the front. He assumed the white blobs surrounding the lighthouse were meant to be seagulls. Resolving not to wear it in Rachel or

Gordon's presence he was going to put it away in a drawer but felt a sudden pang of guilt and slipped it on.

The second contained a book of quotations from his previous assistant, together with a long letter bringing him up to date with news on ex colleagues. A handwritten card wished him well with his writing and hoped the book would inspire him. He had just settled down to read the letter when Rachel poked her head round the door.

'Happy birthday,' she gave him a big hug and kiss then stood back to stare at him.

'What are you wearing?'

'Don't ask, my mum's latest knitting attempt. Gets worse every year.'

'Have you been sick down it?'

'I think they're seagulls actually.' He quickly slipped the jumper off.

'What are you doing, it suits you, very nautical! Here these are for you.'

Rachel handed him an envelope and a large parcel. He slipped open the envelope and pulled out one of Rachel's prints of Aberdysyyni. He opened the card.

To Stephen, happy fortieth, love from Rachel.'

He opened his mouth in protest.

'Actually, I'm only thirty nine, I've got a whole year to go yet.' He examined himself in the mirror. 'I don't look forty do I?'

'Well....'

'I mean forty sounds so old, it's middle aged, you go downhill from there.'

'Thank you Stephen, remind me to book into a retirement home.'

'No, I don't mean you look...'

Rachel handed him the parcel. 'Maybe you'd better open this.'

He carefully undid the string and eased back the brown paper, revealing a large original watercolour of the Lookout, viewed from the beach, with the hills rising majestically above it to meet a wild and dramatic sky. An inscription on the back read

'To Stephen. Your home. Rachel.'

He was stunned into silence.

'Do you like it?'

'It's magnificent! I don't know what to say, thank you so much.'

He carefully put down the painting and hugged a smiling Rachel.

'I mean it, thank you... you're amazing.'

After Rachel had left to open the Gallery, he carefully hung the picture. He couldn't stop gazing at it, she really was a talented artist. He spent a very agreeable day getting ready for the BBQ, which was scheduled for that evening. He moved trestle tables and chairs, which Bob had dropped off the day before, into position and set up the cooking station. Unpacking bunting and lights, also from Bob, he fastened them to the fence and balcony, set out glasses, plates and cutlery and spent much of the afternoon making salads, sauces and dressings.

Having finished his preparations, he walked over the dunes to the beach, looking for the spot the picture of the Lookout was drawn from. He lingered by the sea for a moment, watching the ever-changing patterns as small waves broke on the shore, then wandered back to the dunes and sat down. It was a still afternoon and the sun glistened on the water. His mind wandered over the eight months or so since arriving in Aberdyssyni. So much had changed, he now felt as settled as he had ever felt. Inevitably his thoughts drifted to Rachel. He really valued her as a friend, she was the most fun loving and fascinating person he had ever met, even if her behaviour often bordered on the bizarre. Her zest for life and unquenchable energy were infectious, he felt alive in her presence.

But more clearly than ever he knew he wanted more. He wanted to share things with her that went beyond mere friendship, to experience new things with her, even to build a life together. He was aware of how physically attracted he was to her but his feelings also ran much deeper. He knew he had to share his feelings with her but was terrified of her reaction, what if she felt nothing for him in return? He was also desperate not to lose her friendship- he wondered if she had ever got over Luke- and there was Josh to consider. He closed his eyes, the dilemma swirling round his head.

By six Stephen was showered, changed, and ready for his birthday party. He lit the BBQ and had just poured a beer when a van screeched to a halt. Evans and Anne climbed out clutching bottles of wine. They had barely begun a conversation when a steady stream of guests started arriving. As Stephen began to greet them Evans seized the moment to whisk Anne up the Lookout steps to admire his handiwork.

Next to arrive were Jimmy, the barber, and Bob, the publican, with their wives, closely followed by Billy, for once not wearing his paint splattered overalls. Indeed, everyone had dressed for the occasion, this was a party people had been looking forward to, more bottles of wine were thrust into his hand together, despite his protestations, with birthday gifts.

'Evening Shakespeare,' Gordon's voice boomed. Dressed in a vibrant Hawaiian shirt, he was accompanied by Margaret, who hugged Stephen warmly, and also Brian and Moira, down from Birmingham for a few days.

'Good to see you Gordon, that's quite a shirt!' Stephen smiled as Margaret rolled her eyes.

'You should see the other one's I've got, didn't think you'd mind me bringing Brian and Moira, hope you've got plenty of food, I'm starving, haven't eaten since lunch, none of that fish nonsense though, there's Pasty and Grumpy,' and without drawing breath Gordon was off, pumping Jimmy's and Bob's hands, his voice drowning all others.

Stephen rushed around getting drinks for people and putting food on the BBQ, already feeling overwhelmed, when Sammy and Conrad arrived, Conrad sporting a pink shirt and yellow bow tie, and clutching a bottle of claret. Sammy handed Stephen a box containing jars of Greek olives, vine leaves and feta cheese.

'Just to bring a little sophistication to proceedings,' Sammy winked and helped Stephen find room for the jars on an already fully laden table.

Glenda arrived with her husband, at once commencing a tour of the Lookout with the air of a professional guide. As other guests arrived Stephen frantically tried to balance his various roles of host, chef and drinks waiter. It did not take long for chaos to ensue, flames from the BBQ reducing sausages to smouldering ash while Stephen ran from one job to another like a headless chicken.

Just as he got desperate Rachel and Nick appeared at his side and took control. Nick grabbed the tongs and began to expertly BBQ while Rachel took charge of drinks, mixing cocktails and uncorking bottles like a seasoned bar tender, telling Stephen to relax and circulate.

Gradually Stephen did relax, the evening drifted along in a haze of conversation and laughter, moving from group to group, chatting to his many friends. The noise level gradually increased, a sure sign of how well the party was going, Nick and Rachel ensuring no one went short of food or drinks. At one point Nick brought him a full plate of steak, burger and salad, insisting that he remember to eat.

As the evening drew on the guests stood and watched the red sun sink into the sea and the outside lights twinkled, adding to the convivial atmosphere. Gordon called for silence, ironically seeing he was responsible for at least half the noise and asked fellow guests to raise their glasses to the birthday boy. A raucous chorus or two of *Happy Birthday* was followed by much cheering and shouts of 'speech, speech.'

Against his will, Stephen was shepherded forward. He looked around at his friends, overcome by the warmth he felt, which was only partly due to the wine.

He caught his thoughts, putting them into words.

'I just wanted to say thank you all for coming tonight, and Nick and Rachel for rescuing me, but for far more as well. Thank you for making me so welcome and so much part of this wonderful village, these last few months have been the happiest I can remember. I love you all. Even you Gordon.'

Gordon's splutter of indignation was the cue for more laughter and clapping as drinks were topped up and the party continued.

It was almost midnight when glasses were emptied for the last time and people began to drift off, all declaring it was the best evening they had enjoyed in a long time. Rachel was the last to leave, promising to come back in the morning to help finish the clearing up, although as Stephen glanced around, most had been done already without him realising.

Pouring a final glass of wine and sat on his balcony, gazing out to sea, mesmerised by the flashing of the marker buoy. A perfect evening! A warm feeling of happiness engulfed him. One year today he would be forty, a major milestone in his life. Where would he spend that birthday? What would he be doing? He already had a good idea; plans were taking shape in his mind.

Chapter 17

'What do you mean you're going to London?' Rachel raised her eyebrows in exasperation as Stephen shuffled uncomfortably in front of her. 'You know it's my birthday party Friday night, it's been planned for ages!'

'I know, I know, I'm so sorry, it's just that it's a special event, and I...'

'You mean my birthday isn't a special event?'

'No, I don't mean that, of course it is, and I'll be back for the party, I promise.'

Stephen had been dreading this conversation for much of the past week and true to form had put it off until the last minute. Rachel's birthday party in the Lobster Pot Café had been planned for weeks when, out of the blue, he had received an invitation to a special lunch to celebrate his old company's twentieth anniversary. His first reaction had been to decline, but the more he thought about it the more he wanted to be there, he had been part of the company for almost all of its existence and it was also a great chance to catch up with old colleagues.

'It'll be fine, honestly Rachel, I wouldn't miss your party for anything.'

'You'd better not, and don't forget its fancy dress, super heroes.'

Stephen groaned. Fancy dress was one of his worst nightmares. 'I won't, and it's no problem, the lunch will be over by three, and I won't have a drink. I'll be back in plenty of time.'

'You'd better be Stephen Blanchard, you'd better be.'

As Stephen hurried down the platform at London Euston the clock struck six times. Six O'clock, it couldn't be! The afternoon had started so well, lunch had been a special celebration and he had only intended to have one glass of champagne, but one glass had turned into two, then three then four as he had become immersed in warm conversations with friends and colleagues. By the sixth glass he had completely lost track of time. Eventually he realised he was one of the last in the room, and it was already after five. In a panic he hurried unsteadily to his feet, said his goodbyes and ran to find a taxi.

He sank into his seat on the train, feeling more than a little light-headed, and tried to make sense of the time. Provided he could make his connection at Birmingham he could still make it back to Aberdyssyni soon after ten. If he missed the connection he wouldn't get there before midnight. The idea of having to tell Rachel he was going to miss her birthday party made his toes curl.

He just made it, hurling himself onto the train seconds before it pulled away from Birmingham New Street station. He sank, breathless, into his seat. That had been a close one! The train was less than half full, as the last remaining workers and shoppers left the city to begin their weekend. Stephen relaxed into his seat for the first time since leaving London, secure in the knowledge that he should be back in his village no later than half past ten, plenty of time to join the revelry. It would be later than he had promised Rachel but he was sure she would understand. When the trolley came round he would treat himself to a celebratory drink, in the meantime he just might rest his eyes for a moment or two.

He awoke with a start to find it was dark outside and his carriage was deserted. A quick look at his phone revealed he had been asleep almost two hours. By squinting through the window he could just make out the hills and moorland of the mid Wales countryside. Judging by the time he must be well on the way to Machynlleth, where the train would terminate and he would take a taxi for the last part of his journey home.

Stephen remembered with a groan that the party was fancy dress, his costume was in his bag. Better get changed now, there would be no time later. He walked still a little unsteadily to the end of the carriage and pressed the button to open the sliding door of the toilet, where he changed into his Superman costume, ordered on line in a fit of enthusiasm when the party was first arranged. He pressed the button to open the door. Nothing happened. He pressed it again. Still nothing. Stephen groaned and began to press all three buttons in an increasing frenzy. When that failed to work he tried tugging at the door to open it by hand but it was securely shut.

Stephen checked the control panel and pressed another button, marked 'alarm.' A sign advised him that in an emergency this would enable him to speak to the driver. Reasoning that this qualified as an emergency he pressed it. Again silence. Exasperated he pressed it again and again with the same result.

Superman sank down onto the toilet seat and put his head in his hands. Why did these things always happen to him? He cringed, if Rachel and his other friends found out, the story would be a topic of conversation at the Lobster Pot Cafe for months, embellished by Nick and Gordon until it became folklore. It would not be the first time!

There was only one course of action. Despite his embarrassment he would have to attract attention and await rescue by the train manager and his fellow passengers, although it did occur somewhat worryingly that he had seen no one since waking up.

He knocked on the door, tentatively at first, his cry of 'help' emerging like a small squeal. But no response caused him to bang and shout louder. Still no sound of concerned passengers or staff running to his rescue.

He sank down again and considered his options. Then he heard the recorded announcement.

'We will shortly be arriving in Machynlleth where this train will terminate. Please ensure you have all your personal belongings. Machynlleth, all change.'

Moments later the train juddered to a halt and he heard the doors open. At least now there would be a train check. Confident he would soon be on the final leg of his journey Stephen began to bang and yell again. No answer, this was ridiculous! Then the train doors closed and they moved off again. After a few moments they slowly passed over points then came to a halt. This time the doors did not open. Suddenly there was silence as the train engine was switched off, then the lights went off plunging the toilet into complete darkness.

Stephen scrabbled in his pocket for his phone. This was a complete disaster! Now what? He checked the time, almost ten. He pushed his face against the glass but it was pitch black and he couldn't see a thing.

Against his better judgment he decided to ring Rachel, to try to explain his predicament and seek her advise, although he didn't hold out much hope for sympathy. Rachel seemed to find each of his growing list of predicaments more and more hilarious, especially when he struggled to see the funny side.

He dialed her number and the phone rang and rang. Eventually it was answered although all he could hear at first was loud music and the hubbub of voices, seemingly each competing to be louder than the other.

'Rachel it's Stephen'

'Sorry who's that?'

'Stephen'

'Who?'

'STEPHEN'

'There's no need to shout Stephen, I'm not deaf you know. You'll have to speak up though, I'm at the party.'

'I know you're at the party, I can hear it.'

'Where are you Stephen, you're late, are you on your way?'

'I'm stuck in the toilet'

'You're what? Speak up'

'I SAID I'M STUCK IN THE TOILET!'

'Stephen that is far too much information. I told you not to have that curry last night, now hurry up, you're missing a great party.'

'No liste...'

Sudden silence at the other end. Stephen put down his phone in despair, his head in his hands. He tried banging and shouting, to no avail. He considered his options. He could ring Rachel back but at the moment that was a last resort. Call Network Rail? He had no idea of the number and their offices were no doubt closed for the weekend. Call 999? Seemed a bit drastic and he was worried they would think he was a practical joker, his story was so implausible.

There was no other option. With a resigned air he dialed

Rachel's number again. This time it took even longer to be answered and the cacophony of noise even greater.

'Rachel, it's Stephen'

'Have you finished on the toilet?'

'I'm not on the toilet I'm in the toilet'

'Don't be pedantic with me Stephen, anyway why are you in the toilet? Have you fallen into it?'

He winced as Rachel collapsed in hysterical giggles and now seemed to be sharing the story with Nick, Sammy and Gordon. He could even make out Gordon's loud guffaws, and some comment about being flushed with success.

'Rachel I'm serious, I'm on a train'

'You're in the rain? How can it be raining in the toilet?'

'Rachel listen, please listen. I am stuck in the toilet of a train, locked in'

More giggling as Rachel passed on this latest news.

'Stephen you are so funny, but enough joking, it's a great party. If you've got some stupid plan to surprise me by leaping out of the toilet here do it now. Bye.'

Stephen sank back onto the toilet seat and put his head in his hands. Why him? No point in calling Rachel again, a text was the answer.

He composed it carefully.

'Rachel, I really am locked in a train toilet I think in sidings at Machynlleth. I'm serious. Please alert the authorities post haste'
He pressed send. That should do the trick.

Moments later an incoming reply illuminated his screen

'Shall I let the SAS know as well? Or International Rescue? Stop messing around and hurry up, it's a great party.'

Becoming increasingly despondent Stephen considered his options. There seemed to be no other choice but to dial 999. He reached for his phone and clicked the button. No reassuring light. The battery was dead.

Stephen groaned in despair. It was pitch black, he was in deserted sidings, his phone was dead, his friends were incapable of understanding simple English. It looked like he was here until daylight would no doubt bring rescue. It was going to be a long night.

Smothered in self-pity Stephen sank down onto the cramped floor and made attempts to at least get reasonably comfortable. He was convinced he would be awake all night.

An hour or so later a noise outside woke him up, his body stiff and aching. He heard scrabbling and banging. Probably animals, maybe wild animals, were there still wolves in Wales? Or worse, a ghost! Or even worse still, train robbers! The noise got closer, he thought he heard his name called but bizarrely he could make out some kind of drunken singing, which sounded suspiciously like Rachel.

There it was again. 'Stephen, are you there?' Gordon's booming voice. Then singing. Definitely Rachel. He began banging on the window. 'Gordon, Rachel, help, I'm here.'

There was scrabbling directly below him and moments later he could make out the shape of what appeared to be a giant approaching. A flashlight illuminated the outline of Robin sitting on a very large Batman's shoulders. Closer examination revealed it was Sammy and Gordon.

'I'm here'

'There you are, what are you doing in there?'

'It's a long story'

Behind Sammy and Gordon, Stephen could make out the shape of Rachel, dressed as Wonder Woman. She seemed to be having some difficulty holding her balance and in her hand was a half full glass of champagne.

She looked at him accusingly, her voice slurred.

'Stephen Blanchard, you will go to ridiculous lengths to avoid my party!'

Chapter 18

By common consent autumn does not really exist in Aberdyssyni. If the weather is mild, which it had been this year, the holiday season extends through September and even into early October, culminating in the school's half term week.

After that week, almost overnight, the village empties of visitors and the clocks changing heralds the beginning of winter, typified by winds, rain, occasional breaks in the clouds and dark evenings.

In winter the whole character of the village changes. Locals hurry along the often wet pavements battling with umbrellas threatening to turn inside out in the stiff breeze blowing off the sea. Many traders close down their businesses completely until the spring, those who have enjoyed good summers might head off to warmer climes for a month or two, others bemoan their poor seasons over cups of tea in the cafes that remain open.

There are still regular weekend visitors but now they are more likely to be couples in search of a romantic or relaxing break, with log fires, long walks and pub lunches.

Not all local enterprises are quiet, Billy's painting and decorating business is in high demand in the close season, and so many people are after Evans' time that Anne is forced to impose even stricter limitations on how much she allows him to do.

Rachel has reduced her opening times at the Gallery to just afternoons while Nick opens the Lobster Pot Café from Wednesday to Sunday each week. He and Kelly are able to cope with the reduced levels of business on their own, Gary and Dawn have returned to college. After a shaky start both have made good progress under Nick's tutelage and he hopes they will return in the spring.

Aberdyssyni draws its blinds and prepares for another winter.

It took Stephen a couple of weeks of grovelling, and dinner at the Lobster Pot Café, before Rachel forgave him for missing her party. It had taken calls to the British Transport Police and a further couple of hours waiting before someone from the train company arrived well after midnight to release him. The police officer who attended found the whole episode hilarious, the Superman and the train toilet escapade was soon doing the rounds of the station canteen. Back in the village Stephen was the butt of countless toilet jokes wherever he went. There couldn't be a person who hadn't heard the story! Gordon in particular seemed determined to dine out on it for many months to come.

One late October afternoon Stephen called for coffee at the Gallery and immediately sensed Rachel was upset. She was far from her normal bouncing self and red eyes suggested she had been crying.

'Hey, what's wrong?'

'Nothing.'

She seemed to be avoiding making eye contact with him. Stephen gently took her arm.

'Rachel, come on what's wrong?'

'It's really nothing, it's just me being stupid.'

'Tell me.'

'It's Josh.'

'What's happened, is he okay?'

'He's fine, that's the point, I got this earlier.'

She opened an e-mail on her laptop.

'Hi Mum, I won't be back after Christmas after all. I'm in Peru, helping on a UNESCO project to build a school. I've met a girl called Alessa, she's local, I wish you could meet her, you'd love her. Hope you have a good Christmas, talk before then. Josh x.'

'Rachel, I'm sorry.'

Next moment Rachel folded herself into Stephen's arms, the tears she had been trying to bottle up all morning flowing freely. Stephen wrapped his arms around her and held her tightly. He gently released her and crossed to the door dropping the latch and turning the closed sign. He guided Rachel to a seat.

'It's just stupid, I know it is, it's just that I was so looking forward to him coming back.'

'He will.'

'But when? And I'm not so sure, he's met a local girl.'

'When did you speak last?'

'A month ago, at least, there's the occasional e-mail, I miss him so much.'

'Sounds like he's loving his adventure.'

'What if he doesn't stop loving it, if he settles there, I couldn't bear it.'

'He won't. He'll come home.'

'I don't know Stephen, his Dad was an adventurer, I loved him then let him go, I couldn't stand to lose Josh.'

'You won't.'

'Thank you Stephen.' Rachel kissed him on the cheek... 'you're a good friend.'

She pulled away and wiped her eyes. 'I'm okay, anyway there's always Skype.'

Stephen made them coffee, and when he carried them through Rachel looked a lot better.

She gave him a weak smile, 'let's change the subject, how's the writing, did you talk to that publisher?'

'The one Conrad put me in contact with? Yeah, sent him my synopsis and opening chapters, and believe it or not he's interested, wants to meet me.'

'Stephen that's brilliant, where, when?'

'Next month, in London, I'll catch the train.'

'Make sure you use the toilet before you get on. This is exciting. What's it going to be called?'

'I don't know, maybe *Aberdyssyni Lives*, it's just not a very interesting title, that's all.'

'Have you got enough material to finish it?'

'Not yet, the big bits missing are still about Sammy and Nick.'

'You think there are still mysteries to solve?'

'I'm certain there are. The crates Sammy brings ashore for one thing, I'm certain there was another boat that night at sea. Then there's the Greek connection, both of them, and those missing five years before Sammy came home, so many mysteries!'

'What are you going to do?'

'I don't know, maybe start with the crates.'

'I've got an idea, a plan.'

Stephen listened carefully, half an hour later he left the Gallery full of purpose. When she was sure he was out of sight Rachel reached for the phone.

Stephen arrived at the jetty just before midnight. He looked for the hiding place that gave him the best vantage point, and after some deliberation settled himself uncomfortably behind the dustbins at the rear of the Lobster Pot Cafe. Perfect! There was a mystery to solve and he was the man for the job, Rachel had told him the very same only a few hours earlier. In his imagination he saw himself on the set of a James Bond movie, leaving the casino dressed in a tuxedo, trailing a SPECTRE agent. Piers Bronson or Daniel Craig.

It was a still night, the moonlight illuminating the jetty, casting shafts of light onto the water below. The gentlest of breezes barely ruffled the furled sails of boats bobbing in the harbour.

Footsteps! He had arrived in the nick of time. Craning his neck, he could make out the unmistakable figure of Sammy, dressed in yellow oilskins, walking briskly along the jetty, white beard and weather beaten features clearly visible in the moonlight as he passed Stephen's hiding place.

Sammy reached the end of the jetty and lowered himself nimbly down a ladder onto the deck of the Kerkira. Stephen watched as he unlocked the wheelhouse and busied himself on the deck, tidying ropes, buckets and floats into neat piles, stowing items into a storage box to the stern, whistling as he did so.

Moments later he was back on the jetty, piling lobster pots, coils of rope, floats and bait containers at the top of the ladder, before descending several times, arranging them on the deck, packing them neatly into the hold. As he worked, he sang, in a deep and tuneful voice, loud enough for Stephen to recognise the same song from the Greek night.

Now he stood on the jetty once more, short and stocky, alert, his profile lit by the moon. His mood seemed to change, no longer singing, looking furtively this way and that before untying the rope around a large tarpaulin. He pulled the cover back to reveal a pile of boxes and crates in a variety of sizes. Sammy began to work more purposefully, heaving them to the jetty edge, arranging them in similar sized piles, before struggling down the ladder several times, the contents jingling and clinking. Once they were all on the deck he stowed them into the hold, methodically and carefully, frequently glancing back around the jetty as he did so.

The cargo stowed Sammy busied himself in the wheelhouse and moments later the Kerkira's engines roared into life, shattering the peace of the night.

Once more Sammy climbed the ladder and stood on the jetty looking around before letting out a shrill whistle and beckoning urgently. Craning his neck, Stephen gasped as a diminutive figure, dark clothed and hooded, emerged from the shadows, sprinted across the jetty, followed Sammy down the ladder to the deck and was quickly ushered into the hold, the trapdoor slamming behind him.

Moments later Sammy had cast off the lines and the Kerkira was nosing out of the harbour, carefully avoiding boats at anchor, making for the open sea beyond.

Stephen emerged from behind the bins rubbing his neck, stiff from the uncomfortable hiding position. He pressed Rachel's number on his mobile. He had much to report.

Chapter 19

Stephen was still breathless with excitement when he arrived at Beach Cottage the next morning. He brought Rachel up to date with everything he had seen from his vantage point behind the dustbins.

'There were more crates, lots of them, he was loading them, I bet he's part of an international smuggling ring.'

'I'm not sure there's much need for smuggling these days Stephen.'

'I wouldn't be surprised if it's guns or explosives.'

'Now you're being ridiculous, Sammy would never be involved in that sort of thing.'

Stephen thought for a moment. 'Well, okay, maybe not, but he's up to something.'

'Are you sure he didn't spot you?'

'Of course not, I was the master of disguise, and what about the figure who ran onto the boat?'

'Tell me about that again.'

'Well it was dark but there was definitely someone, he ran right past me.'

'Did you recognise him?'

'No, I told you, it was dark.'

'And you didn't imagine it?'

Stephen snorted in disgust. Imagine it indeed! Would James Bond have imagined it?

Rachel smiled. 'So what next, Interpol?'

'Be serious Rachel, what do you think we should do?'

'Talk to Sammy, ask him about the crates, but maybe don't mention the person, you don't want him to think you were snooping.'

'I wasn't snooping, and suppose he is up to something, he might think I've been spying on him since I moved here, like an undercover policeman.'

'Trust me Stephen, he won't think you're an undercover anything.'

Still feeling a little bruised over Rachel's lack of confidence in his spying credentials, Stephen made his way along the side of the jetty. He knew something was going on, there were too many connections, the Greek link, the crates, the running figure, he just couldn't figure out how it all fitted together. He was miffed that Rachel seemed sceptical.

He found Sammy working on the deck of the *Kerkira,* moored in exactly the same place as the previous night. The fisherman was on his knees, scrubbing the deck. Standing up to get more water, he noticed Stephen above him on the side of the jetty and beckoned him on board.

Dismissing the momentary concern that this could be a trap, his imagination was in danger of running away with him, Stephen made his way gingerly down the ladder and jumped onto the deck. His mind spun as he tried to work out ways to get the conversation round to last night's events.

Sammy resumed his scrubbing.

'How's the book going Stephen?'

'Yes, good, Conrad's story is finished, and Alfred's. I still need some more though; I need your help.'

'Go on.'

'When we were out fishing you told me your story, but you missed out those five or so years after the Merchant Navy. What were you up to?'

Sammy carried on with his work, not looking up.

'Just this and that.'

'And the connections to Greece, you and Nick, the singing, the dancing, Nick's visitors.'

Sammy paused and straightened his back, stretching.

'What did I tell you that night that you had to do?'

'Find it out for myself, not just ask.'

'Well there's your answer.'

Sammy resumed his scrubbing. Stephen groaned in frustration.

'So did you go fishing last night?'

'Of course, every night I can.'

'You wouldn't have taken anything with you, would you? Or

anyone?'

Sammy put down his brush and stood up, Stephen was sure he caught a quick look of concern.

'What do you mean, what have you seen?'

Stephen faltered. 'Nothing, it's just that, it's only...'

'Were you spying on me?'

'No, absolutely not, not at all.'

'That's as well, they used to hang spies back in the day. Anyway, I've got work to do.'

Back on the jetty, Stephen made his way thoughtfully to the Lobster Pot Café, still shaken by his encounter with Sammy. Was that a threat? Was Aberdyssyni the sort of place they still hanged spies today? Better be careful, he'd obviously put the wind up Sammy.

Nick was in the kitchen when he arrived, he motioned Stephen to a table, joining him with coffee. Stephen reasoned once more that a direct approach was best.

'Nick, I need your help, it's about Sammy.'

Nick raised an eyebrow. 'Go on.'

'I think he might be smuggling.'

'Smuggling?'

'Yes, something happened yesterday evening.'

'Go on, I'm intrigued.'

'Well, I was hid...I mean walking by the jetty and I saw something.'

'Saw what?'

'Sammy was loading crates onto the *Kerkira*.'

'Really?'

'Yes really', Stephen said, a little tersely. Why did people seem to doubt his eyesight? 'And a man as well.'

'He loaded a man on as well?'

'No, he ran on.'

Nick sat back in his chair, trying to make sense of Stephen's story.

'So who was this man?'

'I don't know do I? Maybe a fugitive.'

Nick seemed to be struggling to stop a smile.

'Nick, don't laugh, this is serious.'

Nick leaned forward; beckoning Stephen closer with a conspiratorial air.

'Are you sure about this?'

'Of course I am, what shall we do?'

Nick leaned further forward and lowered his voice to a whisper.

'At the moment nothing, if you're right we don't know what we are dealing with, this could be a dangerous situation. We need to keep our wits about us, let's keep a close eye on things over the next few days, tell no one.'

Stephen nodded vigorously, at last there was someone who believed him and he could trust. Nick was right, better to lie low and observe, this could be dangerous, who knows what desperados they were dealing with.

Just then Kelly arrived at their table, smiling brightly.

'Hi Stephen, it's good to see you.'

Stephen rankled inside. How could she be so brazen after what he'd seen in the restaurant? He turned his back on Kelly, pointedly staring out of the window.

Taken aback, Kelly shrugged at Nick, collected the empty cups and headed for the kitchen.

Stephen leaned forward placing his hand on Nick's arm.

'Nick, you know I'm your friend, don't you?'

'Thanks Stephen, and I'm yo...'

'I mean any time you want to talk about...you know...things, I'm here.'

With that he stood up, shot what he hoped was a knowing and supportive look, and made his way out of the restaurant, leaving Nick shaking his head in bewilderment.

At the beginning of November Stephen left Aberdyssyni on the early train, before it was light. He had a busy day ahead. By late morning he was in central London, ready for the meeting with the potential publisher.

A very constructive meeting was followed by an agreeable lunch. He discovered that the publisher's father had worked with Conrad many years previously and held him in the highest esteem. Stephen went out of his way to emphasise he wanted the book judged on its merits, not looking for favours based on Conrad's connections. He agreed to deliver a first draft of his manuscript by Easter, pushing to the back of his mind his issues in pinning down Sammy's and Nick's stories.

By mid-afternoon he was in Birmingham in the back of a taxi, on his way to his old company. He had one more important task that day. His ex-boss greeted him warmly and they spent time catching up on news. Before they finished, he was handed an envelope, which he opened tentatively, inside were details of the value of his share options he had accumulated over the years. He did a double take when he saw the total, it was far more than he expected, reflecting the success of the company. This windfall would be a real help in realising the plans shaped in his mind.

Stephen had explained the main purpose of his visit in an earlier phone call and was shown to a small meeting room stacked with the latest video conferencing equipment. Half an hour later he emerged, pleased with progress.

It was a very satisfied Stephen who arrived back in Aberdyssyni that evening on the last train. He recalled his anticipation and concerns when he had first stepped onto the same platform almost ten months previously- so much had happened since.

In the middle of the month Stephen asked Conrad to join him for lunch at the Lobster Pot Café, to thank him for the introduction to the publishing house. Over a fine meal they reflected on each of their pasts and the circumstances that had brought both of them to Aberdyssyni.

Over coffee Conrad relaxed in his chair, fixing Stephen with a twinkling eye.

'Now then dear boy, what about you and Rachel?'

'How do you mean?' Despite his best efforts Stephen couldn't stop blushing.

'When are you two going to be...what do they call it these days? An item.'

'Conrad, I don't... I mean...I'm not sure if...'

'Just don't leave it too long dear boy, you two are well suited, we all think so.'

Stephen felt an urgent need to change the subject.

'What about you, Conrad, what's your plans?'

'Well dear boy, I'm seriously considering retirement...'

Over the next few days Stephen pondered on Conrad's comment about he and Rachel, particularly not to leave things too long. He knew Conrad was right, but prevarication was borne from a fear of ruining a close friendship, which he greatly valued. He knew he must say something, Christmas was the ideal opportunity, he would invite Rachel for Christmas lunch at the Lookout.

He called next day at Beach Cottage to issue his invitation, but he was too late, another invitation had already arrived. Rachel handed him a printed card.

'Stephen and Rachel, please join us for lunch on Christmas Day at the Lobster Pot Café. Aperitifs 1pm. Dress to impress and bring your dancing shoes. Nick and Kelly.'

Rachel was smiling broadly. 'What a lovely invite.'

'Yes, but isn't it strange it's addressed to both of us?'

'Why's that Stephen, don't you want to be seen with me?'

'No it's not that, it's just that...'

'Shall we just go and enjoy the day?'

'But what about Kelly, after her and Jed were...'

'Come on Stephen, let's not spoil the day, it's really none of our business.'

Stephen considered this for a moment.

'Okay, you're right, and it does sound wonderful. We might even be able to unravel some of the other mysteries.'

'We might Poirot, we might.'

Over the next few days the more Stephen thought about Christmas Day at the Lobster Pot Café the more excited he became. At the end of November, he received two phone calls within a few hours of each other. Now his plans were really taking shape.

Chapter 20

Christmas Day began very strangely for Stephen. He was stood on the deck of the *Kerkira,* motionless on a clear, blue ocean, a warm sun above, Rachel in the wheelhouse, her back turned. Beside her, Sammy, in full Greek national costume, surveyed the horizon through a telescope. Putting down the telescope he pointed to the water, Stephen watched as crate after crate drifted past. He reached down heaving one onto the deck. Inside were strange looking bottles filled with a sweet smelling liquid.

Suddenly the figure in the wheelhouse turned around and Stephen saw it wasn't Rachel but Conrad, dressed as a policeman with a large pink bow tie which was spinning madly. Smiling chillingly at Stephen he moved towards him, speaking through lips that didn't move.

'I'm arresting you dear boy, it's the Greek connection, the Greek connection.'

Stephen stared down at the crate by his feet. Now it was full of Christmas decorations, brightly coloured baubles and a silver reindeer.

Stephen awoke with a start, pitch black still outside, the covers pulled over his face. It took a few moments to realise he wasn't on the deck of the *Kerkira,* but safe in his hammock on Christmas morning. It was just after 7am, stretching out, he enjoyed the warmth of his bed, listening to drizzle outside and the distant sound of the waves, clinging to the last vestiges of the dream as it drifted away.

His mind drifted back to previous Christmas mornings, the excitement and magic of waking as a child and finding Santa Claus had been, hangovers while back from university after nights out, the tension between Helen and him over which set of parents to spend Christmas with.

All that was in the past and he anticipated the day ahead with total pleasure Christmas Day at the Lobster Pot Café with his friends, Nick's cooking, his and Rachel's joint invitation, the surprise he had planned for the day. A shiver of excitement passed through him.

By eight he was dressed, lighting the stove. He looked proudly around his home. A real Christmas tree stood in the corner, he and Rachel had fetched it and a similar one for Beach Cottage in her Land Rover, decorating it together with brightly coloured baubles. Next to it his Christmas cards, from family, friends and ex work colleagues, but also from local people who were no more than passing acquaintances in the village. He had been surprised to receive them, unaware that Nick and Gordon had elevated the local author in the Lookout to celebrity status.

There was only one gift to open this morning, a familiar parcel from his mother. He tentatively pulled out a red jumper probably two sizes too big with a snowman on the front. He placed it quickly in his drawer next to his still unworn birthday gift. He phoned his parents to thank them and exchange greetings. The sentiment was heartfelt. In those few dreadful hours earlier in the year he had doubted his father would be around for Christmas.

The direction to dress elegantly had caused Stephen some consternation, he feared Rachel would be little help, instead seeking advice from Conrad, who he regarded as the very pinnacle of elegance. This had not helped much, Conrad assuring him somewhat cryptically 'it's not what you wear it's how you wear it.'

After some debate he settled for polo shirt, chinos and jacket, and grabbing an umbrella he headed for Beach Cottage, wishing a very Merry Christmas to an elderly couple, and a young family with children wobbling on new bicycles. Beneath his arm he clutched two parcels, one in line with instructions received from Nick, and the other a gift for a special friend.

Rachel greeted him at the door, throwing her arms around him for a Christmas kiss, dressed in an old peasant blouse and what appeared to be dozens of coloured rags tied together to form a skirt. Stephen assumed she must have spent the morning on one of her DIY missions or an early spring clean of the cottage, strange activities for Christmas Day.

Rachel led Stephen through to the kitchen where Bryn greeted him with customary enthusiasm, Stephen pushed him away, anxious to avoid covering his elegant attire with hairs or muddy paws.

Rachel passed him a bottle of champagne. 'Will you do the honours?'

'Isn't it a bit early?'

'Nonsense, it's Christmas Day.

They clinked glasses and toasted each other's health. Draining his glass Stephen felt delightfully light headed, viewing the long day ahead and Nick's customary hospitality with some trepidation.

He handed Rachel her parcel. 'Merry Christmas.'

Rachel opened the wrapping carefully and pulled out a long, slim box. Inside was a gold bracelet.

'Stephen, it's beautiful, you shouldn't have, thank you.'

She slipped it on and kissed Stephen again.

'That's really special, I mean it, you shouldn't have.'

'I wanted to, it means a lot, you mean a lot, I've loved this year, I wante...'

He broke off as Rachel passed him a package of his own. Inside was a carving of a Red Kite, a common sight over the village, its wings spread in flight.

'Thank you, it's stunning.'

They refilled their glasses and chatted about the day ahead. Stephen frowned, 'I hope it's not awkward with Kelly.'

'It'll be fine, forget it.'

'Have you heard from Josh?'

The look of sadness on Rachel's face made him kick himself for asking.

'No, nothing, I was hoping he'd call or at least message seeing it's Christmas, but he must be busy, and there's the time difference. It's just that today is...special, it's his birthday, he's twenty one today.'

She broke off and brushed a single tear away from her eyes.

'Anyway let's enjoy the day, and remember you need to talk to

Sammy and Nick, find out all you can, but be subtle, you don't want to arouse suspicions.'

They discussed the directions they had received from Nick on gifts. Each guest was to bring one item suitable for any other guest, the two rules being it must not be expensive, and must be special to the person bringing it.

Stephen had thought long and hard before deciding to put together an album featuring old photographs of Aberdyssyni, it seemed a most appropriate gift. Rachel picked up a parcel the size of a shoe box, despite Stephen's curiosity she would not reveal what was inside. She also had an envelope containing a gift for Nick and Kelly to thank them for hosting the day, all the guests had contributed.

Stephen glanced at his watch.

'Nearly time to go, I'll wait here while you get changed.'

Rachel gave him a quizzical look. 'What do you mean?'

'I mean get changed for the party, it said be elegant.'

The quizzical look was replaced with a frosty glare.

'I am changed and I am dressed elegantly thank you very much.'

She smoothed down her skirt and pulled on a coat.

'Come on, if you can bear to be seen with me- get changed indeed!'

They strolled to the Lobster Pot Café, exchanging season's greetings with people they met on the way, braving the drizzle for a bracing walk by the water. Climbing the stairs, they looked around the restaurant, tastefully decorated with a stunning Christmas tree. A large circular table had been placed in the middle of the room, laden with plates, sparkling wine glasses, colourful crackers, party hats and streamers, eight places had been set around a centre piece of twinkling yuletide candles. To the far side of the room an area had been cleared for dancing, with a marvellous display of helium balloons to each side.

They were first to arrive. Nick and Kelly were there to greet them, Nick resplendent in a white dinner jacket and bow tie, while Kelly wore a short black cocktail dress. Remembering his promise to Rachel, Stephen greeted Kelly with a brief kiss on the cheek. Nick kissed Rachel warmly and both he and Kelly congratulated her on her choice of outfit. Stephen ignored Rachel's withering look- there was no accounting for taste!

Next to arrive were Conrad and Sammy, their flushed faces suggesting they had also indulged in an early Christmas drink. As predicted, Conrad was indeed the height of elegance in a velvet smoking jacket, and a pink bow tie remarkably similar to the one in Stephen's dream. Beside him Sammy looked a little uncomfortable in a jacket of his own.

Nick poured bubbling champagne and the six of them chatted animatedly together, their chatter soon drowned out by the arrival of the final guests as Gordon burst through the door, Margaret trailing in his wake.

'Merry Christmas boss,' Gordon boomed, pumping Nick's hand, 'and to you Shakespeare, sorry we're late'. He made his way around the group as an Emperor might greet his subjects, dispensing kisses and handshakes in equal abundance, hugging Rachel and Kelly until they thought they would burst! He wore a voluminous black dinner suit with a brightly patterned waistcoat. It was the bow tie, however, that transfixed Stephen, bright red with snowmen on it and flashing blue lights. Next to him Margaret was dressed demurely in blue.

Now everybody had arrived Nick led them to the balcony. The day had brightened up considerably and they gazed out across the estuary, at dog walkers on the beach. Nick popped the cork on more champagne and replenished glasses, raising his to propose a toast, but Gordon got their first.

'If I may boss, on behalf of us all we'd like to thank you and Kelly for your invite, Merry Christmas!'

The echo of 'Merry Christmas' came from all sides and there was much clinking of glasses. The party had begun!

It was soon time for presents. Back in the restaurant each person had deposited their gift into a sack under the tree, which was now overflowing with eight brightly wrapped packages of varying shapes and sizes. Nick called for attention to a chorus of catcalls.

'Ladies and gentlemen...'

'And Shakespeare,' yelled Gordon from the back.

'Ladies and gentlemen,' Nick continued with some difficulty, 'it's time to exchange gifts.'

Cue spontaneous applause and more whistling.

'Remember the rules, every person picks a gift, don't take your own assuming you can remember which one it is...'

Hoots of derision.

'...Once you've opened your gift you must identify who chose it. Now who's going first?'

There was much shuffling before Margaret was propelled to the front. After deliberation she selected a long, heavy box. Inside was a magnum of champagne.

'From Conrad, maybe?' she suggested tentatively.

Conrad smiled and nodded, as Margaret returned to her place to applause.

Conrad was next. With much 'excuse me dear boys' he picked a flat parcel containing chefs whites and hat. The jacket was embroidered with 'Lobster Pot Café.'

'Thank you, dear boy.' Conrad correctly identified Nick. 'But I can't even boil an egg. Mind you they might fit my housekeeper!'

Nick selected the next parcel, opening the Aberdyssyni photo album, which he studied carefully.

'Rachel?' he suggested. She smiled but shook her head.

'Stephen, of course, thank you so much, that's really special.'

Stephen went next, opening his gift carefully, pulling out a small, brightly coloured bouzouki.

'Another Greek connection.' He looked questioningly at Sammy, when would the mystery end?

They took a break to study gifts and sip champagne before Sammy came forward, rummaging in the half empty sack. Rachel joined him, guiding his hand to one particular parcel, prompting a chorus of boos, whistles and cries of 'leading the witness.' Rachel grinned sheepishly.

Sammy opened the package and gazed in wonder at a wooden carving of the *Kerkira*. It was perfect down to the last detail, its name stencilled on the bows. Sammy turned it over and over in his hands, examining it lovingly.

'It's beautiful,' Nick said, not only on behalf of the speechless Sammy but everybody.

Rachel stepped forward, opening a basket full of spring bulbs.

'That must be from you, Margaret,' she smiled, 'thank you so much. They'll look a treat in the spring.'

Just two gifts remained. Kelly came forward and selected two parcels tied together. The first contained a DVD of '*a collection of the best Manchester United goals ever.*'

'Thank you Gordon,' she laughed, 'it's just what I always wanted.'

'Well Nick did say to give something special to me,' Gordon defended himself.

Opening the second package Kelly pulled out a leg of lamb to more general amusement.

'Just you left then Gordon,' Nick motioned him forward, 'and you can work out who it's from.'

Gordon rummaged in the bottom of the sack and pulled out an envelope.

'Thank you Kelly,' he said, ripping it open, reading the card twice before handing it to Margaret.

'You'd better read them what it says dear, I think I need a drink!'

Margaret read out loud.

'*A gift voucher for a facial and beauty treatment at the Tallgryn Spa. An hour of indulgence from our trained therapists.*'

There was an explosion of laughter as Gordon opened and closed his mouth, for once at a loss for words.

'It'll be great Gordon,' Nick comforted him, 'while you're enjoying your treatment Kelly can watch the football.'

Champagne was sipped and gifts admired. There was much laughter at Gordon's expense, while Sammy's carving was passed from hand to hand for closer examination. Nick and Kelly disappeared to the kitchen announcing that lunch would be served in twenty minutes.

'I hope it's turkey,' Gordon remarked, none too hopefully, 'fish is all very well but it's Christmas Day after all.'

Stephen wandered over to the window where Rachel was gazing out to sea, lost in thought.

'Are you okay?'

Rachel turned. 'Yeah, I was just wondering what Josh is doing.'

'I know, I'm sorry.' He slipped his arms round Rachel. She leaned her head back against him.

'It's okay. Come on, lunch time.'

Stephen kissed her gently on the head, it felt the most natural thing in the world. He glanced at his watch and the door.

The moment was interrupted by Nick emerging from the kitchen to announce lunch, the news greeted with loud cheers. He motioned his guests to the table, place names by each setting, Stephen found himself sitting between Gordon and Margaret.

Crackers were pulled, hats placed on heads and jokes exchanged to great merriment. Gordon, recovered from the shock of his gift, adopted the role of master of ceremonies, combined with that of sommelier as he dispensed wine and wise cracks in equal measure.

Starters arrived, plates of mussels, and the chatter died away as the serious business began. Rachel made a point of opening her napkin.

'Just being careful Stephen, don't want to get my skirt dirty, I need it to change the oil in it tomorrow.'

Stephen chose that moment for a coughing fit and turned to Margaret who was consumed by fits of giggles.

'Are you okay?'

'I'm shorry', she hiccupped, I don't normally drink. That champagne has gone straight to my head, is there anymore?'

Meanwhile Gordon engaged Nick on the subject of traditional Christmas food.

'Boss this fish stuff is all very well, but after all Christmas is

Christmas, it's about turkey.'

'Gordon, you seem to have made short work of your mussels though,' Rachel observed from across the table to general agreement.

More wine was poured and the conversation became even more animated as guests contemplated the main course to come. Nick and Kelly reappeared bearing plates of salmon in sauce with an assortment of vegetables. These were laid in front of seven people but Gordon's place was left empty. Nick and Kelly sat down re-joining the conversation.

Gordon looked forlorn, 'but...Boss...'

'Is there a problem Gordon?'

'It's just that I've got no lunch.'

'I'm sorry Gordon,' Nick struggled to keep a straight face, 'but you said you didn't want any of the fish stuff and there's only fish, don't worry there's pudding later.'

Gordon looked aghast, 'I didn't say that did I?' He looked round the table for support, but the rest of the guests rallied to Nick's side.

'I'm afraid you did, dear boy,' Conrad nodded sagely.

'Hang on Gordon,' Nick headed for the kitchen. 'I'll see if I can rustle up a cheese sandwich to keep you going.'

Gordon was left shaking his head murmuring 'a sandwich, a cheese sandwich.'

Moments later Nick re-emerged, a broad grin on his face, carrying a giant plate laden with roast turkey and steaming vegetables. He laid it down in front of Gordon to a chorus of cheers.

'Boss, boss,' Gordon smiled broadly, picking up his knife and fork with the look of a man whose Christmas's have all come at once.

For a while the only sounds were the clatter of cutlery and clinking of glasses as people enjoyed their food. Eventually final mouthfuls were consumed and Nick and Kelly congratulated on the delicious meal.

Stephen was increasingly aware that all was not well with

Margaret, her hiccups becoming more frequent, each followed by a slurred 'shorry.' She dropped her knife on the floor several times, struggling to retrieve it, resuming her seating position only through pulling herself up Stephen's leg hand by hand, much to his acute embarrassment.

'I'm so shorry,' she apologised, 'it's the wine and you've got much nicer legs than my husband, is there another glass, I am enjoying myself.'

Only Gordon was still eating, manfully tackling his potato mountain. Never one to miss a gambling opportunity, Conrad opened a book on whether Gordon could empty his plate, the smart money was that he would. With one final effort he finished the last mouthful and sat back with a deep sigh of satisfaction to a round of applause.

'Boss,' he finally managed to say, 'I don't suppose there are seconds by any chance?'

After a much needed break pudding was served together with dessert wine. The light lemon mousse tasting so delicious that even Gordon forgot to bemoan the absence of Christmas pudding. Conversation began to flow again around the table, more mellow as the afternoon drifted by and darkness descended, Stephen doing his best to ignore the persistent tugs on his sleeve from Margaret who was sinking ever lower in her seat.

'I do like you,' she slurred, 'you're so handsome, not like my fat oaf of a husband, if you and Rachel weren't together, I'd be after you.'

Stephen opened his mouth to deny the implied relationship, but Margaret was on her feet, staggering in the general direction of the toilet, giggling and singing as she went.

As coffee was served, Gordon, in his self-appointed role as master of ceremonies, climbed to his feet, banging his glass on the table for silence. He thanked Nick and Kelly once more for their hospitality and wonderful food before regaining his seat to rapturous applause.

Nick rose to reply, thanking everyone for their kind comments before announcing that, in the best tradition of Lobster Pot Café Christmas events, it was up to the newest guest to make a maiden speech.

To much further applause Stephen reluctantly climbed to his feet. In that moment he realised just how much he loved living in his new home, how he felt he belonged. When he spoke, it came from the heart.

'Nick, ladies and gentlemen,' he began to much encouragement, 'it's difficult to find the words for what's happened to me. A year ago I'd met none of you, today I'm amongst friends...'

He ignored Gordon's 'speak for yourself.'

'...since I arrived you have made me feel more welcome and happier than I can ever remember. You're very special people and I'm proud to live amongst you. There's one person here who I especially want to make happy today, we'll know later if I've succeeded. Thank you from the bottom of my heart.'

He sat down to warm applause from all, catching a quizzical look from Rachel, then stood once more, retrieving an envelope from his jacket pocket.

'Nick and Kelly, thank you once more for today, this is a small token of our appreciation from all of us. We know things are difficult for you right now, hopefully this might help.'

He handed Kelly the envelope, who shot Nick and Sammy a questioning look, receiving shrugs in response. She pulled out the card and read it two or three times to herself, her face turning a beetroot colour. She handed the card to Nick trying desperately to supress giggles. He read the card out loud, struggling to keep a straight face.

'A candlelit dinner for two with champagne at the Dinas hotel, followed by a night in our four-poster bed, and breakfast in bed. A romantic escape for a special couple.'

Nick's face contorted in what appeared to be a last attempt not to laugh. Stephen glanced at Rachel raising an eyebrow.

This was not the response they had expected.

'Why thank you Stephen, Rachel, thank you everyone, a most umm... unexpected surprise. Sammy, did you know about this?'

Before Sammy could answer all the lights suddenly went out, leaving the room in almost total darkness. Nick and Sammy went to find a torch and check the fuse box, Margaret, who had been dozing, grabbed Stephen's arm.

'Postman's knock, what a wonderful idea, can we go first?' Nick and Sammy were back, placing more lighted candles on the table.

'Don't worry, problem with the fuses, help is on the way.'

The room looked beautiful bathed in candlelight and the buzz of conversation resumed. Fifteen minutes later Evans appeared at the door, tool box in hand, a party hat on his head. He, Nick and Sammy headed for the fuse box.

Too much was playing on Stephen's mind and he couldn't let it rest. He noticed Kelly disappear into the kitchen holding a candle and followed her, he went up and took her by the arm.

'Kelly, what's going on?'

'What do you mean?' Kelly seemed surprised, uncomfortable with Stephen's grip of her arm.

'We saw you with Jed having dinner, Rachel and I were there, you...you kissed. What were you thinking of, what would Nick say?'

'It's okay, he knew, he wanted me to go, he lent us his car.'

Stephen had been expecting denial or anger, maybe even contrition, this was unbelievable, Nick and Kelly must have a very modern relationship. Kelly pulled her arm away, leaving Stephen bemused.

As he followed Kelly from the kitchen the lights came back on, Evans and Nick reappearing to cheers and applause.

'Come and join us Evans,' Nick beckoned, 'grab a glass.'

'Don't mind if I do, just a quick one though, the missus is waiting in the van.'

'What, for goodness sake, go and get her!' Nick rolled his eyes.

Seats were pulled up between Conrad and Rachel as Evans

and Anne returned. Stephen had wanted to bring Rachel up to date with the latest developments but she was soon enveloped in conversation. Across the table Stephen watched uncomfortably as Kelly whispered in Nicks ear, gesturing towards him, this was getting more confusing all the time. Nick's face broke into a broad grin, he beckoned Sammy over and whispered to him, both dissolving into laughter.

What on earth was going on? It was all too much for Stephen who wanted to say something but was hampered by Margaret, who was now asleep on his shoulder. Before he could move her Nick stood up, banging the table with his glass.

'Ladies and gentlemen,' he announced as conversations died, 'certain misunderstandings and even accusations this afternoon (he looked pointedly at Stephen) suggest that I may have been a little economical with the truth earlier this year. It appears that people around the table have believed Kelly and I are lovers and that she has been two timing me.'

He paused as Kelly, bright red again, dissolved into uncontrollable giggles. Stephen and Rachel gazed at him in rapt attention, hanging on to every word. Conrad raised an eyebrow, a look of amusement on his face, Gordon was opening and closing his mouth again, gripping his coffee cup. Evans and Anne looked bemused while Margaret snored gently.

Nick continued. 'Confession time, Kelly isn't my partner, she's my daughter.'

Stephen and Rachel exchanged looks of complete bewilderment while Conrad's eyebrows reached the very top of his head. Gordon let his coffee cup fall from his hand, the handle parting company from the cup as it crashed to the table. Only Sammy was unperturbed, his face etched in a broad grin.

Stephen was first to break the silence.

'But...we thought...I mean...'

'Things are not always what they seem,' Nick interrupted, 'I admit I may have misled you a little at first, but you did put two and two together.'

'...and made five dear boy,' Conrad murmured, 'well, well, well.'

'But Jed… the restaurant,' Stephen was still shaking his head, 'we thought…'

He looked to Rachel for support but she was already on her feet, breaking into laughter, hugging both Nick and Kelly in turn.

'You monster,' she punched Nick playfully, 'you really got us this time.'

'My dear boy, who would have guessed,' Conrad added.

Gordon managed to find his voice at last, 'boss, boss, boss.'

The table dissolved into chatter and laughter; the remaining plates cleared away. Stephen's head was spinning, now there were even more unanswered questions!

As if reading his mind Nick appeared at his side, guiding him over to another table where Rachel, Sammy and Kelly were already seated.

'I guess we need to fill in a few gaps Stephen, you deserve to know about the Greek connection, and Sammy's mysterious night time activities. Come and sit over here, it beats scrabbling behind the dustbins outside.'

As the others put on music the five of them settled round the table.

Nick took a sip of wine and continued.

'You see originally there was no Nick Thorpe, there was Nicolas Theodopoles, but the story starts even earlier, back in the war.'

Chapter 21

By 1943 Allied forces were deeply involved in fighting the Second World War on many fronts. American troops were gathering in Britain preparing for the D Day invasion, in January they carried out their first bombing raids over Germany. Hitler was advancing on the Soviet Union. In Africa Montgomery's Eighth Army had driven Rommel back to the Tunisian border, acts of atrocity were being carried out in the Pacific against Allied servicemen- the war in the Atlantic continued remorselessly.

In occupied Greece, partisan activity against the occupiers was growing by the day with attacks on German patrols, storehouses and communications. The power of the German army made this guerrilla activity an unequal war, in October the Germans lost nineteen men in an attack that left over seven hundred and fifty Greeks dead. In all, thousands of Greek civilians were killed in reprisal actions as they fought to resist almost overwhelming odds.

Such was the scope of the war the British government were able to devote very little time to events in Greece. One small section of the Ministry of War in Whitehall was responsible for maintaining contacts as best they could with the partisan movement. A small group of British agents were supporting the guerrilla activity as best they could. Some contact was maintained between London and the men on the ground through Imperial cable routes via Malta and Gibraltar.

By early 1944 things were becoming increasingly desperate for resistance fighters on the Ionian island of Corfu (or Kerkira to give its Greek name). Contact had been lost with two British agents, raising fears that they had been captured. It was agreed that another operative must be landed on the island, who could blend in with the local population, make contact with the resistance fighters and seek to locate the missing agents.

Eventually an agent was selected. There was much opposition at first from superiors who were shocked at the choice, but they were the perfect fit, with Greek family connections and a fluent grasp of the language. Minimal training was undertaken but the need was great and the agent insistent they were ready, and in February they boarded a transport plane on a quiet Norfolk airfield. They refuelled in Gibraltar then at dead of night made a long slow sweep over the island. Torches flashed from the ground to mark the target area for the drop and moments later twenty two year old Sylvia Duffy's parachute opened safely in the dark night sky.

On the ground the first person to meet her was the leader of the resistance fighters, twenty five years old Demetrius Theodopolis, dark skinned and good looking, although this was the last thing on her mind as they quickly gathered in the parachute. Minutes later they were crowded together in the cab of an old pickup truck bumping over tracks on their way to the farmhouse that served as the local headquarters of the partisan movement.

Sylvia Duffy was the youngest agent operating behind enemy lines and one of the very few women in active service. Her maternal grandfather was Greek, she inherited looks from his side of the family as well as fluency in the language. At the outbreak of the war she joined the WAAF determined to play a bigger part in the conflict, why should only men see active service? The invasion of the country she regarded as her spiritual home strengthened her resolve, persistence eventually brought her to the attention of the authorities. A few weeks of training in espionage, self-defence and parachuting followed, she was an impatient pupil, desperate to see real action, her departure could not come soon enough.

Over the next few weeks she accompanied Demetrius wherever he went, taking part in a successful mission to blow up an ammunition dump, planting explosives in the path of troop laden lorries and watching with foreboding from the hills high above the capital as one thousand seven hundred Greek Jews were loaded like animals onto a ship at a beginning of a journey that would end at Auschwitz.

The group tried without success to locate the missing British agents before events overtook them in late 1944 as allied troops liberated the island. A few weeks later Demetrius and Sylvia held each other on the harbour side in Corfu town before she boarded a ship bound for Southampton.

Back in Britain Sylvia received a medal for her bravery, months later celebrating VE Day on the streets of London with thousands of others. Unable to get Demetrius out of her mind she returned to civilian life. They re-established contact finding the weeks waiting between each letter excruciating. When Demetrius tentatively suggested she consider returning to Corfu she needed no persuading. Weeks later she was on a ship in the Mediterranean heading for Athens where another boat took her to Corfu to find Demetrius waiting on the quayside. His mother and father took her in like their own daughter and within weeks the couple married in a traditional Greek ceremony.

Mr Theodopolis senior, also Demetrius, was in his early fifties and already a successful businessman. He owned two motor yachts, which he had somehow managed to conceal from the occupiers during the war, resuming his business ferrying passengers and goods between Corfu, the other Ionian islands and the Greek mainland.

The family lived in a large stone walled villa south of Corfu Town, Sylvia settling in with her new husband into a completely different life than she had experienced in post war Britain. Just over a year later the couple celebrated the birth of a daughter, Anne-Marie.

Demetrius had joined his father in the family business, proving himself every bit as resourceful as he had been in the war. The business expanded quickly and over the next few years opened up new routes not only with the Greek mainland but also Italy. The younger Demetrius still thirsted for adventure and not all cargo carried was legal, there was much money to be made running contraband goods to and from the mainland.

Anne-Marie proved to be a challenging and rebellious child, Sylvia found it increasingly difficult to control her, while

Demetrius, immersed in the business, had little interest, believing it was a woman's job to bring up a child.

At nineteen Anne-Marie disappeared, and when she finally reappeared, she admitted she was pregnant. Despite furious questioning from her father and tears from her mother she refused to reveal who the father was. In 1966, she gave birth to a baby son, Nicolas.

The next year was traumatic for Sylvia. Anne-Marie showed no interest in her young son, preferring the company of various male friends. Before Nicolas was even a year old she was gone, apparently heading for a new life in Athens, leaving Nicolas to be brought up by his grandparents. Sylvia doted on the boy, and his grandfather treated him as his own son. Nicolas in return worshipped Demetrius, spending as much time with him as he could, joining him in his office or on one of the many boats in the rapidly expanding business empire. The Theodopolis Shipping Company was now a growing and important corporation with a fleet of vessels ploughing the Mediterranean and Aegean.

While accepting that Nicolas would one day inherit the business, Sylvia was adamant he should first complete his formal education, arranging for him to attend boarding school in England from the age of eleven, returning to Corfu each holiday. Over the five years he was there, Nicolas missed his grandparents (in reality he regarded them as his parents) but also fell in love with England, proud of his joint nationality (something Sylvia had insisted upon) and already as proficient in English as he was in Greek, again due to his grandmother. He learned about English culture, visited many parts of the country on school trips, and loved playing rugby and cricket. He grew into a tall, good looking young man, speaking English with hardly the trace of an accent.

At sixteen he returned to Corfu ready to join the family business. His grandfather, now in his early sixties, began the long job of schooling him in the various aspects of commerce, delighted to have such an eager pupil. Nicolas was also headstrong, with a need for adventures of his own, and a few months later would be involved in an incident that would change his life forever.

At around the same time a young Sammy Owen arrived in Corfu, recently discharged from the Merchant Navy, also on the look out for adventure. He eventually planned to return home to Wales but was in no hurry to do so. With money in his pocket, he rented a one room apartment in the tiny fishing village of Ipsos, directly across from a small stretch of water linking to the southern coast of Albania, a forbidding mountainous country closed to the outside world.

Finding work as a local fisherman and learning sufficient Greek to get by, Sammy was fascinated by the Albanian coast, questioning his new friends about the country. He was warned to stay away, with stories of Albanian naval patrol boats which shot on sight, and of Albanian and Greek gangs involved in the dark world of smuggling and people trafficking, who would do far worse to people who crossed them than shoot on sight!

This did nothing more than fuel Sammy's yearning for adventure, he began to make excursions of his own in the dead of night, venturing closer and closer to the Albanian coastline, while keeping as low a profile as possible.

What Sammy did not know was that a younger man, only seventeen and equally adventurous, was fascinated by the stories of local gangs and had taken to going out at night in a small speed boat, exploring the Albanian coastline for himself. Too young and headstrong to share Sammy's sense of danger, his luck soon ran out. Spotting the lights of two boats ahead, he ventured too close, a shout from one of the boats followed seconds later by the burst of automatic gunfire. He desperately tried to escape but it was too late, his fuel tank exploded, knocking him unconscious and throwing him into the sea. The other boats fled the area, leaving him for dead, fearing arousing the interest of an Albanian naval patrol boat. Nicolas would have indeed died that night were it not for the prompt actions of Sammy. Observing the incident under cover of darkness, he sped to the spot, where Nicolas, badly dazed, was seconds from drowning when Sammy hauled him out of the water.

Back at Ipsos the burly Sammy carried Nicolas to his apartment. Realising a visit to hospital would alert the authorities he tended to the young man's burns himself, nursing him through the night back to consciousness. The next day, bundling the much recovered but still shocked Nicolas into a borrowed van, he drove him home.

That night saw the beginning of an unbreakable bond between Nicolas and Sammy that would last a lifetime, although neither knew that within a few years Nicolas would be in a position to repay Sammy for saving his life. In the meantime, a grateful Demetrius and Sylvia went some way to thanking Sammy by giving him a job in the family business.

Sammy enjoyed the new challenge and worked hard, he became fluent in Greek and began to develop a love and appreciation of the country's history and culture- its art, poetry and music.

Nicolas now threw himself wholeheartedly into his work, anxious to prove himself to the grandfather he adored. For his part Demetrius, now in his early sixties, was delighted to have him on board. Forgiving Nicolas for his stupidity that night at sea, Demetrius remembered what a headstrong young man he had been. Although he was many years from contemplating retirement, he wanted to ensure his grandson would be fully equipped to one day take over the reins of the business.

Over the next few years Sammy and Nicolas were inseparable, often together in bars and restaurants across the island, competing for the most attractive local girls and increasing number of visiting tourists. Although settled into his job Sammy's adventurous spirit had not been quenched, intrigued by the thrills and money to be made from smuggling between the island and Albania, despite Nicolas's warnings of the dangers of being caught by the authorities, or even worse by the gangs who controlled the illegal trade, he took to sailing at night to deserted coves on the Albanian coastline, making contact with a local gang. He began to make regular trips under cover of darkness, even smuggling Albanians across seeking a new life in the west. The work was well paid, even though he was undercutting the rates charged by the Greek gangs.

Although Sammy was aware of the dangers, he was also foolhardy, inevitably eventually overstepping the mark, muscling in on a deal already agreed with a Greek gang by offering a lower price. The Greek gang leader became aware of the usurper and Sammy's fate was sealed. When he arrived back on the Corfu coast three henchmen were waiting. Bound, gagged and bundled into the back of a lorry, driven to a remote farmhouse in the middle of the island. He was held prisoner, the gang determined to find out the extent of his dealings before doing away with him.

Nicolas, having heard no word from Sammy for a couple of days, began to search for his friend. He and especially his grandfather was well known and respected by local villagers and he gleaned various pieces of information, eventually discovering Sammy's whereabouts. He had no hesitation on what to do next, involving the police would have severe implications, not least he was worried about how many of them were in the pay of the gang leader. This was something he must do alone.

That night, taking a family jeep and a revolver, he climbed high into the hills, abandoning the vehicle a quarter of a mile from the farmhouse and continuing on foot. Kneeling behind a rock he surveyed the scene through binoculars. A single bulb illuminated the kitchen through the open door. Sammy was slumped at the table, hands tied behind his back, guarded by two men, both armed. He inched slowly closer, taking care not to be seen, clutching his gun. He had never fired a shot in anger, but he knew he would not hesitate to use it to save his friend.

Just yards from the kitchen door he crouched behind a stone wall. After a short while one of the men looked out, said something to the other then lit a cigarette and wandered over in Nicolas's direction, oblivious to his presence. He waited with bated breath as the man walked past him. Leaping up he slammed the butt of the revolver down as hard as he could on the man's head, who dropped like a stone without a sound. Nicolas dragged him behind the wall, knowing he had to act quickly before the man regained consciousness. Holding his weapon, he crept up to the door. The remaining guard had his back turned, reading a newspaper. Sammy gave a look of shock when he saw his friend, who motioned him to be quiet. Nicolas moved swiftly across the floor and before the man realised what was happening, he brought his weapon hard down on the back of his head. Just like his friend the man slipped to the ground, unconscious.

Nicolas pulled out a knife and cut Sammy's ropes. He got unsteadily to his feet, rubbing his wrists. Noticing his friend was shaking Sammy took control. He grabbed Nicolas by the arm- they must move quickly!

Together they ran back to the jeep, passing the first guard, who was beginning to regain consciousness, knowing they had to get away as fast as they could. Reaching the jeep, they heard shouts behind them, both guards were running towards them. Shots ran out, narrowly missing the pair. Flinging themselves into the vehicle, Nicolas threw it into gear. Behind them a lorry engine burst into life and more shots ricocheted off the jeep. They roared down the steep track along the side of the hill, the lorry in pursuit, as more shots rang out Sammy grabbed the revolver and returned fire.

As the track descended it began to snake around the hill, hairpin bends, a sheer drop to the left with no safety barriers. Nicolas threw the jeep round the corners, the wheels skidding on the gravel. Ahead was a tight right hand bend- accelerating he negotiated it with inches to spare. Behind them they heard the screech of brakes, watching mesmerised as the lorry failed to steer round the bend. The rear wheels skidded as the driver fought to regain control, it was too late, the wheels slipped over the edge and in slow motion the lorry toppled over and over falling hundreds of feet into the valley below where it exploded into flames.

Both Nicolas and Sammy were shaking. They knew they had to get away, it would not be long before the gang were alerted and would come after Sammy. The only two people who could identify Nicolas were dead, they couldn't have survived the crash and fire, but now he had to get Sammy off the island.

It was almost dawn when they arrived in Ipsos. Sammy collected a few belongings and his passport while Nicolas knocked up the owner of a local restaurant to use the phone. Using his many family contacts, he put into action arrangements he had made earlier. Half an hour later they skidded to a halt on the harbour side in Corfu Town where a boat was already waiting, Sammy would be taken to the mainland where a car would drive him to Athens. Nicolas and Sammy embraced; it was time for Sammy to go home. It would be over twenty years before the friends met again.

Nicolas knew it was time to get his head down and immerse himself in the family business. First Demetrius insisted that the young man complete his education in preparation for the future. Now very close to his seventieth birthday, Demetrius had no intention of stepping away for many years- it was time for Nicolas to become involved.

It was not only the business that occupied Nicolas's mind. His grandfather carefully engineered an introduction to Christina, two years older than Nicolas, the daughter of a fellow business associate and family friend. Demetrius saw it as the perfect match and also believed Christina had the makings of an astute businesswoman. For his part Nicolas fell in love with the beautiful raven haired girl, within a year they were married and two years later Christina gave birth to a daughter whom they called Kelly.

Barely weeks passed after the birth before tragedy struck the family, Sylvia dying after a short illness at the age of seventy-one. Nicolas was devastated, he loved his grandmother, he owed her everything, she had also been the mother he never had. He hoped it might slow Demetrius down but the old man coped with his own grief by throwing himself into the business.

As the years passed Nicolas also became more and more immersed in the business as it grew to become a major shipping company. As Demetrius predicted it was Christina, however, who had more of a head for business, taking a seat in the boardroom next to Nicolas, becoming an increasingly important voice in Demetrius's ear. Though glad of her involvement, Nicolas was also concerned at her ruthless ambition to build the business by any means, regardless of who got hurt on the way. He tried to raise the issue with his grandfather but the old man was blind to it.

Nicolas disliked the ruthless cut and thrust of the business world, not for him the palatial head office now relocated to Athens where Christina grew in influence every day. He was happiest out in the business, on the bridges of the various vessels as they plied their trade across the Mediterranean and beyond, getting to know not just the officers but the crew as well.

As years passed Nicolas began to hear disquieting stories of some of the company's business practices, certainly unethical and bordering on the illegal. Time and time again he fought with his conscience. Kelly was now in her early teens already growing into as beautiful a young woman as her mother. He adored her, but things were far from well between him and Christina, not just because of their differing views on business practices. In 2007 they divorced, much to the anger of Demetrius, now in his mid-eighties but still refusing to let go, who insisted Christina retain her place in the boardroom.

Things came to a head one day in a ferocious boardroom argument over a particularly acrimonious takeover, Demetrius siding with Christina, the other directors falling into line behind the old man, making Nicolas's position impossible. It was time for change.

The next day Nicolas travelled home to Corfu, driving high into the hills to the now burned out shell of the farmhouse where he and Sammy had cheated death. He spent hours sitting on a rock lost in thought. As the sun sank in the west, he made his decision. This life was no longer for him, he was ready for a brand new start, to fulfil his promise and look up an old friend. It was time for a new identity- as he left the hill that night Nick

Thorpe was born.

His mind made up, just two conversations remained. He tried to explain his decision to his grandfather who would have none of it. His place was running the family business. The conversation with Kelly was no less emotional, but at least she understood. He hugged his daughter promising to meet again soon.

Nick arrived at Heathrow in late 2007, Sammy was there to meet him, delighted to be reunited with his friend after so many years. Together they drove to Aberdyssyni.

Nick settled easily into his new home, the only drawbacks being the cold and the rain! Sammy arranged for him to rent a flat above a shop premises owned by local bookshop proprietor Conrad Hamilton. Already a proficient cook he found work as a sous chef in a local hotel, progressing within two years to head chef, gaining a reputation for his Mediterranean dishes.

As much as he enjoyed his role at the hotel, he yearned to open his own restaurant. Perfectly positioned right by the harbour was a dilapidated building run half-heartedly as a tearoom by an elderly couple- it was the perfect location. Nick and Sammy met with the owners and presented a generous business proposition. A few months later Nick was the owner of the business.

On a proud first day as proprietor the two friends sat on the balcony thinking of possible names. They gazed down at lobster pots piled on the jetty. A few minutes later they toasted the success of the Lobster Pot Café!

Over the next couple of years Nick worked hard to build up the business, from the beginning determined to focus on seafood with a Mediterranean twist. His reputation grew steadily and soon the restaurant was thriving.

Although he settled in easily Nick missed his daughter dreadfully. After graduating from university, she was working as a tour guide in Athens. He learned that Christina was now running the family business. Demetrius, now well into his nineties with failing health and back in Corfu, still took an interest in developments, often asking after his grandson.

That Christmas Nick travelled to Athens to spend time with Kelly. He asked her to come back to Wales with him for a few months and she readily agreed, intrigued to learn more of her father's life. Early in the new year, almost the same day Stephen arrived, they travelled to Aberdysyni, Kelly settling into the cottage overlooking the water that was now Nick's home, anxious to work with him in the restaurant. Sharing same wicked sense of humour, it had been Kelly who had persuaded Nick to create an element of mystery around their relationship.

In the summer Christina rang with the news Nick dreaded, his grandfather was slipping away. She begged Nick to return home, to the family business or at last to make his peace. Unable to resolve matters over the phone Christina travelled to Aberdyssyni with the family lawyer. They argued furiously, witnessed by Stephen, Christina demanding that Nick return to the business. Kelly was visibly upset seeing her parents argue so vehemently.

Nick knew matters could not rest; he must make his peace with his grandfather before it was too late. Next day he flew to Corfu, sitting at his grandfather's bedside, holding the old man's hand. With tears in his eyes he gently explained how Demetrius had been his world but he couldn't come back. His grandfather nodded, squeezed his hand then fell asleep.

Demetrius died two days later, at peace with the world at last.

Nick finished his story and took a large sip of wine, lost in his memories. Stephen and Rachel sat spellbound, for some moments nobody spoke, gazing out of the windows at the water. It was early evening and dark outside. Nick squeezed Kelly's hand.

It was Rachel who broke the silence, wiping away tears.

'That's the most amazing story I've ever heard, you were always so secretive about your past, thank you for sharing it.'
Stephen looked at Sammy.

'What about the crates, that night at sea, the voices, there's something still going on isn't there?'

Sammy smiled.

'I may have been back here many years, that night at the farmhouse seems like a different lifetime, but it's in the blood, I'm just keeping my hand in, just a bit of fun.'

He paused, Stephen waited for him to continue, well aware of the importance of silence.

'Container ships dock across the Irish sea all the time, friends of mine over there like a bit of fun as well, so a few boxes disappear and find their way to me. Just food and drink, nothing dangerous, reminds me of Albania, stops me getting old.'

'But the figure on the quayside, he ran onto your boat, I was hiding, I saw...'

He broke off as wide grins break on the faces of the others.

'Didn't you recognise Billy?' Nick's smile turned into laughter.

'Billy...you knew...'

'We knew Stephen, you're not exactly the most secretive of secret agents.'

Stephen looked dumbfounded. He turned to Rachel for support, then the penny dropped.

'It was you, you set me up!'

Feeling lightheaded due to a combination of alcohol and all he had been told, Stephen looked around the room, Evans deep in conversation with Gordon, Ann by his side, lecturing her husband on his drinking while consuming a large schooner of sherry.

Nick jumped up, 'come on- party games!' People were divided into teams, balloons were distributed and a race began, members required to pass the balloon down the row between knees. There was great hilarity as Stephen's team finished a distant second, Gordon finding the task impossible.

As the evening wore on a soporific atmosphere descended on the assembled company. Nick put on more music and the dancing began, as friends jived, twisted and rock and rolled. They moved around the dance floor swapping partners, Stephen quickly realising that a military two step with Gordon was not a good idea. In contrast Evans and Ann glided elegantly in a waltz, reliving their Butlin's days.

As the evening wore on the tempo changed to slower music, Rachel moving across the room leading Stephen firmly by the hand to the dance floor. Then they were in each other's arms and it just felt so right. They kissed, hesitatingly at first, then more deeply, Stephen's heart pounding, there was so much he wanted to say despite his jumbled thoughts.

He pulled Rachel closer.

'Do you think you and me should...maybe it's the right time to...'

He was interrupted by a loud knocking at the door. Outside stood a young man, with long auburn hair past his shoulders and piercing blue eyes. Rachel stared in amazement, lost for words, then gasped.

'Luke, it can't be, Luke, no Josh, JOSH, I can't believe it's you!'

With a squeal of delight, she threw herself into her son's arms, the next few minutes a confused mass of hugs, tears, questions, more hugs and tears, Rachel hanging on to Josh as tightly as she could. There was something at the back of her mind, something she must tell him. Eventually it came to her

'Josh', tears of happiness streamed down her face, 'happy birthday, happy twenty first birthday!'

Chapter 22

It was New Year's Day, cold and icy, a bitter wind blowing off the hills. Stephen, Rachel and Josh walked arm in arm along the beach, dressed warmly to protect them from the cold. Running ahead Bryn bounded along, barking madly, his ears pinned back by the wind, zig-zagging wildly from side to side, setting off in vain pursuit of a flock of gulls.

The three of them laughed and joked as they walked. They had stayed up late the night before, seeing in the new-year at Beach Cottage in front of a crackling fire.

Rachel and Josh had spent nearly all of the past week talking, they had so much to catch up on. Rachel could not believe how her son had changed in the more than two years he had been away. The eighteen year old she had waved goodbye to in Portsmouth had grown into a young man the image of his father. This likeness, coupled with a drink or two, caused her momentary lapse on Christmas Day.

She delighted in showing Josh off to her friends, walking around the village, hanging on tightly to his arm, glowing with pride.

Remembering back to Boxing Day, the three of them had sat at Beach Cottage and Rachel had demanded that Stephen tell her the whole story of his part in Josh's return. Stephen had been painfully aware of how much Rachel was missing her son, her tears that October morning had convinced him to try to do something. His contacts back in his old company proved to be invaluable, they traced Josh's e mail to an internet café south of Lima, and a short time later Stephen made the journey to Birmingham. Making use of the company's state of the art video conferencing he had spoken to Michael Sanchez, the company's man on the ground in Peru. Michael relished the opportunity to play detective, tracking Josh down through calls to UNESCO then travelling to the small town, finding Josh playing pool with friends in a bar. Days later, in a pre-arranged telephone conversation, Stephen explained to Josh how desperately his mother missed him. The young man had been shocked, agreeing to return home in time for Christmas. What Stephen omitted to add was that he had wired Josh the money for the flight home. In a final conversation the young man confirmed that he would arrive at Heathrow early on Christmas Eve, take a train to Shrewsbury, spend the night with his grandparents and borrow their car to drive to Aberdyssyni Christmas morning.

Inevitably things did not work out as planned. His flight was delayed by some twenty hours, and only touched down at Heathrow early Christmas Day morning. No trains were running leaving Josh with no choice but to hitchhike to Aberdyssyni. There was little traffic and progress was slow, a succession of lifts followed, drivers fascinated by his story. It took him over twelve hours to complete his journey.

Over the days that followed mother and son had the chance to understand how each had been feeling. Josh had not appreciated how much Rachel had missed him. Relishing the adventure, he lost track of time, with months too quickly turning into years. Stephen's call had been a stark reality check. Realising how much he missed his mother he had no hesitation in returning. It was wonderful to be home.

Rachel asked him tentatively about the future, the last thing she wanted was to tie her son down. Travel was in his blood; he was still young enough to seize every opportunity. He confirmed he would return to Peru in mid-January to complete his contract but would be home again by summer, after that he had no immediate plans but going to university would be a possibility. He also had the small matter of the ten thousand pounds inheritance on his twenty-first birthday.

Josh asked his mother about Stephen, really taken that he had cared enough about Rachel to contact Josh, he probed and teased mercilessly but was unable to extract much from her. For her part Rachel waited anxiously for Stephen's plans for the future, he had intended to stay a year, and that was almost up. Would he leave his friends behind, maybe even returning to his old company? The thought of life without Stephen made her ache.

She knew Stephen had feelings for her, intuition confirmed by Nick and Conrad, it had been amusing waiting for him to say something, she loved his shyness and awkwardness, but now it was time for her to take the initiative. She was more and more sure there was something special between them, experiencing feelings she last remembered watching a street performer in Shrewsbury.

They headed up the beach Stephen looking up at the Lobster Pot Café, now closed for winter. He smiled; the restaurant already held so many memories. As they walked he became lost in thought, shocked at how much he had changed from the Stephen who stepped from the train almost a year ago. Where had the year gone? He thought of the Lookout, his home for the last year, transformed by Evans, of Sammy, Conrad, Gordon, Glenda and all his other friends, of Nick's amazing story. He felt so much part of their lives.

Most of all he thought about Rachel, casting sideways glances at her as they walked back along the beach. The wind ruffling her already tousled hair, eyes sparkling with happiness. She meant more to him than he cared to admit, tonight it was time to resume the conversation interrupted on Christmas Day.

At the end of their walk a tired and happy Rachel and Josh returned to Beach Cottage, while Stephen headed for the Lookout. Josh was intending to spend his evening catching up with old school friends, and Stephen had invited Rachel to dinner. He hurried home to commence cooking.

Stephen hummed to himself as he prepared the meal, sipping a glass of wine, watching the light fade outside. He was looking forward immensely to the evening ahead, he had a lot of news for Rachel. He carefully laid the table in front of the window, lighting a candle whose flame danced and flickered in the window's reflection, casting soft shadows across the room.

Rachel arrived promptly at seven, clutching champagne and looking stunning in an elegant blue dress and simple make up.

He kissed her cheek
'You look amazing.'
'Thank you Stephen I can make the effort occasionally.'

Later Stephen cleared away the dinner plates and returned to the table with the champagne. Having spent a delightful meal chatting about the past year, Stephen was unable to take his eyes off Rachel, his heart thumping. They sipped their drinks looking out over the estuary to the sea beyond, lost for a few moments in reflection.

It was Rachel who broke the silence.
'We're rubbish at it aren't we?'
'Rubbish at what?'
'Telling each other how we feel.'
Stephen thought for a moment before replying.
'It's because I'm scared.'
'Scared, why?'
'You know, of getting it wrong, ruining a beautiful friendship.'
It was Rachel's turn to reflect.
'I'm scared as well, scared you're going to leave.'
'Leave, why would I do that?'
'You only ever came for a year.'
Stephen gazed across the table at Rachel.
'How could I leave? I love this village, my friends, you...'
'Stephen...'
'Anyway, I've got an announcement to make.'
Rachel held her breath as Stephen continued.
'There's a good chance 'Aberdyssyni Lives' will be published, I want to write more, where else could I do it? But I need more as well, I need to put down roots.'
'Go on.'

'This morning I exchanged contracts on a business venture.

Conrad's going to retire, meet the new owner of Aberdyssyni Books.'

A broad smile broke over Rachel's face as she took in the news.

'That's wonderful Stephen, at least you won't have to steal your own books!'

'That's not all. I'm also buying the rest of Conrad's business; I'm going to be the owner of the Gallery as well. That makes me your landlord and you mine, perhaps we should come to a better arrangement.'

Rachel leaned across the table and took Stephen's hand, squeezing it gently.

'Tell me what you started to say on Christmas Day, before we were interrupted.'

They sat and talked about the future long into the night. Far below them the tide turned back up the estuary. It swept past the marker buoy, sending out its comforting green flashing light under the cold winter's sky.

Printed in Great Britain
by Amazon

14975338R00122